THE BLACK KACHINA

ALSO BY JACK GETZE

Austin Carr Mysteries
Big Numbers
Big Money
Big Mojo
Big Shoes

JACK GETZE

THE BLACK KACHINA

Down & Out Books
3959 Van Dyke Rd, Ste. 265
Lutz, FL 33558
www.DownAndOutBooks.com

Edited by Chris Rhatigan
Cover design by Eric Beetner

ISBN: 1-943402-69-8
ISBN-13: 978-1-943402-69-4

For my friend, Maggie Kilgore

"Today's Salton Sea was formed in 1905-07 when the Colorado River broke through irrigation floodgates near Yuma. Since then, Hoover Dam and other dams have supposedly tamed the rampages of the Southwest's mightiest river. However, the ghosts of Lake Cahuilla and its ancestors born of the river still brood over the valley."

—Lowell and Diana Lindsay,
The Anza-Borrego Desert Region.
A Guide to the State Park and the Adjacent Areas,
Second Edition, 1985.
Wilderness Press, Berkley, CA

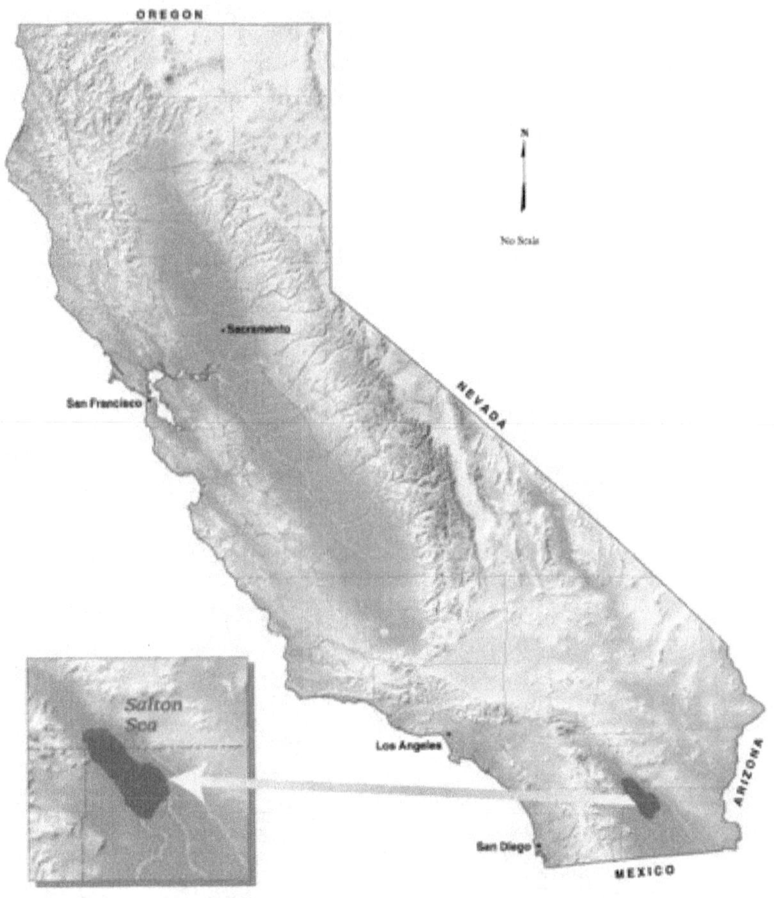

OREGON
NEVADA
ARIZONA
MEXICO
Sacramento
San Francisco
Los Angeles
San Diego
Salton Sea
No Scale
N

ONE

United States Air Force Lieutenant Colonel Maggie Black had been surrounded by men since her freshman year at the Air Force Academy in Colorado Springs. She'd been seventeen years old. By twenty-four, she'd been flying F-15C Eagles over Iraq, one of a handful of female American combat fighter pilots. These years of experience with men had taught her a few things, too, including some guys didn't like women flying fighter jets and a few didn't like women doing anything except baking cakes and spreading their legs. But most men, especially those in the service, cared only how you performed on the job. Another lesson of her male-dominated environment, Maggie could easily read when men excluded her, or left her out of an information loop, and right that second, checking out this El Centro, California aircraft control tower, all eyes on her, all eyes male, Maggie's mild concern for her silent B-52 test plane converted to serious worry.

"Eagle Six Four, this is Hard Candy," the tower radio officer said. "How copy, over?"

Again, there was no answer but static.

Through the Naval Air Facility's floor-to-ceiling

wraparound glass, Maggie had watched in awe as inky thunder clouds blossomed above this desert-based air gunnery range near California's Salton Sea. Multiple streaks of copper lightning sliced between the darkest clouds she'd ever seen. There had been no storm warning from the flight station's weather people. Clear skies had been predicted.

"Where *are* they?" Maggie said.

"Radar says forty miles to the northwest, turning for a run down the gunnery range."

Maggie's assigned radio officer sounded nervous. Zuniga, she thought his name was. She side-stepped closer to him. "You're telling me our B-52 lost radio contact when she flew near that God-awful black thunderstorm?"

"Yes, ma'am."

Maggie placed her paper coffee cup out of the way, then gently knocked her artificial left hand—a twelve-thousand-dollar BeBionic she'd purchased herself—into the non-opposed thumb position. Aligned with her individually motorized fingers, the jointed thumb could now tuck neatly into the pocket of her khakis. "Well, let's keep trying."

"Yes, ma'am. Of course. Eagle Six Four, this is Hard Candy. Please respond. You need to increase altitude, over."

Silicone gloves were mandatory to keep moisture and dirt from her prosthetic hand's parts and electrical connections. Although her BeBionic came with many flesh-colored, life-like covers—even separate male and female versions—Maggie preferred the plain, jet black glove as a reminder to herself and others. She didn't want her prosthetic mitt looking *too* real.

"How low are they?" she said.

"Two thousand feet."

"*What?*"

"Yes, ma'am. Two thousand."

Maggie told herself to stay calm. The bomber's pilot, Air Force Major Anthony Pinella, had been flying B-52 Stratofortresses for seven years, and while there was truth in the joke the sixty-year-old bombers flew like eight locomotives pulling ten thousand garbage cans, Maggie knew Tony Pinella. Rain and lightning wouldn't put a man like Tony off his game. He could fly the Stratofortress through a car wash. Still, he was operating close to the Pinyon, Vallecito, and southern Santa Rosa mountain ranges—peaks that reached over four thousand feet.

The radio officer gasped. His fingers reached for the radar screen. "*Shit!*"

Maggie frowned. "What's the matter?"

Her friend Pinella's cold war era B-52 jet bomber carried a crew of five, men and women with spouses and children and brothers and sisters, moms and dads. Also on board was an expensive piece of experimental weaponry Maggie and her team had designed, plus whatever remained of Maggie's Air Force career.

"Eagle Six Four, this is Hard Candy." The radio officer's voice had jumped half an octave. Sweat beaded his forehead. His fingers reset controls and dials that

Maggie didn't understand. "Eagle Six Four, this is Hard Candy. *Please respond.* Over."

"I said what's the *matter?*" Maggie pressed the radio man's shoulder with her right hand, her real hand. His tan uniform slid smoothly under her fingers, like polished wood. Maggie liked her uniforms stiff, too, but Zuniga's contained more starch than a truckload of potatoes.

"They're gone." Zuniga lurched forward. "They—" His voice warbled. "They dropped off radar."

Maggie groaned. She'd seen cemeteries full of death during her military action in Iraq. But non-experimental aircraft weren't supposed to crash on this wide open, Southern California desert test range. These training facilities were known worldwide for their year-round good weather.

"Eagle Six Four, this is Hard Candy. How copy, over?" Zuniga's voice begged for an answer, but nothing came back but static.

Maggie faced a room of anxious gazes. She bumped the volume on her voice. "Let's get two rescue teams ready. Right now."

The Chinook throbbed, hissed, and thrashed, poking Maggie's senses every second of the flight. She fought the distractions by monitoring the topography below the chopper on her BlackBerry, glancing only occasionally at the young men and women beside her. The Naval Air Facility emergency crews wore orange jumpsuits and blue helmets. Their black boots, sacks, and bundles of equipment jammed the chopper's cabin.

Maggie fought an old feeling. Sinking despair. What the hell had happened to her simple, fairly common weapons test? She tried to push the negative voices from her head but couldn't. *You lost your mother, you lost your hand, you lost your F-15. Now you lose the Air Force's experimental weapon with two hundred pounds of explosives? You lose everything! You're a loser!* Did everybody go through this mental crap when life went badly, or was it only her? Right this second she felt like she'd never done a damn thing right in her whole life.

Maggie sucked in a slow breath and let the air go at an even slower pace. She needed to get a grip, do her job. Maggie Black was no loser. She'd earned Burbank High School's highest grades her senior year. Class valedictorian. She'd entered the U.S. Air Force Academy when she was barely seventeen. She'd been a naturally great pilot, too, earning the second-best scores in her class of cadets and then later, easily meriting a slot in Ace Billy Payton's squadron during the Iraq War. Many years after that, when her plane's hydraulics had taken a fluke, small-weapons hit, she'd flown the F-15C hundreds of miles upside-down and survived a nasty bailout.

Maggie Black was no loser.

Above the Carrizo Badlands, the two helicopters maybe ten minutes out of their El Centro Naval Air Facility, one copilot spotted a tower of black smoke to the north. Maggie's phone caught the attention of the rescuers on each side of her, especially after the helicopter banked hard right toward the Fish Creek Mountains.

Maggie and the brightly clad Navy search and rescue crew jumped from the chopper onto a sparse and rugged desert landscape one hundred yards below a still-smoking crash scene. Tony Pinella and his B-52 had plowed directly into the side of a desert mountain—pale, sulfur-colored rocks piled to the height of a skyscraper.

Maggie saw no piece of wreckage bigger than a couch, nor any sign of the air-to-ground cruise missile carrying her experimental weapon. The plane's devastation was jaw-dropping and complete. One hundred and eighty-five thousand pounds of rolled steel, plastic, rubber, aluminum, and other sundry elements, plus forty thousand gallons of fuel. What had been a massive subsonic bomber, forty feet high, one hundred and fifty-nine feet long and one hundred and eighty feet across, was now a junkyard in the blackened V of intersecting rock formations.

Maggie's phone buzzed as she joined the search. It was her commanding officer, Brigadier General William Payton, his call a reminder there were nonhuman consequences to the crash of her B-52, consequences like her selfish career problems she'd dismissed earlier.

Maggie left a group of rescuers and hurried to a lonely spot where she could speak without being overheard. The house-sized boulder at her back contained long-embedded ancient shells inside a darker layer of stone. Two buzzards circled in a dark sky.

"Hello, Billy," she said. "I was going to call you when I knew more."

"The NAF flight chief called me, said our plane crashed. Any survivors?"

"We just arrived at the crash site, but I can't imagine anybody survived," she said. "They don't get any worse. Right into the side of a mountain. Our borrowed B-52 is blackened scrap."

She heard her old friend curse. They'd met at the Air Force Academy and under Billy's leadership years later, Maggie had joined the large, second wave of female fighter pilots trained when women were approved for combat. With Billy as her wing commander, she'd piloted an F-15C Eagle on forty-seven combat missions over Iraq.

"What about our experiment?" Billy said.

"Scrap, too, it looks like. I see nothing resembling our cruise missile, nothing left bigger than a piece of furniture around here."

"Jeez. Maybe Pinella deployed our missile when he saw they were going to crash. Get those explosives away. The missile had emergency parachutes, right?"

"Yeah, but I doubt he had time. Besides, we'd already know it. We installed a separate transponder on the weapon. There's no signal."

"Shit."

Oh, yeah. A whole big smelly pile of the stuff. She and General Payton had seen their share of crap flying over

Iraq, three times drawing an anti-aircraft missile lock-on, having to destroy an enemy radar site. This was way worse. None of their combat team had suffered a scratch during the war. Tony Pinella and his crew were dead.

"Listen, Maggie, I need proof our exploding air to ground missile isn't on the loose, okay? Find me pieces at least. I'm going to have some congressman grilling my ass tomorrow or the next day. The crash of an Air Force test plane will be on TV soon, I promise you."

"We'll find it," Maggie said. "I'll give you a call as soon as we do."

Not a scratch during the war. Maggie had lost her hand afterward, when she'd been reassigned to the 22nd Fighter Squadron at Spangdahlem Air Base in Germany. Small arms fire during a postwar mission over Iraq had caused her F-15C to crash in the German countryside, destroying a barn and wiping out half of a popular farmer's cattle herd. Her commanding officer at the time had questioned Maggie's piloting in his incident report, said she could have avoided most of the damage. The bastard. His comments were the result of Maggie having ended their romantic relationship. He'd even showed her the negative report, offered to change the wording if she'd resume the affair.

He would always be *The* Bastard.

"It'll be dark in a few hours," Billy said, "I'm going to give you tomorrow as well. But if you don't get that missile back, find some wreckage to show those pricks on the Armed Forces Sub-Committee, you can drag your ass up here to Edwards and explain to *my* CO in person. Got it?"

"Yes, sir."

Maggie had suffered a recurring dream since her wartime crash, but that night the repeat arrived in particularly vivid format. In the dream, or nightmare as the images turned out, Maggie's arm was whole again. Maggie reclaimed the title of complete and uncut, a woman with all her parts, all her charms, all her natural born self. And Whole Maggie did what she loved best— fly an F-15C Eagle, soaring between white clouds in a soft blue sky.

Flying, floating, weightless.

Above the earth and free, twisting and banking faster than the wind.

Then suddenly out of control.

Flying was like heaven to Maggie, soaring like the birds, and she first woke up from the dream breathless and sweaty, still lost in the flying. But seconds later, when her consciousness came all the way back, a stinging heartache grabbed her. Maggie's left arm and hand were missing two inches below the elbow. The normal, four-limbed human she'd been born no longer existed.

Maggie Black was forever different.

TWO

Asdrubal Torres often used his weekends to hike and forage in the barren mountains and deserts near Southern California's Salton Sea. The plants and rocks and creatures had been sacred to his mother's Cahuilla people for thousands of years, and by living alone among the dry land's natural inhabitants, fasting, sometimes drinking a *toloache* to invite the spirits, he rejoined a natural, harmonious world the white man had nearly destroyed.

With no elephant tree bark for his *toloache* one Saturday, Torres walked to a harsh, secluded mountain valley where a few of the sacred and dangerous trees still grew. The sky was blue and clear, and the air warm but not hot. He found himself singing one of his mother's old bird songs as he made his way along a dry creek bed dotted with golden-flowered manzanita bushes. He'd heard his mother sing the song many times, although she had never explained its meaning, nor was he certain of all the words. But even when humming, the rhythm and melody played happily inside him, a sign perhaps of his own contentment at the beginning of another vision quest.

His happy mood vanished as he approached the ancient and revered trees. Hearing voices, he crept to where he could scale the arroyo's bank and observe from behind a house-sized stand of the prolific manzanita. Had he angered the spirits with his song's unremembered words, his humming? His mother's warnings about the power of these trees had alerted him to an "ever-present spirit" that threatened violent death.

What he saw made the blood roar inside his ears. Two teenagers—boys he recognized from his own reservation—not only relieved themselves on this rare and sacred desert stand of elephant trees, they inexplicably laughed while doing so. Their urine collected near the snakelike exposed roots spreading from the largest tree's bulbous trunk. Grandmother of this whole stand, the tree these boys had selected to poison with their waste was at least five hundred years old. Perhaps one thousand.

Could these ignorant children be unaware of the blasphemy they committed, the risk they took with their lives? His fingertips pressed white against his palms. How could any Cahuilla, even drunken teenagers, defame the sacred trees of their forefathers? Many Cahuilla enemies—Serrano, Yuma, and Mojave braves—had died from arrows tipped with poison from these elephant trees. His mother always used great care to honor and praise those departed souls and the courage of the warriors' tribes whenever she collected bark.

The boys ceased their laughing when Torres appeared from behind the big yellow bush. "You urinate on your own spirit, fools," he said. "The power of every ancient Cahuilla warrior lies—"

"Fuck yourself, *culo.*"

The world stopped spinning for Asdrubal Torres. Staring at the sneering, disrespectful boy who had cursed him, Torres saw in that single moment the decline of his entire Cahuilla nation. The indications had been all around him for decades. Important activities of their ancestors, like cultivating desert plants, or traveling to the oak groves to gather acorns, were now considered a waste of time. The tribe rarely prayed together or cele-brated the most blessed Cahuilla traditions. *Puul, net,* and *ngengewish* were words rarely spoken. His clan of Cahuilla people drove foreign cars, ate cheeseburgers and worked for the tribe's gambling casinos.

He slipped the hunting knife from his belt and showed the blade to the taller boy, the one who cursed and called him *culo,* or ass in Spanish. Torres clenched the knife so hard, muscles in his right arm trembled. In his heart, he believed that unless he acted right then and with every effort and all means available, Cahuilla culture would be lost forever. To do nothing would be the same as acknowledging his people never existed. All in that moment. All in the way these boys ridiculed and cursed him. Young braves from his own reservation.

He *had* to do something.

The blasphemous teenager laughed, his teeth wide and white. "What do you think you're going to do with that knife, old man? Give yourself a haircut?"

His younger friend yapped like a small dog, and the

laughter set off an explosion inside Torres. Perhaps the fierce spirit of the elephant tree seized him through *toloaches* he had ingested over the years. Or maybe the failures of his personal life piled up all at once. For certain, he remembered his jaw rattled when he tried to speak again to the boys; also, that the trembling in his arm spread throughout his body. When the earthquake reached his toes, he lunged at the boys like a hungry spider, his long knife slashing.

After praying for the dead boys, cleaning up, acquiring his bark, and thanking the elephant tree for a piece of its skin, Torres hiked north to a secret trail in the tall pink mountains. The hidden path wound across valleys, up rocky canyons, and through half an acre of jumping silver *cholla* cactus, eventually reaching a boulder only visible after navigating the maze of white spines.

He would find no drunken teenagers here.

On the sacred rock, which was taller than himself and wider by a factor of ten than anything he could embrace, an ancient Cahuilla artist had pecked and scratched intricate designs—a tangled pattern of lines, plus seven stickmen riding four-legged beasts and carrying long knives. These petroglyphs could have been chipped into the rock as late as 1774 when the first white man, Spanish explorer Juan Batista de Anza, traveled through this pass on his way to Los Angeles. But, of course, who really knew? The Spanish had been exploring the land east of the Colorado River for two centuries before that, and the idea of men with long knives riding animals could have been a tale passed across the desert for generations before de Anza.

He sat cross-legged in his traditional place of power beside the sacred art. In preparation for drinking the hallucinatory *toloache* and his quest, he prayed as he traced the ancient stone lines with his fingertips.

Oh, Great Spirit, thank you for letting me be part of this mysterious world today. Thank you for all the people, plants, animals, creatures, and spirits I share this life with. Know that my heart is grateful. Should you grant me yet another day on this earth, I pray your love and wisdom will guide me.

Despite his decades-long hope the spirits would show him a solution to his people's decline, Torres never specifically prayed for such a gift. His mother had taught him not to ask for favors. If you wanted things, she said, you must search inside. Ask the Great Spirit only for guidance. His mother had taught him that daily prayer to thank the Creator for another day of life was every human's duty.

Though he did not ask for direct help, Torres sensed that day would be different, that the spirits had already intervened in his life and would further enlighten a path for him. An idea or a plan would come. The day had been special from the beginning, and surely the two boys had been a sign, perhaps a sacrifice that would somehow show Torres how to guide his people away from the white man's world of greed and conquest.

He crushed a tiny bit of elephant tree bark with his thumb and forefinger, then placed this non-deadly amount into his mother's stone bowl with a quantity of dried datura root and other ingredients, some preserved and a few collected that day. He mixed and drank the *toloache*, then closed his eyes and began to chant, a call to the animal spirits who lived nearby.

In time, they all came to see him, too. First the mouse, who told him not to leave his place of power. Then the rabbit, who explained it was safe to travel, but not slowly, and not in the direction Torres had planned. And the coyote, who urged him to charge and bite if he was hungry enough.

Little sound accompanied Torres's hike up the pile of pink rocks white men called the Santa Rosa Mountains, nothing but wind across his ears and the talking of crows and hawks. The black-feathered birds chattered more than necessary, but Torres had learned to take comfort in their nervous vigilance. Mountain trails could be dangerous, particularly under the spell of a *toloache*.

Reaching a prominent western cliff overlooking the Salton Sea and the Coachella and Imperial valleys, the view was like standing on the rim of a giant serving dish, the Salton Sea but a tiny patch of blue at the very center of the dish's bottom. North and south of the distant blue lake, two green quilts of farmland stretched the length of both valleys. Once the site of a great inland sea named for his people, now the white man's cities sprouted inside this green slime like poisonous mushrooms.

He gazed at the imprint of ancient Lake Cahuilla that marked the mountains below him like a ring on a bathtub. He wished he had known the lake in those days, perhaps 1492 when the first white man, Christopher Columbus, sailed to America. The fresh waters of Lake Cahuilla then were full of fish, and the surrounding reeds and grasses teemed with life. Torres's people would have expected the water to last forever, like the moon and the stars.

Standing high above today's Salton Sea, a puddle compared to ancient Lake Cahuilla, Torres removed all thoughts from his mind, even the internal dialogue people used to soothe themselves. As he had a thousand times over, he asked the spirits for guidance.

Seconds or minutes later—the *toloache* made gauging time difficult—a cold wind brushed the back of his neck. He spun toward the western mountains and the forest named for the white man's dead president, Cleveland. There, the yellow sky had grown dark. Black clouds covered the mountains and lightning fired in the cracks of the storm. Thunder rumbled as the rain and blackness raced toward him.

Were the spirits talking?

A sound startled him, and he stared again at the trail where shafts of sunlight still remained. Dream or reality, he could not say, but into this surreal brightness walked a man-sized Nataska, the black ogre kachina of Hopi legend—the kachina, or spirit, known as The Punisher of Wicked Children.

An invisible hand probed Torres's chest. His heart seemed to pause beating. He knew of the spirit Nataska from his mother, who carried both Cahuilla and Hopi blood. But this black ogre kachina frightened him more than the doll he had seen as a child, more even than his Hopi grandmother's terrifying stories of Nataska eating children who misbehaved. The Nataska before him now displayed long sharp horns protruding from his red scalp, and oversized eyeballs that radiated black-light purple. The rows of jagged, triangular teeth inside his long, reptilian mouth resembled those of a great white shark.

Though frightened, Torres refused to run. He understood the black ogre's presence must be connected to his earlier misadventure at the elephant trees. Had Torres himself not punished two wicked children there? Obviously, this kachina was part of a vision the *toloache* and the spirits had prepared for him.

The long-toothed vision pointed his legendary saw toward a depression in the earth, a dark shadow on the trail. A clean-edged rock there caught Torres's eye, a hand-worked piece of flint. Nataska nodded, encouraging Torres to retrieve the arrowhead or broken spear point, and as Torres reached for the hand-sharpened rock, perhaps a talisman hewn by an ancient warrior, a strange hiss stabbed his ears. As he touched the pointed flint—the very same instant—a numbing explosion of air and sound knocked him flat against the earth.

Sweat poured from his skin. He could barely draw breath. What was that earsplitting slash of air, that black, winged shape that had raced above him? He sensed some gigantic predatory bird swooping down to eat him. He cried out in panic.

Noise and the giant bird passed, yet fear so gripped him, Torres at first refused to behold the manmade nature of his imagined predator. Only when the plane was miles away, brushing a rocky mountain, did he understand. The huge military bomber had passed only a few hundred feet above him at the exact instant he touched that rock.

Oh, Great Spirit, what a sign!

In the storm-darkened sky, only lightning showed the aircraft's downward path, and he witnessed the crash like an old, silent film—in blinking pictures that caused the aircraft to lurch and shrink and end in fire. After passing above Torres in the southern Santa Rosa Mountains, the plane had touched one Fish Creek mountain peak and exploded behind another one many miles away and off to the west.

The fire winked at him through a cloudy sky. He cried no tears for the men he assumed were inside, or their families, and yet he felt distraught. His body withered from foot to scalp as he had at his mother's funeral. Why? Of what sadness had he been thinking before the coolness of the sudden storm touched his neck and Nataska had appeared in the shafts of light? What despair stayed with him still?

The dead Lake Cahuilla...how the white man's slime and poisonous mushrooms now covered the bed of an old lake. Among his clan, he had listened to many stories of the abundant game and happy life their ancestors had lived around the old lake's shores.

Could the day's events have been coincidence? Those blasphemous teenagers. The visit of Nataska. The flint. The crash of the plane. And this overwhelming grief he still felt for the lost Lake Cahuilla. Surely, everything was connected. Surely, the spirits offered him a message.

He squatted on the mountain trail to rub his new flint. On-again, off-again showers soaked his clothes and chilled his skin. But the flint warmed in his hand, the rock becoming so hot he cupped his palms to catch the next rain. When his hands filled with water, taming the flint's unnatural heat, Torres grasped the message of his visions. To heal his tribe, he must fill the valley below with water as he'd filled his hands with rain.

Torres rose to his feet and danced. What joy he would experience destroying what the white man had built. What happiness and unity he could build for all indigenous peoples by returning Lake Cahuilla to the Cahuilla.

Yes, he would need help. Much. And his dancing slowed as he considered the task's difficulty. Las Vegas, Phoenix, San Diego, and Los Angeles relied heavily on Colorado River water, so the dams and waterways were strong and well protected. The world, and everyone in the Coachella and Imperial valleys, had learned a serious lesson in 1905-07 when the Salton Sea had been created.

The fertile commercialized land of both valleys rested several hundred feet below sea level, and was still subject to flooding from a redirection of the Colorado River. It had happened in 1905. The white man had built many dams, canals, and reservoirs to safeguard his families and farms since then.

But did the difficulty matter? By directing his visions and tampering with nature itself, the spirits clearly had gifted him this exact responsibility. Torres need not worry how impossible his charge, or even what exactly to do next. He had been chosen. The people and answers he needed already struggled to find *him*.

THREE

Two broad-shouldered nurses in white jeans and white golf shirts employed chains, levers, and pulleys to lift Jordan Scott's grandmother from her steel hospital bed. The expensive apparatus groaned and squealed as if it were alive, swinging Grandma Scott over soiled sheets into a wheelchair. The extra service cost eight hundred dollars a month, but without the daily transfer, Jordan knew Grandma Scott would be tattooed in bedsores.

She grinned when she saw Jordan, a full set of bright white teeth, too, Grandma Scott never having smoked. Her smile still dazzled him. Jordan's father had been Grandma's only child. Jordan had no family now but Grandma. He hugged her shoulders.

She patted his hand. "Your grandfather came to visit last night. He said he's an angel now, and that I'm about to join him."

Jordan's gut twisted. His grandfather had been an "angel" for more than a decade. "You just had a bad dream, Grandma." He grinned. "I'm guessing you need to cut back on the zombie TV shows."

One little busted blood vessel had knocked Grandma Scott permanently off her feet. He'd seen the old photos of her surfing back in the 1960s, riding stormy eight-footers off Wisconsin Street in Oceanside. Only four years earlier, at sixty-six, his grandmother had been the local women's senior golf champion. One stroke ended everything but bed for his grandmother.

"It was no dream," she said. "Your grandfather reminded me of something I must do. Something you'll have to help me with."

Grandma hadn't been what you'd call lucid since her stroke, but dreaming about her dead husband, talking about her own death, this was new. Jordan wondered how to handle her as he wheeled her past the crowded television room.

"What did Grandpa remind you to do?"

"Return the basket your great grandfather stole from the Cahuilla Indians. Do you remember it? Your grandfather and I always kept it under the square piano? You used to crawl around on that rug often enough."

A picture flashed in Jordan's head, a sepia shot of his grandparents' old square piano and something underneath, behind the piano's brass pedals—a woven brown and black basket covered with Native American designs. The thing was bigger than an automobile tire. Grandma had always kept stacks of magazines inside it.

"I remember the basket but I never heard any story before," Jordan said. "Grandpa's father stole it from the Cahuilla Indians? Barton Scott? The railroad engineer who became a federal judge?"

"That's what your grandfather said. He planned on returning the basket to those California Indians but never got to the job. Makes him feel guilty. Me, too. Those lovely Cahuilla might need it for something spiritual, something important."

Odd Jordan hadn't heard this tale before. While alive, Grandpa had loved to tell stories, especially about his London-born, cowboy father, Barton Scott. Another thought occurred to Jordan: A large antique Indian basket might be worth some cash.

Grandma touched Jordan's arm. "Will you take back the basket for me, love?"

"Sure, Grandma. Funny thing, I was assigned a story near the Salton Sea as I pulled in the parking lot here. A military plane crash. U.S. Air Force, they think."

"Oh, I'm sorry to hear that."

"Yeah, the crew was killed. Each one means a whole family torn apart."

"A sad story to write, I'm sure."

"Covering the military feels like a diary of death sometimes. But while I'm down there, I'll stop in one of those Cahuilla Indian casinos. Couple of them have museums. I'll find someone who'll know which band of Indians the basket belongs to. Where's this antique treasure now?"

"You'll find it with all the household things you arranged storage for, I'm sure. But don't you get any ideas about selling it, Jordan Scott. That beautiful basket is worth a considerable sum, I'm sure. But we will not take money for returning what was stolen."

Since Jordan's parents and his older brother Ryan had been killed in a car crash twelve years earlier, Grandma was his only family. The stroke had been a financial strain, and his reporter's salary wouldn't help much once Grandma's capital ran out. Jordan already paid a thousand bucks worth of her monthly bills. If she lived another six years, Grandma's principal would be gone and Jordan wouldn't have saved enough.

He loved her dearly, but if this Indian basket was worth *real* money, he wasn't so sure he'd be carrying out Grandma's wishes.

Rain transformed Jordan's headlights into a curtain of glare, obscuring the painted business sign and any address number. He parked his leased Ford Escort and hopped out into the storm anyway. If the car's navigation said he'd arrived at the Lakeside Band of Cahuilla headquarters in Southern California's Anza-Borrego desert, good bet he was there.

Filing his stories by e-mail in El Centro and driving up here had taken longer than he'd expected. The highway alongside the Salton Sea had been thick with trucks and the steepness of Highway 76 as it ascended the Santa Rosa Mountains surprised him. Finally, the bleak beauty of the Anza-Borrego Desert State Park had been undiminished by the heavy downpour. He'd pulled over twice to absorb the desolate-but-beautiful views.

Jordan lifted his grandmother's basket from the backseat. Tightly woven of brown reeds, the perfectly round container was three feet in diameter, eighteen inches tall, and decorated with black zigzags, squares, a large bird and a series of stickmen. Nothing special as far as he could tell, except for the size.

With the basket over his head as a makeshift umbrella, Jordan ran toward the doublewide trailer this band of Cahuilla Indians called home. Jordan leaped and hopped athletically across the lot, hunting for dry ground. Being a top baseball pitcher in high school didn't help much with the jumping, though. By the time he'd reached the trailer's hand-built porch, maybe a quarter-pound of mud decorated his jeans.

Inside the doublewide, a young woman in a sleeveless red blouse glanced up from her computer. She remained seated at her neat steel desk, checking out Jordan first and then what she could see of the basket. Her straight, shiny black hair fell in a ponytail to her waist. A thick-linked necklace of turquoise and silver circled her throat.

He placed Grandma Scott's artifact on a long reception counter. "I'm Jordan Scott," he said. "I called about the basket."

The room was set up with three desks around the perimeter, a water cooler and a rectangular coffee table against the empty wall. A white plastic coffeemaker, red plastic cups, and the usual assortment of sugar, creamers, other additives and utensils adorned the well-organized table. The air smelled of pine and a taste of the electric storm Jordan must have brought inside with him.

The young woman's gaze had fixed on Grandma's basket. Her dark eyes grew slightly larger and a gap opened between her lips.

"Are you the lady I spoke to on the phone?" he said.

Her gaze remained on the basket, but she tugged a cell phone from her slim-fit gray slacks. She was taller than Jordan had expected, close to six feet, like him. Her fingers danced across the buttons of her cell phone.

"Ma'am?" he said.

She snugged the phone against her ear and whispered. After a moment, she let her gaze meet Jordan's. "I'm sorry, Mr. Scott, but I had no idea you were bringing me something so old and so special. I have to talk to our chief."

Jordan glanced at Grandma's basket. What if Grandma Scott's Indian artifact was worth fifty thousand dollars? Or a hundred? He had seen such things on that television series, *Antiques Roadshow*. Maybe he should walk out now and take the basket to an antique dealer in San Diego or Los Angeles. Would Grandma ever know?

Nice, Jordan. Still. They needed the money.

No chance. Grandma had been firm about taking money in return for what had been stolen. And as usual Grandma was right.

The young woman in silver and turquois closed her cell phone. "The chief is coming right over."

Once his hands touched the woven basket, the Cahuilla chief never stopped fondling the black designs. Like a lover caressing his partner's tattoo, the chief traced the images over and over with his fingertips. "Where did you acquire this?"

"It's my grandmother's," Jordan said.

He tried to remember the chief's name. Damien? Ronald? Some newspaper reporter he was. He remembered the young woman's name. Charlotte. The rain outside infiltrated through open windows and made the room feel sticky.

"How did she come to have this basket?" the chief said.

"She told me her stepfather, my great grandfather, had stolen it, so my grandmother asked me to give the basket back to the Cahuilla Indi—uh, Native Americans."

The chief stared at him. Reynaldo, that was his name.

"Indian works fine," Chief Reynaldo said. "Indians, Native Americans, First Americans. They're all the white man's words. My people call ourselves *wiwaiistam*, so please, do not hesitate to say Indian. We all know exactly who you mean. It says Cahuilla Indians on the sign above this trailer and all of our businesses in town."

Chief Reynaldo had eyes like a raptor and skin stained dark leather. He wore his silver hair in a ponytail longer than Charlotte's. Except for the hawk gaze and extended hair, he looked pretty normal in his suit and white dress shirt, plain brown leather shoes, but Jordan couldn't ignore the chief's eyes. They focused on him as if roasted news reporter might be the tribe's next meal.

"Your grandmother possesses a very old basket," Chief Reynaldo said. "Perhaps even a *puul's*, our word for shaman, or medicine man if you watch old movies. I've never seen anything like this, nor can I translate the story these markings on it tell. Of itself, however, the presence of a Golden Eagle indicates this was either a chief's or a *puul's*."

Jordan coughed. "Charlotte suggested it might be valuable."

"I did?" she said.

"Certainly Indian artifacts have a value with collectors," the chief said, "although few outside of California have heard of the Cahuilla. Better for you if Grandma's basket were Navajo."

Jordan waited for more information. You never learned anything while you were talking, an adage he'd picked up from his first-grade teacher, Mrs. Rampart, not journalism school.

The chief smiled at Jordan's silence, his first, although the man's yellowed teeth failed to diminish his predatory appearance. "Why would you care about value? You said your grandmother wanted to *give* it back."

Jordan kept his mouth shut.

The smile on Chief Reynaldo's lips faded. "As surely as the basket has value, so, too, has it been stolen. A chief or *puul* would never trade or make such a gift, especially to a white man."

Jordan's neck stiffened. He sat up straighter. "Maybe, but that basket's been under our family's square piano for a hundred years. There's no one alive who can say for sure how my great grandfather got it."

The chief pointed to the basket's markings. Woven with blackened fibers, the dark images were crude, meaningless to Jordan. Stickmen working, or carrying something. The scenes were akin to a bad diagram in some foreign-produced instruction booklet.

"Did your great grandfather work for the railroad?" the chief said.

Jordan nodded. "Yes. He was an engineer. He helped survey land for new track after a big flood in the early nineteen hundreds."

Chief Reynaldo's fingers curled against his palm. "Oh, I know well of the flood. I also know your great grandfather must have been a murderer."

FOUR

Two hundred miles northwest of her El Centro NAF station, arriving at Edwards Air Force Base in a downpour, Lieutenant Colonel Maggie Black broke one of her most cherished personal rules: When the driver opened the back door of the Air Force's gray, four-door sedan, Maggie offered him her hand, a request for help getting out.

Normally, Maggie couldn't afford to appear weak or act like a lady, particularly in uniform and under pressure. And today Brigadier General Billy Payton might kick her butt from one side of Edwards to the other, and everyone knew it. But also today, Maggie's artificial arm throbbed like a diesel engine. And another severe, low-pressure weather system had aggravated her back and leg stiffness, a chronic reminder of the plane crash and bail out that had consumed her left hand and forearm. Colonel Black presented her hand to her driver because pride and discipline didn't matter if you needed physical assistance.

"Can I ask you a question, Colonel?" her driver said. Peterson his name was. Airman First Class. A toothpick and a boy, in his early twenties.

"I think you just did, Peterson." Underneath the driver's umbrella, water splashed her ankles as Maggie tugged and straightened her dark blue Air Force uniform. "But sure, go ahead. Ask me another question—as long as it's not why the pilots call me Bullseye."

"No, ma'am," he said. "That's because your F-15 trainer took an unarmed Sidewinder missile right up the—"

Maggie made him stop by raising her hand. She stared at Peterson's fuzzy-skinned cheeks. He'd been a good boy on the way here. Driving slowly, letting her puff a cigarette without complaint, and staying mostly quiet. "Then what's your question, Peterson? And make it quick."

"Why are you taking so much heat for that plane crash? Those B-52s are like sixty years old, on their way out of service. I just wondered—"

"It's what the Stratofortress was carrying that has me in the soup," Maggie said. "But I can't explain—not until you're old enough to buy me a Bushmills. Which, now that I think about it, will be never."

Blushing, Peterson escorted her up the wooden steps, carefully using the umbrella to keep her mostly dry. "Good luck, ma'am."

"Thanks." She snatched the umbrella from him.

A pang of guilt tickled her. She'd been popular in grammar school, elected to student office at a young age, probably because she'd always spoken up when others were timid. Maybe she'd been big for her age, too. But by the sixth grade, her leadership abilities had turned her into a bit of a bully, Maggie needing Bobby Augusta to straighten her out one day on the playground. Oh, Bobby had suffered a shot or two himself, but she'd been forced to surrender, both to Bobby's fists and his fact-based taunts. Bullying accusations had upset her from that day on, even when self-diagnosed. Peterson hadn't really done anything to be browbeaten, or insulted, or whatever the hell she'd done. She was nervous about this meeting.

She hesitated at the doorway. "Peterson."

"Yes, ma'am."

"Sorry to be so grouchy. I must be worried about seeing the general. I know he's going to kick my ass, and he does such a fine job."

Peterson grinned and saluted.

Inside General Payton's suite of trailers, her old wing commander and friend from the Air Force Academy yelled at her from inside his private office. "Goddamn it, Maggie. It's been three fucking days! Where the hell is that missile?"

He couldn't even see her yet.

Maggie got her Bullseye nickname like her driver said, above the skies of Arizona while taking part in a training mission the Air Force called a 2v2, which in Maggie's case pitted two F-15Cs against two F-15Es in a mock dogfight. Maggie had brought her damaged aircraft in for an emergency landing, and later that day, located the offending pilot for a verbal assault of her own. *That* turkey had deserved a little bullying.

Maggie strode into Billy Payton's office, the largest of three boxy rooms inside the prefabricated, one-story building. More like a trailer park, really. Portraits of various Air Force fighter jets dominated the drab green walls, the F-15 displayed most prominently. Although the current fleet was being replaced by the much newer F-35, Maggie had been proud to fly the older twin-engine, all-weather tactical fighter. What fighter pilot wouldn't? Designed by McDonnell Douglas, now part of Boeing, the F-15 had logged over one hundred aerial combat victories with zero losses.

"Could I at least sit down before you start cursing at me?" she said. "My legs and back hurt like hell."

He waved her toward a chair. Brigadier General William "Billy Boy" Payton also felt the heat of her lost experimental weapon, Maggie realized. The sweat clung to his forehead forming rice-sized beads. Clipped newspaper stories about the plane crash and pink message slips covered his desk, several of his to-be-returned phone calls due the FBI. She'd learned to read upside down and backwards as a weekly newspaper trainee one summer in high school.

"Why can't you find the damn thing?" Billy said. "What happened to the son-of-a-bitch's transponder?"

"It's not working. In fact, I found out the transponder—probably all the electronics—went offline before the crash."

"*Before* the crash? How is that possible?"

"Lightning took out the ship's communications, all their instruments, all the electronics," she said. "So far, the Navy's special investigators think that's probably what caused the crash. The transponders must have been disabled as well."

General Payton pushed away from his desk and lumbered to the window. The rusty one-room air conditioner spurted only puffs of cool air inside the stuffy office. Damp marked the back of Billy's shirt. The general had always been a big sweater. "So you found every piece of a B-52 bomber but nothing of our test missile?"

"Not yet."

"Why the hell not? It's huge."

"The weapon must have fallen off before the crash," she said. "Those Fish Creek Mountains are like a moonscape. There are holes, ravines, rock forma—"

"Maggie, it's a cruise missile. The thing is bigger than my brother's 1967 Cadillac, the one with tail wings."

Billy's profile had changed considerably in the years Maggie had known him. Thin to round. Her old drinking buddy and one-time lover—her first—from the Air Force Academy obviously had never lost his longtime attraction to ice cream.

"I'm doing everything I can," she said.

A top scholar, Maggie had been a virgin when she'd met and fallen for senior cadet Billy Boy Payton. Though they'd remained good friends, her future wing commander's piggish infidelities back in those days made Billy the last military man Maggie had slept with. Well, except for that cute Australian pilot she'd met in the stateside hospital. And, of course, The Bastard.

"Let me ask you," Billy said. "Could a stranger have

already found the missile and stolen our experimental weapon?"

A sharp pain caused Maggie to rub her forearm near the black BeBionic hand assembly, her fingers massaging flesh above where a rod fit into a socket below her elbow. "Anything is possible," she said. "I don't know. That electrical storm could have knocked it—"

"An electrical storm? Honey, wait until you see the *shit* storm that missile brings down on us if you don't find our experiment soon. You and I will be testifying before both houses of congress until the day we die."

She glared at him. "Call me honey again, you might not be testifying in one piece."

Billy waved at her. "I forgot. Sorry."

Billy's leadership had helped bring Maggie much success in her early Air Force career. Forty-seven patrol and combat missions on his wing had fueled a quick rise. But nobody called her honey. Not even Billy. Was there a more dismissive word in the English language? Maggie could do—and previously had done with Billy—a five-minute rant on baby, sweetie, and honey.

"I don't know what else I can do," Maggie said. "I have every helicopter and light plane in the county looking, every man I can find on the ground. I even convinced governor whack-job in Sacramento to send me two National Guard regiments."

"Could a civilian actually move a cruise missile?" Billy said. "Damn things weigh three tons, don't they?"

"More. Seven thousand pounds with our experimental charges. But all it would take is a heavy-duty boom lift on the back of a six-wheel tow truck. You see them all over Southern California's highways. Ford and General Motors sell them off dealer lots. Maybe they'd need a covered trailer to carry and hide the missile for towing. I'm hoping."

"So you have thought about it," Billy said. "You *are* worried about someone grabbing a couple hundred pounds of the newest, most powerful military explosive?"

Maggie sighed. She had worried about every conceivable possibility over the last few days. A few inconceivable, unless you believed in alien kidnapping. "I have to consider theft, sure," she said, "but I don't think it's likely. We'll find that missile. We're working back along the flight path, on foot, yard by yard."

"Except you told me the electronics were out and communications disturbed. So how could you even *have* an exact flight path?"

Maggie shrugged. True. That was the problem. Base radar only narrowed the search to three hundred square miles of the rockiest, rain-and-wind-cut, vegetation-challenged topography she'd ever seen. The Fish Creek Mountains. The surface of the moon looked easier to explore.

"We estimated on a map," she said. "We're doing the best we can."

The general picked up one of the pink message slips from the FBI. "It'll be the end of both our careers if that thing blows up and kills someone. You know that, correct? I authorized the construction of your prototype three-stage bunker-buster. I also borrowed a retiring B-52 from the Air Force's Global Strike Command and begged the Navy to use their desert air facility down there in El Centro. But I won't be the—"

"If there's a way I can take full responsibility, Billy, let me. I appreciate the opportunity you gave me after the accident in Germany."

He waved her off. "Just find that damn missile."

The two old friends stared at each other. There wasn't much else to say. Maggie had lost the missile. She'd better find it, and quickly. Figuring Brigadier General Billy Payton was about to dismiss her, she lifted her umbrella from the back of the chair.

"How are you and your old man doing?" Billy said. "You were barely talking when I saw you in San Diego last year."

The subject surprised Maggie more than the new friendly tone. "Pop's doing better since Christmas," she said. "I'm not sure why. Maybe after thirty-eight years, the old man is learning to live with the fact his daughter is not the marrying kind."

Billy grinned. "Well, give him a break. Every man wants grandkids."

"He should adopt."

Billy laughed. "Hang on while I call Duffy. Let's see if he wants to ask you anything himself."

While General Payton called his commanding officer, Maggie picked up the folded newspaper on Billy's desk. She wanted to show him she wasn't concerned. In reality, she imagined herself being grilled by the U.S.

Senate while her father and friends watched on live television. Some nasty old senator would ask her how the experimental missile she designed had killed a family of God-fearing desert hikers.

Or had blown up a loaded school bus.

Ten paragraphs into reading the *San Diego Sun-Times* story, she decided she liked the writer's objectivity. Nothing but reported facts and named sources about the crashed plane. Old school journalism, not the agenda-driven news you normally read today, attacking the military and corporations for existing. The reporter had done his homework on B-52s and the El Centro Naval Air Facility, too. No inflammatory speculation. Maggie had enjoyed journalism class in high school and had taken an elective course at the Air Force Academy as well. She often checked local bylines. But she'd never heard of staff writer Jordan Scott.

FIVE

Along with heat in his cheeks, a natural curiosity that blossomed in Jordan Scott's high school journalism class now flamed in response to Chief Reynaldo calling his grandfather a murderer. Hard to believe his great grandfather Barton Scott had been *any* kind of criminal. Except times were different a century ago, rural California like any other part of the fast-changing-but-still-wild west. Many men carried weapons and delivered their own justice.

Jordon spoke slowly and evenly. "Why would you say that?"

"Because railroad people and traders the railroad introduced sold our ancestors blankets and pillows infected with smallpox," Chief Reynaldo said. "When most of us died, they stole our water and mineral rights and much of our government-awarded land."

Jordan nodded. "The San Diego school system taught California history. I know why the Cahuilla resent white men—like every other indigenous human on the planet. But I can't believe my ancestor Barton Scott was a murderer. He ended up a federal judge. Plus, the smallpox epidemic was all over by 1906 when my great grandfather was hired to survey the new track."

"Perhaps," Chief Reynaldo said. "But possession of this basket strongly suggests violence. No Cahuilla would give such a gift."

Jordan shook his head. "You're leaving something out. What does this basket have to do with violence, or the railroad?"

Chief Reynaldo glared back. His eyes devoured Jordan like black holes sucking stars. Jordan shifted his gaze to Charlotte when she cleared her throat.

"He does not want to tell you," she said, "but I believe my father thinks you may have brought us a legendary basket, the famous water basket of Chaco Cruz, one of the Cahuilla's most famous *puuls*."

Chief Reynaldo grunted. He pushed his chair back and stood. "This white man does not need to hear about our legends. He cannot understand. He will only laugh and remain ignorant. It is what they do."

"Stop," she said. "You sound like a racist. This man must hear." Her gaze locked on Jordan. "With this very basket, Chaco is said to have created the Salton Sea."

Jordan's face wrinkled. "I don't understand? How could he do that?"

Chief Reynaldo sighed. "See."

"Shush, father. Let me speak." Charlotte shifted her chair closer to Jordan. "Chaco Cruz attempted to recreate an ancient lake that once existed in the valley—Lake Cahuilla. He is said to have used this basket's magic over a century ago to divert the Colorado River."

Jordan couldn't hold back a smile. "You're talking

about the flood of 1905 to 1907, when an irrigation experiment broke down under a river surge?"

"That is what the white man saw," Chief Reynaldo said. "But the Salton Sea's creation last century was no accident. There are old photographs of the great Cahuilla shaman, Chaco Cruz. He was real, and so are the stories about Chaco tapping the water spirit back in 1905. He constructed this basket to convince the Colorado River to refill Lake Cahuilla as it has done over and over throughout time. My great grandfather was there, and he told my grandfather, who told my father, who told me. The truth has been passed down. Chaco Cruz's magic worked."

"But the flood eventually stopped," Jordan said. "The Salton Sea is, and was even in 1907, only a tiny remnant of the old Lake Cahuilla."

Chief Reynaldo leaned in. "You know more than most, Jordan Scott, but you *see* only a piece. The flood stopped because Chaco Cruz, his two men, and his magic basket went missing in the desert. The railroad likely hired assassins—perhaps your great grandfather. Certainly he or someone he knew killed our tribe's greatest *puul*."

Driving home to San Diego, Jordan struggled with the desert mountain roads as well as the idea his great grandfather might have been a killer. A legend was all Charlotte and her father had been talking about, really. Probably pure bull. But if the tribe believed it, truth didn't matter. Who knew what really happened in 1907? It wasn't like Jordan could look up old television footage. Firsthand accounts didn't jump out from a computer search. Every story on the flood he could find said irrigation control mistakes had caused an accident, a levee breakthrough that railroad and farming interests had needed more than two years to patch. Another thing the stories often mentioned about the century-old flood was the Salton Sea's surface. The lake existed two hundred feet below sea level. Things could have gotten so much worse for the Imperial and Coachella valleys if the railroad hadn't eventually stopped the water flow.

Rain slammed Jordan's windshield. The wipers shot him only brief glimpses of the slick asphalt. Traveling south on California State Highway 79, maybe halfway back to Highway 8 and the straight line home to San Diego, Jordan braked and pulled over when the roadway became obscured. He figured showers that heavy couldn't last long. Better safe than sideways.

He opened the driver's window, but rainwater flew in sideways, enough to change his mind about fresh air. He buzzed the window back up and used his cell phone to dial his boss, Sam Carson, at the paper. Beyond the highway, behind a stand of tall palms, a curtain of ten or more separate lightning bolts flashed from sky to desert floor. Long blue-line jewels zigzagging through the blackness. He'd never seen anything like it.

"The copy you sent earlier today looks good," Sam said. No hello, of course. "Why are you still in the mountains?"

As city editor of the *San Diego Sun-Times*, Sam Carson kept Jordan and the other reporters on a tight rein. What else from an ex-Marine who raised quarter horses and entered the San Diego County bronco-riding tournament every year?

"How'd you know I was in the mountains?" Jordan said.

"I hear thunder, the rain on your roof. You hit the biggest storm out there in ten years."

"Thanks for the assignment, boss."

Sam grunted. "Seriously. You okay?"

"I'm good. I had to pull over for a minute. I couldn't see where—"

The car's interior filled with white light. A punch of air knocked the Ford sideways and an explosion of sound rattled the windows. Jordan's stomach somersaulted. Streaks of lightning danced in the palm trees across the roadway.

Ears numb from the thunderbolt, he watched through dreamy eyes as the palms burst into flames. The bushy tops fired up like matchsticks, their bulbous crowns exploding atop the long bare poles.

"Jordan?"

It had been on a night like this when Jordan's brother, Ryan, and their parents had died in an automobile accident, a collision with a truck. Ryan's baseball team had played that weekend in Yuma, and Jordan had been sick, unable to travel with the family. His Grandma Scott lived on the beach in Del Mar in those days, twelve years ago, and Jordan had spent the weekend with her.

He'd been asleep in the big upstairs bedroom when she'd woken him with the news. He'd never seen his grandmother cry before or since.

His motel room line rang, tugging Jordan awake. Dull gray light filled the sparse cubical, and rain drops rattled the horizontal window overhead. He rolled onto his side and checked the digital clock while he pawed for the phone. Nine-thirty. Oops. He lifted the receiver knowing his editor must have tracked him down.

"Yeah?" Jordan said.

"Why aren't you interviewing somebody important?"

It was Sam Carson. Jordan rubbed his eyes. "What's going on?"

"Were you sleeping?"

"I didn't get back to El Centro until late. I had to check something at an Indian casino in Palm Springs. Then I ran into that storm, remember?"

"Listen, I'm emailing you a *New York Times* story. The wrecked B-52 was carrying some kind of experimental weapon."

"Text me a link. Was it a nuke?"

"I shouldn't think so. But whatever the plane was carrying, if it makes a boom, it's a story. Now get out of bed and see what you can find. The Air Force is directing everyone to their public relations people at Edwards, but *The Times* says the experiment was operated from a base near the border with Mexico."

"Could be anywhere," Jordan said. "There are so

many military air strips in the Southwestern desert, especially—"

"I need copy by six. And charge your cell phone." Sam Carson clicked off.

Jordan rolled out of bed. The grayness of the room seemed wrong, dreamlike. The motel's off-white tiled floor smelled of pine disinfectant, and the furniture reeked of cigarettes. *The San Diego Sun-Times* paid its reporters a travel expense rate of $110 per day, so Jordan had never stayed at a Ritz-Carlton. But he knew the best Mexican food spots in California. Chicken tacos with green chili sauce in particular.

The motel phone rang again. Sam was always hanging up and calling back.

"The big angle is what the hell was onboard that plane, obviously," Sam said. "But I also want to know why the Air Force was using a sixty-year-old airplane to carry anything. I thought that ageless B-52 fleet had finally been retired."

"Good idea. I was thinking I'd better work a feature angle, too. Some TV station is likely to beat us on any breaking stuff. We can—"

"Don't get beaten," Sam said. "You're the reporter who broke that page one Air Force story last summer. That's how you got this job, remember? Now get back on the phone or nose around the air bases there, find someone who worked the crash site. Where's that big source of yours from last year? Call me tonight after you file."

"Okay, I have to—"

Sam was gone again.

Jordan had been lucky last summer on that Air Force story. Jordan's high school catcher and friend had grown into a senior Air Force mechanic who knew dozens of pilots. Tim McCordy. He and Jordan had been playing golf last August when Tim told him that a missing fighter pilot was bipolar, with several erratic episodes in his past. So following the discovery of the crashed fighter plane, Jordan's tiny, practically unheard of online news page had been the first to print the truth: The Air Force pilot had most likely committed suicide by crashing his plane into a mountain.

There was a chance Tim might know something about this crashed B-52 and missing weapon as well. Jordan hadn't talked to his longtime friend in a few weeks, though this wasn't unusual. The Air Force sometimes sent Tim's crew all over the world if an emergency required top technicians.

There was no answer when he called, so Jordan sent an email and left a voice message. "Hey, Tim. It's Jordan. Hope your mom's doing better. I've been assigned to cover the B-52 crash at the Naval Air Facility in El Centro. If you know any pilots or ex-pilots who might know something—even just who I should talk to—I'd appreciate a call back. As usual, I'm offering two box seats at Dodger Stadium, whatever visiting team you want. Call me."

Jordan flipped on the hot water for a shower and unwrapped the paper around a scrap of hotel soap. This plane crash was a major assignment now. He'd be up against *The New York Times*, *The Associated Press*, *The Los Angeles Times*, and all of Southern California television, probably the networks for a day or two.

He adjusted the temperature and shifted under the stream of hot water. He felt ready for the challenge; maybe destined for it. He'd been a high school freshman when his family had died, the "little brother" of popular senior baseball star Ryan. At the time, Jordan figured the kids acted mad at him because he'd survived and Ryan hadn't. When Jordan grew up, he'd understood the kids hadn't been angry: They'd avoided him because they hadn't known what to say to an orphan. But by then the experience had already shaped Jordan into a lifelong observer—maybe the best raw material there was for a newsman.

SIX

Maggie found a solid patch of grass behind her El Centro apartment's oleander bushes. The space was over one hundred feet from her ten-unit apartment house's rear entrance, the legal distance from her building's smoke-free premises. The oleanders were lovely, too, the profuse blooms fire engine red. Two food-stinky garbage containers nearby provided the single drawback. Depending on the wind, or course. Maggie wondered sometimes if her whole life wasn't controlled by unseen air currents.

In the past she'd strolled on the sidewalk to smoke, always in her civilian clothes, usually wearing jeans and her Warrior-Airman-Wingman, Under Armour T-shirt, flagging back at people who drove by and waved, or even commented. Surprising how many strangers felt compelled to say something about her smoking, although Maggie had no problem with their disapproval. Hell, she wanted to stop smoking as much as anybody, but she was determined to quit her way, by reducing her cigarette consumption slowly over time. Sneers and jeers never had much effect on Maggie. Not once she'd made up her mind.

She slipped her BeBionic left hand into the opposed thumb position, selected the tripod grip to hold her cigarette and fired up another Marlboro Silver. It was only six-thirty, a bit early for number six of the seven smokes she'd planned to allow herself each day this month. But considering everything that had happened—the crash of the aircraft with Tony Pinella and four others aboard, the disappearance of her experimental weapon, the long drive to Edwards Air Force Base for Billy's semi-reasonable ream job—well, an extra cigarette or two didn't seem so bad.

Maybe not the Navy SEAL way, Maggie breaking her own rules and making excuses, showing a lack of discipline. But Maggie lived in the real world. A human world. And she owned some discipline. Enough to spare. Those freaking SEALs were crazy anyway. Especially the ones who'd chased her and a friend all over Berlin one weekend.

She punch-dialed the newest phone number on her BlackBerry.

"Hello?" the Air Force major said.

"Hey, Bob, it's Maggie. I know you would have called if anything turned up, but I figured I'd better check in anyway. You guys find anything this afternoon?"

"Just more remains, Maggie. No sign of your missile, shell or the payload."

Bob McKenzie was a redhead with freckles who easily qualified as one of the nicest guys on the base, really pitching in to help her since the crash. Today when Maggie had been called away, he'd handled all her personnel record-keeping responsibilities.

"When did you break off today's search?" Maggie said.

"About two hours ago. Everybody had been in the air since dawn."

Maggie drew on her Marlboro. Her lost experiment and the B-52 crash put the NAF rescue and recovery teams on permanent duty, or so it seemed. She imagined dozens of husbands and wives at home cursing Colonel Black's every new order. Maybe she should print up posters with her face imposed over a bullseye, sell them in the NAF parking lot. Could be a big money-maker.

Take a Whack at Bullseye Black.

"Thanks for covering my ass today," Maggie said, "and I hope you told those search and rescue crews how much the Air Force appreciates their extraordinary efforts. You and your wife, I owe a fancy dinner out. I'll be there tomorrow so you can get back to your regular duties. Six o'clock outside the flight center?"

"Yeah. I'm guessing the civilian crews had no luck today either?"

"No, not a sign," Maggie said. "And I can't imagine where the hell that cruise missile went. I'm open to suggestions. Anything."

Bob sighed. "That bastard fell straight down an old well, or somebody saw it and picked it up. My only two thoughts, Maggie."

"Not much else, is there?"

"I can't think of anything."

"Me either. Well, thanks again for your help. I'll see you tomorrow."

"See you."

Finishing her cigarette, Maggie's stomach rumbled. Obviously dinner was on her agenda, and maybe something good, something to take her mind off this tragedy and her sense of failure. Even for an hour; let her subconscious work on the problem. Maybe she'd have a finger or two Bushmills, too. She'd been drinking and eating primarily with the recovery crews—water, soft drinks, delivered sandwiches, salads, tacos, and pizza. She'd carried a few pieces of fresh fruit from home, but she longed for a delicious, relaxing meal. Her parents had taught Maggie to enjoy restaurants at a young age.

Maggie headed back inside her apartment and shed her uniform. Maybe after a shower, she'd drive to the one decent French restaurant in Imperial County. The chef there wouldn't make Maggie's favorite meal, *beouf bourguignon*, but he excelled at almost everything. Maybe tonight he'd prepare local chicken, or fresh seafood from San Diego.

Reporter Jordan Scott didn't really think Colonel Black would shoot him, but the idea crossed his mind. Because San Diego was home to all kinds of military, Jordan had interviewed dozens of admirals, colonels, and generals— more men than women, but plenty of both—and each had been humorless. They'd all wanted to control the interview, ask and answer the questions. Any of them would be extremely pissed at the surprise Jordan planned. And if she'd advanced over people like the kind Jordan had met, how tough was Maggie "Bullseye" Black? Tough enough to carry a weapon?

Jordan laughed and turned to the kid Terry beside him. "So...give me the vest."

Inside the French restaurant, waiting for the kid to hand him the sleeveless red waiter's shirt cover, Jordan mulled his plan. As always, the first rule of news reporting, you had to listen after you asked a question. Understand the answer. After that, the thing that got you noticed was persistence. When an individual, government agency or private institution stonewalled the media, ace reporters found a way through the brick and mortar.

Terry peeled off his red vest. But he kept the garment in his hand. "You're not some terrorist, right?"

One of the French restaurant's busboys, the kid had already taken fifty bucks from Jordan. Waiting for an answer to his terrorist question, Terry added, "You don't look much older than I am."

"Would you like to see my Sheriff Department's ID again?"

"The thing is, this is going to cost me the job. I know I said I was going quit anyway, but—"

"Let me guess," Jordan said. "Fifty bucks doesn't seem like enough."

Terry the horse-trader nodded.

Jordan dragged two more twenties from his wallet. It wasn't easy. They were heavy. He waved them in the air, refusing to hand them over until he had a solid grip on Terry's red vest. The material was hard and rough on his palm—like canvas. But with his own white dress shirt and black slacks, Terry's red vest made Jordan a perfect match for the restaurant's other servers. He hoped Colonel Maggie Black would appreciate his extraordinary efforts, give him a story.

Terry pointed with his forehead to a cork-lined waiter tray beside them in the busy kitchen. A single golden drink in a rocks glass and a bowl of mixed nuts took up a quarter of the tray's space. "That's her double Bushmills," Terry said. "She's sitting by herself at number twelve. The farthest table from the kitchen."

"She's wearing her Air Force uniform?"

"Yup. She's only a *Lieutenant* Colonel but you still call her Colonel."

"I know that."

Jordan lifted the tray with two hands, and marched into the dimly lighted dining area, the cork platter with the Colonel's drink and his own head held high.

Like he owned the place.

Maggie couldn't make up her mind. She'd come to Le Belle Ami having decided on her second-favorite dish—*poulet à la Provençale,* or chicken breast tenderloin sautéed with garlic, leeks, tomatoes, capers, and white wine. But Jacques, the chef and owner, offered a special tonight that sounded delicious—*truite aux amandes,* or fresh wild trout with almonds and brown butter, the mild but delicious rainbow trout allegedly caught this morning in the California Sierras and trucked to El Centro on ice for her dining pleasure.

Odd that she couldn't make a choice. What was the matter with her? Maybe she couldn't make up her mind because she had wanted another drink for ten minutes. Where the hell was that waiter with her Bushmills? She wheeled to stare at the kitchen doorway, and everything hit her, a mild temper flare becoming an ache in her chest, tear-filled eyes and invisible hands at her throat. Maggie blinked. And blinked again. She'd seen pieces of Tony and his crew at the crash site. Some you could tell what part of a human they'd been before, others you couldn't. Each and every one would torture her dreams for months or years. Maybe her lifetime. The smells today had been especially gruesome. Damn. Damn. Damn. She'd lost her virginity to a Casanova pig, Billy. She'd lost her hand, an F-15 fighter, and a top-rank career to a stray AK-47 bullet. And now she'd lost five lives and a multi-million project to a purple storm with copper lightning.

Where was her freaking Bushmills?

Maggie shook off the self-pity as she always did— with a focus on the now, a determination to keep putting one foot in front of the other. Screw the weapons program. Screw the congressmen. Screw trying to reclaim her double-crashed career. In fact, screw the Air Force if she had to. If she couldn't find that experimental weapon, she'd move on and find something better. Fly commercially maybe. She'd already earned her prosthetic waiver from the Flight Standards District Office in San Diego. In one way, Maggie was ready for a change. Flying combat for the military had been better than fun—her life's dream—but desk work, budgets, and personnel management sucked, even while working for the United States Air Force. Plus, she hadn't met a new man in two years who didn't look like a desert animal—hard-skinned, spiked, and poisonous.

Finally, her Bushmills appeared to be zooming in for a landing. A different waiter came through the doorway with her drink, this one older than the last kid but still young, and much more handsome, intriguing to Maggie in dark-rimmed glasses and longish hair. He made her smile, too, walking toward her table with a grin and the tray held high, carrying her drink like a court attendant bringing the queen her crown.

Jordan Scott used his grin as a mask. The woman's uniform and black glove gave Lieutenant Colonel Maggie Black a real military hard-ass look. Darn near *Dr. Strangelove*, Jordan being a fan of the old movie. And the Colonel couldn't have become an Air Force combat pilot being soft and gooey. It was a tough assignment, getting this battle-hardened woman to talk, but Jordan knew his only weapon was charm. He maintained the wide smile as he set down her drink and nuts.

He'd worked the phones all day. Nothing had turned up until his friend Tim McCordy called back. Tim said a one-armed, female Iraq combat pilot named Bullseye

Black had visited Brigadier General Billy Boy Payton at Edwards that day, Tim knowing this personally because his F-15 mechanic crew was stationed back home at Edwards this month. Tim had seen Colonel Black himself when she'd once checked out the new F-35s. She was cute, like everybody said, but kind of old. From other pilots, Tim learned Colonel Black was in charge of the experiment the B-52 had been testing when it crashed, and also that both the experiment and Colonel Black were stationed at the Naval Air Facility in El Centro. She'd been called on the carpet before General Payton that day, the rumor was, General Payton being the boss of all Air Force weapons research. Tim didn't know what the B-52 had been about to test, but he'd sure pointed Jordan to the person who could. All Jordan had to do then was find this Colonel Maggie Black.

Jordan had read four newspaper profiles of Margaret Black that afternoon, including two from 2003 when she'd been a relatively rare female combat pilot. Two stories mentioned she hated cooking. One claimed she practiced judo and loved eating out, especially at French restaurants. A story about her research in the *El Centro Gazette* a year ago also mentioned French cooking.

Sure, it was a long shot Colonel Black would be dining in a French restaurant that night, but then again Tim's information suggested she'd probably had her ass chewed good by her boss that day—after a long trip to Edwards, too—so why not try a few joints? There were two authentic French places in El Centro, another in the neighboring town of Brawley. Jordan found her on the third try, within sixteen minutes of beginning his telephone calls. "Excuse me, ma'am (or sir), did my big sister Colonel Black make us reservations tonight?"

Now, four hours after hearing her name, Jordan stood beside Colonel Black's table at La Belle Amie restaurant. He didn't expect a detailed explanation of what the Air Force searched for in the Fish Creek Mountains. But the Air Force's statement that they'd lost something "classified but non-nuclear" no longer passed the sniff test, not with Jordan, his editor Sam Carson, or much of Southern California's population. All Jordan hoped for was some proof the weapon wasn't nuclear. That would be news.

Colonel Black stared at him. She was much better looking than the snapshots he'd seen online. Pretty blue eyes. And she didn't look that old to him. What was his friend Tim talking about? She frowned when Jordan plopped in the seat across from her.

"Sorry to bother you, Colonel Black, but my name's Jordan Scott. I'm a reporter with *The San Diego Sun-Times.* Will you tell me, on or off the record, what kind of experiment was aboard that crashed B-52 bomber?"

"Your name is Jordan Scott?" Colonel Black tilted her head quizzically, deepening a small line in the center of her forehead. Her chin, a sharp V, protruded an extra half-inch, reminding Jordan of that ruler queen elf in the first *Lord of the Rings* movie—Galadriel.

"Yup," he said. "That's me."

Why had Colonel Black repeated his name? Did she know him? Maybe she'd read one of his stories about the crash, seen his byline. That made sense. Most people never noticed bylines but Colonel Black was involved with the crashed plane and might have paid attention. She looked smart, too—like she remembered things. She stared at him.

"Scott with two tees." He smiled and tried to be otherwise appealing, a technique that along with his gentle demeanor worked better for him at gathering information than confrontational or ambush-style journalism. Jordan befriended and relaxed people into talking too much. He didn't bully them.

The Colonel clasped her Bushmills and lifted, pausing with the rim at her lips. "I've never heard of you, or *The San Diego Sun-Times.*"

SEVEN

Colonel Black's skepticism caught Jordan off guard. Or was she poking fun? A smirk twisted one corner of her mouth. He glanced around the semi-dark restaurant, admiring the softly lighted, post-impressionist artwork on the papered walls, Jordan stalling until he recalled a phrase he'd heard his editor use: "Thirteen Pulitzers over the last half century. We cover Southern California from the desert to the sea."

Colonel Black grunted, but beneath the sweep of hair that covered half her forehead, the Colonel's eyes sparkled. Individually, her features weren't spectacular—the mouth too large, the nose shaped like a ski-jump—but taken together, most men would call Colonel Black pretty, especially when she smiled. Wasn't Cate Blanchett the actress who had played Galadriel? There *was* a resemblance, at least when the actress was younger. Maybe the Colonel's features seemed unspectacular to others because she wore little or no make-up.

"Let me ask you a question," she said. "Who told you I knew anything about that crashed Stratofortress?"

"A friend of mine in the Air Force."

"What's her name?"

"It's a him and I promised him anonymity. Try to say that three times fast."

"Where's he stationed?"

"I can't tell you," Jordan said. "But his motives aren't bad. He's not trying to hurt the Air Force. Like everybody else on this planet, Colonel, my source wants to know what the hell disappeared from that bomber."

"I'm sorry, young man, but you'll have to get your information from the people at Edwards Air Force Base. I believe there's a General William Payton in charge."

"So it *was* a nuke, wasn't it?" Jordan said.

"No, it was not."

"Convince me."

Colonel Black chuckled, then tasted her Irish whiskey again. Jordan liked her easy laugh, the obvious sense of humor. The woman was remarkably relaxed and comfortable for a lieutenant colonel in the United States Air Force, at least in his experience. When the Colonel smiled, showing lots of gum above her small white teeth, even the rows of medals on her uniform seemed friendly. The *Dr. Strangelove* image had faded fast, despite the black glove on her left hand.

She said, "How is it that a twenty-something reporter for a San Diego paper tracks me down at dinner, but *The New York Times*, *Newsweek*, and fifty other reporters don't even know I exist?"

"I have good Air Force connections," he said. "Long tentacles that reach—"

"Big testicles did you say?"

Jordan laughed with her. He liked Colonel Black.

Colonel Maggie. He liked her a lot. He could imagine her being popular in any group of soldiers or people, male or female, young and old. She was warm and open and honest; probably too old for him, yeah, but he could see himself asking her out, giving her a shot. That she hadn't sent him away yet suggested she might be enjoying his company, too. Now was the time to steer her back toward the lost missile, the missing experiment and Jordan's story.

"I'm serious about you convincing me the missing weapon isn't nuclear," he said. "Explain to me why it can't be. If I could understand why *you* believe that, I could convince our readers and maybe calm some of the fear that's keeping kids out of school."

It was true. His paper had reported more than two thousand Imperial and San Diego County school children had stayed home from school Monday and Tuesday. Experimental weapons were a frightening subject, especially when millions of Americans no longer trusted their own government and the military. Jordan didn't agree with that fear, but he understood it.

Colonel Maggie rattled the ice in her empty second drink. "I wasn't honest before. I read one of your pieces in the *Sun-Times* earlier this week. It was clearly written, at least. And generally fair, although you could have explained why it's important for our country's military to test their weapons in secrecy. People forget our enemies read the news and watch television."

Jordan nodded. He sensed momentum shift in his favor. When Colonel Maggie turned to wave for a waiter—the lady could hold her whiskey—Jordan yanked his narrow reporter's notebook from his back pocket.

"Let's put the next round on a new tab," Colonel Maggie said to the waiter. She pointed her finger at Jordan. "His tab. Mr. Scott, give this young man your credit card, please, your drink order if you're having something, and perhaps that silly vest as well."

Jordan had forgotten. He glanced down at La Belle Amie engraved over his heart.

"You don't need it, do you? Or is there someone else here you wanted to barge in on?"

Ninety minutes later, using her gloved artificial hand to hold her credit card receipt, Colonel Maggie Black signed with a tight, polished script. Jordan paid his own list of charges, and noticed his signature erupted outside the rectangular box. He wondered who showed the worse personality disorder.

They'd split the eighty-five-dollar check, even though Colonel Maggie had Bushmills, trout, and white wine. Jordan had consumed two beers. Sam would cancel his expense account.

"I'd better not see my name in the paper," Colonel Maggie said. "If I do, there'll be B-52s flying over *your* house. Understand?"

"A highly placed Air Force source?" he said.

"No good."

"A high-ranking military officer?"

"How about military source," she said.

"Military source with knowledge of the experiment, you have a deal."

She scowled. "I suppose that's vague enough."

Jordan rose when Colonel Maggie did. She offered her right hand and gripped his fingers like a man, not a lady or the iron worker he'd half-expected. Colonel Maggie was tough, a real soldier, a *leader* of soldiers. But the woman had a figure underneath that uniform, and when her grin flashed pink gums at him, she was all woman.

"You are a charming young fellow, Mr. Jordan Scott. But I would prefer we have no further contact. Please don't call me at the base or leave messages with your name attached, understood?"

"Of course."

Maggie picked up her purse. Big, black, and heavy, Jordan wondered if she packed a pistol. He had to believe she did. Most likely her weapon would be the common military sidearm these days, a Beretta M9. Or maybe Colonel Maggie carried a .357 Magnum like *Dirty Harry*. He could believe almost anything about Colonel Maggie Black. What a piece of work. Smart and well-traveled, at least compared to Jordan, this lady in the blue uniform was also a pretty stick of dynamite. Jordan glowed inside, getting a good story tonight and being won over by this Colonel Maggie person. Maybe he should have passed on the second beer. Because of his alcoholic father, Jordan had never been much of a drinker. Glowing over sources wasn't good.

Colonel Maggie stared into his eyes. "I hope my trust in you is well-placed."

"It is, ma'am."

"Goodbye then, Mr. Scott. Thanks for paying half."

Jordan waited until the Colonel left the restaurant before taking out his cell phone. He speed-dialed the newspaper in San Diego and Sam Carson's extension. The paper's evening deadline had passed, but his editor might be working late tonight for the online edition. Jordan captured a deep breath.

"Do *not* tell me you have a story," Carson said.

"If the lost missile carried a nuclear device, they would have found the thing in minutes," Jordan said. "They can pick up that kind of radioactivity from the air now."

"*The New York Times* published that yesterday."

"They speculated. Okay, how about this—Southern California, especially the border area, is full of very sensitive, privately run nuclear detection equipment. At least four local private companies have monitoring contracts with dozens of detection sites near the border. I have names, locations. There's no way a nuclear bomb could stay secret this long."

"Who told you this?"

"An Air Force colonel involved with the missing experiment. I believe her, Sam."

"Can we use her name?"

"No. But this is good info. No nukes."

"What the hell is it then?"

"It's an old cruise missile, a version especially suitable

for this Air Force experiment, and that's also why they were using the old B-52. Stratofortresses, or B-52s, are already fitted for this type of air-to-ground cruise missile. An AGM."

"If it's not a nuke, what's inside this AMG or whatever? What's the weapon?"

"My source won't tell me—yet. But she knows. I think she built it. And she likes me. Give me another day, I'll find out what that missile was carrying."

"Damn," Carson said. "Okay, give me fifteen hundred words on the private nuke detection locations and the missile. And email your copy directly to me."

Behind her tall, silent, and poisonous friends, the red oleanders, Maggie smoked her last cigarette of the day. What a coincidence seeing Jordan Scott's byline that morning then having the man hunt her down inside an El Centro restaurant that night. The guy was an old-fashioned reporter. Knew how to work the phones. And the internet, apparently. That old interview she did with *Newsweek* with the French restaurant quote had come back to haunt her again.

In this case, maybe haunt wasn't the right word. She had to admit she'd enjoyed talking with Jordan Scott. She puffed her smoke. Actually, Jordan not only ranked high on Maggie's list of semi-fair journalists—at least as far as her lost-missile story went—but the young man was *really* hunky. She liked the glasses and scruffy five-o'clock shadow and his dark blue eyes, the way he combed his longish hair now and then with his fingers. His black sports jacket hung well on his shoulders, too. Washed, fitted clothes. Clean hair and hands. Jordan cared what he looked like.

Kid had a decent ass in those slacks, too.

She laughed. Jordan had to be ten years younger. And such a charmer, like her Uncle Dennis. The kind she always fell for. She smiled remembering her fourteenth birthday, how her father's younger brother promised something special and delivered big time by taking Maggie up in his Cessna, letting her actually work the controls. The beauty of flying, the endless freedom and choice of movement had thrilled her, changed her life, really. Like a bird, she'd been bound by nothing on earth but her heart and her will.

Good old Uncle Dennis. A charmer, but not really like Jordan. Her Uncle Dennis Black was a mutual fund wholesaler, wining and dining investment firms' big hitters, earning a percentage of the assets he collected for his money management company. Rich and handsome, Dennis was a playboy—even at sixty—and though Maggie loved her uncle and the smart, beautiful younger women he sometimes brought to Christmas dinner, Jordan seemed a different kind of man.

Jordan must know how old she was. Her graduation info had been included in two of those old interviews and news stories. He probably considered her a great news source, but personally like an older aunt. Or something worse. Or maybe she was being too hard on herself. Jordan had definitely stared at her a couple of times that night, gazed at her the way men do. That casual but completely physical appraisal.

Eyes to ankles.

EIGHT

Near dawn, Torres surrendered any hope of sleep. Though home in his own El Centro bed and pleased his digestive troubles associated with the *toloache* had worn off, his mind worried. What had been real last weekend and what had not? He claimed as prizes only visions of a rather famous Hopi kachina—Nastaska, the Black Ogre—two bloody murders, and a strange dream about ancient Lake Cahuilla.

Perhaps he had badly prepared the *toloache*. That he, the half-breed child of a white man, had been chosen for the important and sacred task of refilling Lake Cahuilla, well, to put it mildly, the proposition seemed ridiculous. Even were such a thing true, he couldn't imagine in a practical way how to proceed. In those first moments out of bed, the weekend's events seemed preposterous.

As per his routine, he made coffee then selected his clothes for work, matching a UCLA regimental-striped tie with a plain white dress shirt and the gold threads in his favorite blue Canali suit. He laid out his choices on the bed, drank two cups of coffee, then woke himself completely under a hot-then-cold shower.

The telephone rang as he toweled himself in the bedroom. It was his tribal chief and friend, Reynaldo.

"Eddie Ordonez and his cousin ran off from their grandmother's house in Ocotillo Friday," Reynaldo said. "They're probably sleeping off the tequila with whores in Mexicali, but if the boys don't show up at school today, or don't call home this morning, I'd like you to lead a search party."

Ordonez. Yes, that had been the boys' family name. Torres knew he'd recognized them from the reservation. While it had been unnecessarily wicked to kill those young men, as explanation to himself, Torres believed angry spirits near the offended elephant trees had used him as a tool for revenge. The boys should not have urinated on those ancient and sacred plants.

"I can't ask anyone but you to lead the search," Reynaldo said. "Eddie's mother thinks they went into the badlands hunting for elephant trees, and you know where they grow."

"Of course I will help," Torres said. "Let's hope they were not caught in a canyon during this weekend's violent storms. A dozen flash floods ripped through the desert Friday and Saturday. As is often the case, it could be their bodies are never found."

"Let's hope they show up this morning. If not, and we search, remind me afterward that I have something truly amazing to show you. Something unrelated to the Ordonez boys."

"What is it?"

"I want to surprise you. See the look on your face."

* * *

Monday through Friday, Torres was equipment department manager for his father's private business, Woodward Construction Company. The job was his because Asdrubal Torres was a bastard son of the owner, Woody Woodward, and because a handsome salary came in lieu of daddy's name or love.

Only two or three people knew the address of his rented two-bedroom apartment in town, and only Reynaldo had visited. Torres wasn't a particularly popular person. His love of silence and solitude were qualities uncherished by most Americans or even the visiting foreigners he'd met. Thus, the sight of Reynaldo waiting at his door following their afternoon search for the missing boys surprised him, though not as much as what Reynaldo held in his sinewy arms.

The tightly woven Cahuilla basket, a perfect circle, was easily larger than the circumference of an automobile tire. Torres had seen a California Indian basket of such size only once before, on a college excursion to the Southwestern Museum in Los Angeles.

"What is *this*?" Torres said.

"The surprise I told you about, my friend. Chaco Cruz's water basket. The legendary magic that created today's Salton Sea."

Dizziness nearly pushed Torres to his knees. Reynaldo knew Torres often spent weekends on vision quests for knowledge. They had shared an interest in such things and Cahuilla history since they'd been teenagers. But there was no way Reynaldo could know about the events of last weekend, the visions that still engulfed Torres' thoughts. Was there?

"How could this be?"

"Ha. You should see the look on your face," Reynaldo said.

Torres could only gape and wonder.

"I do not know why," Reynaldo said, "but the basket has returned. And though we are both tired from the search today, let us go inside your apartment. I want to show you these markings."

Reynaldo set his prize down on Torres's kitchen table. What a gift from the Great Spirit, should Reynaldo be correct. This basket was exactly the thing Torres needed for the attempted recreation of ancient Lake Cahuilla. He should never have doubted the weekend's experiences.

Torres touched the rim of the century-old container. The basket was woven of sumac with black images constructed of the same wood, but dyed with elderberry like other Cahuilla baskets he had seen. The drawings clearly told a story. No one depiction matched another, yet all showed men handling a large basket—apparently a miniature image of the giant basket resting before them.

Reynaldo pointed at several markings. "Like the legend says, the illustrations on the basket are specific instructions on how to carry out the basket's purpose."

Torres nodded.

Reynaldo touched his arm, a familiarity to which Torres normally would have objected. Elation about the basket so gripped him, however, he squeezed his chief's forearm in return. The visions of the past weekend were not false. The death of those boys had involved a rich purpose. Their wicked deaths were part of the Great Spirit's plan.

He lifted Reynaldo's hand from his arm. "Do you understand what this means?"

"It's incredible history for our children," Reynaldo said.

Torres stared at his tribal brother, his chief. His feet would not be still. He leveled a finger at the basket of Chaco Cruz and two sets of stickman images. "See how these men fill the basket in one location and then, over here, dump out the water in another?"

"Of course," Reynaldo said. "And are these markings not clues to each location? These look like ocean waves."

"To recreate Chaco Cruz's magic, we would have to be exact."

"What are you talking about? Recreate his magic?"

Torres smiled. "Just a dream. Let's discuss it later. I want to know where this basket came from."

Reynaldo shrugged. "A young man named Jordan Scott showed up at the tribal office and claimed his great grandfather worked for the railroad during the flood in 1906 and '07. He said the old man admitted to his ancestors the basket had been stolen."

Torres shut his eyes. Chaco Cruz's water basket had to be his. The basket's magical reappearance meant the refilling of ancient Lake Cahuilla was not a *toloache-*

induced dream, but a goal actually within his reach. The Great Spirit would not have sent the prize were it not meant for him, Asdrubal Torres. He could not tolerate any interference either. Would his friend and chief have the stomach for what Torres had been chosen to accomplish?

How deeply should he take Reynaldo into his confidence? His plan to refill Lake Cahuilla might cheer his sad friend. As clan chief, the Ordonez boys' mothers had counted on Reynaldo to locate their missing children.

"We must study the basket and these images carefully," Torres said. "I had a vision this past weekend that may help explain the basket's reappearance. Let me make fresh coffee. I will call in sick to work. In fact, perhaps the time has come for that vacation my father keeps suggesting I take."

Torres answered his cell phone ten minutes later. His father's secretary.

Before answering, Torres waved at Reynaldo. "Please do not leave. This won't take much time. My father."

"Where the hell were you all day?" his father said.

"The dentist."

"All day?"

"I had four cavities and a crown fitting." Torres winked at Reynaldo.

"Jeez. Well, we need you here. No vacations either."

"Why not?"

"The Air Force needs a bunch of crap and we can't

translate your written-in-Greek equipment schedules. I need to figure out which construction sites I can pull the equipment from."

"What kind of equipment?"

"Boom lifts, trucks."

"What's going on?"

"Something to do with that crashed bomber."

"Crashed bomber?" Torres glanced at his friend Reynaldo. So, the low-flying aircraft this past weekend had not been a vision, a product of his *toloache*. He had begun to assume otherwise, although the basket's arrival should have warned him.

"Don't you watch the news?" his father said. "An old B-52 went down in the storm. Some kind of a military test."

"I have already spent considerable funds on my travel plans," Torres said. He had always been an excellent liar, probably a genetic gift his father. "You told me to take time off so I am leaving for Tokyo tomorrow."

Torres wondered what kind of test the lost plane had carried.

"You're going nowhere until the Air Force is through with us," his father said. "General Billy Payton called me himself. I do him a favor, maybe we get the next construction contract at Edwards. Now get your ass in here."

As his father ended the call, Torres recalled an image from that magical night. He'd seen the plane touch a mountain, the contact tilting those enormous wings, diverting the aircraft's direction. The steel beast he'd first imagined to be a hungry bird had traveled miles and miles before crashing into a second desert peak.

Torres unrolled a topographical map on his kitchen table and covered the city of Yuma with the tip of his index finger. His gesture blocked the intersection of Arizona, California, both states' Mexican borders, and the Colorado River. From Yuma, he traced a line west into California. His finger slid past the Imperial Sand Dunes to a desolate stretch of Highway 8 alongside the All-American Canal, an eighty-mile-long aqueduct that delivered Colorado River water exclusively to California's Imperial Valley.

"Here," Torres said.

Reynaldo studied the map intently. He seemed to instinctively understand the channel's importance, how the canal sustained half a million acres of prime farmland and was literally the world's largest irrigation ditch. More than twenty-six thousand cubic feet of water flowed through the channel every second, a current strong enough to drown dozens of would-be immigrants from Mexico every year.

"What do you mean?" Reynaldo said.

Torres tapped his finger twice, calling Reynaldo's attention to one Highway 8 turnoff that lead only to an All-American Canal service road. "Here is the place I think we should strike."

"Strike?" Reynaldo said. "Strike what?"

Reynaldo bent forward, briefly dropping his long

silver hair beside his face, blocking Torres's view of the chief's hawkish eyes, cheeks and his craggy but majestic nose. If only the chief's heart were as fierce as his appearance.

"We want to close the All-American Canal," Torres said.

Reynaldo straightened at the waist. "The canal is heavily patrolled. We could be imprisoned. And for what? This brings us no closer to carrying out the basket's instructions. Is this quest of yours truly a path with heart?"

"Of course it is," Torres said. "And by damaging the All-American Canal, we will force its temporary closure, thereby directing greater quantities of water south. We will be able to work the basket's magic near where our great grandfathers did. This marking on the basket clearly shows a white man's construction, a wooden dam. They gathered the Colorado River water from where the dam broke—the Mexican cut."

"Are you certain? These markings seem to be ocean waves."

"Yes, and they lie between the pick-up spot and the dumping ground. It will require time to understand, though not long. The Great Spirit has already been generous."

"Chaco's magic might be worth a shot, but how would you disrupt the All-American Canal."

"A bomb."

"Plant a bomb on the All-America Canal? We know nothing of such things."

"It will be dangerous, of course."

Reynaldo frowned. "How could we possibly acquire the explosives?"

"You know I work for Woodward Construction company. There is an inventory of such things."

"In today's world they are closely guarded. Even for you, the owner's son."

Thunder cracked. Rain hammered the tile roof of Torres' Spanish-style apartment complex. "I will talk to Henry. He can easily obtain knowledge of nitro-based dynamite, and how to prepare, place, and discharge a device. He claims to have the basic skills already. Our employer provides everything, including drilling equipment that will allow us to place the explosives deeply enough to damage the canal."

Reynaldo stared at him, motionless like a hunting egret. "How will you deal with the canal's security? You know I oppose violence. The Border Patrol will never let you set up drilling equipment."

"We will carry no weapons, I assure you. We will gain access through official paperwork, everything arranged with the canal operator. You will see. There will be no violence."

"Yours is a fine dream, Asdrubal, but only a dream," Reynaldo said. "A century ago, it took almost three years for the river to fill today's Salton Sea. Ancient Lake Cahuilla would take a half a century or more to replenish."

"Why not follow the instructions on the basket and see what happens?" Torres said. "Let the water spirits struggle with the impossible. Perhaps, as was the case over a century ago, the white man will make another mistake."

NINE

The twin-engine Chinook helicopter served as Maggie's workplace again the next morning, her team scouring Southern California's low desert from the Carrizo Badlands north to the Fish Creek Mountains. But the object of their hunt—the Air Force's vanished precision-strike, air-to-ground cruise missile—continued to evade detection. Colonel Maggie Black's flying bomb was Absent Without Leave.

On lunch break, Maggie and the Chinook's various crews enjoyed semi-edible Mexican food prepared and packaged for them back at the NAF facility. Maggie had given up on her under-spiced chicken tostado and gazed longingly at the ten-gallon stainless steel coffee pot tucked in a corner of the open-sided mess tent when an email buzzed her thigh. *Jordan?* How the hell had the reporter gotten her email address? She thought about deleting him, but read the message instead. He asked if Maggie would call him back when she had a few minutes. He needed "clarification" on something she'd said.

Maggie stuffed the phone in her khakis. Time for coffee, not young handsome reporters. She needed to worry about her missile and figure out where the hell her weapon could have gone. If the experiment had exploded, there should be some trace, and she needed that proof. She was obliged to find *something*, even the tiniest of pieces. By today's estimate, nearly ninety percent of the debris field had been collected, packed, and trucked to Edwards.

Maggie grabbed a paper cup and worked the ten-gallon coffee urn handle. What would she do for a paycheck if the Air Force forced her retirement? The pension wouldn't be much. As her cup filled with brown liquid, Maggie imagined Jordan's blue eyes—like deep ocean water. She brushed the vision away, but saw his eyes again as she sipped the fresh coffee. What was it with that guy? Did he think his eyes were so blue and pretty he could call an Air Force colonel at work?

She slapped a white plastic top on her cup and lugged her coffee outside the mess tent to a smokers patio the size of a ping pong table. She hesitated two more minutes, lighting her third Marlboro of the day and enjoying a few puffs. Jordan Scott. The man had some nerve. The man had some blue eyes. She punched in the telephone number he'd given her, Maggie knowing her private line would no longer be private.

"Oh, hey," Jordan said. "Thanks for calling me, Colonel. I forgot what a great voice you have. You could do radio or—"

"What did you need me to clarify, Mr. Scott? I'm very busy."

"Well, it's a bit awkward, so I'm just going to blurt it out, okay?"

Oh my God, what was he going to say?

"When we said goodbye last night, you smiled at me," Jordan said, "and well, I felt something. You know, like a spark."

"Gack." Maggie spit a mouthful of coffee onto the patio's cement slab. The one other smoker stared at her.

"Are you okay?" Jordan said.

She gasped. "Sorry. I gagged on my coffee. I don't think I could have possibly understood what you said. Correctly, I mean."

"I said I felt a spark, as in maybe we liked each other. Feelings, you know. An attraction. Maybe if—"

"I think you might want to get yourself tested for drugs, Jordan. Someone might have poisoned you."

"You didn't feel anything…at all?"

She *had* felt it. Definitely. "I'm sorry, but no. I did not."

Jordan sighed with exaggerated disappointment. What a ham. But then hadn't she answered his question a bit too quickly. A little over-acting herself? Of course she had. The timing was terrible, but this thing with Jordan was interesting. No matter what happened between them from here, she hadn't had this much fun with the opposite sex in a long time. He was strange young man. He made her laugh.

"It surprises me you'd say you felt nothing," Jordan said, "because I'm pretty sure you were flirting with me last night. That was a *very* friendly smile you gave me.

Plus, you just called me Jordan."

Maggie nearly gagged again, but she managed to twist her throat into a cough.

"Did you choke again?" he said.

"Excuse me, Mr. Scott, but I have work to do. This conversation will have to wait."

"So you admit there's something to talk about? Why don't we have dinner tonight? Same place, same time."

"I'm too busy. And frankly, I don't think I'm interested." That gave him a little rope if not hope.

"I've been thinking about your missing weapon," he said. "I have an idea or two that might interest your staff."

"No. It's inappropriate we talk about Air Force matters, let alone see each other socially. I'm sorry, Jor—Mr. Scott. You must excuse me."

"Maggie, wait. Let me—"

She disconnected and for the next few hours ignored his calls and texts. He quit trying around three-thirty while she was back up searching in the Chinook. Okay, the man was cute, smart and more than a little sexy. But Maggie had to be ten years older. Most important, there was no way Jordan was romantically interested in her or any woman in her very late thirties. The guy was a newspaper reporter, out for a story. Simple as that. Who did she think she was, some movie star? She wasn't a real woman he wanted to charm. For newspaper ace Jordan Scott, Colonel Maggie Black was just another news source.

She'd called it from the beginning: Jordan was a

charmer like Uncle Dennis. The guy wanting information as well as—whatever. She had to admit his attentions were fun. Exciting and stimulating, for sure. Those blue eyes had been convincing about his attraction at the restaurant. If she were honest, Jordan made her feel young—and sexy.

She hoped he hadn't given up.

Maggie visited an El Centro sporting goods store on the way home from her NAF office, bought herself one of those fold-up canvas and aluminum soccer-mom chairs. The liquor store also earned a place on her itinerary, Maggie snagging a new bottle of Bushmills and an extra pack of Marlboro Silvers. The desert weather had turned oddly cooler, and her plan for the night included sitting outside behind the bloody oleanders again to drink Irish whiskey, smoke cigarettes, and not go to bed until she'd deduced, inferred or otherwise extrapolated into which rabbit hole her experiment had fallen. Time was running out for Maggie Black and her Air Force career. Billy Payton would call in a few days, tell her someone else was taking over the search, probably the FBI. The local news media had juiced their coverage of the plane crash since the lost-weapon angle had been revealed, and now every morning brought new imagined disasters, the latest involving school children, buses, and the upcoming senior prom season.

* * *

Touring the Borrego Badlands, inside a sandy and flat dry wash, Henry edged the six-wheel tow truck around sandstone boulders and narrow gullies. The ultraviolet lantern Torres held out the passenger's window cast a lavender glow on the arroyo's rugged sides. Two coyotes yapped at them steadily, stalking the truck from bush to bush above the wash.

"They seem to be following us," Torres said.

"If they do not stop soon, I will kill them."

Henry was in a bad mood, probably because he didn't believe Torres about finding an experimental weapon. He'd expressed numerous and compelling doubts. Hopefully, Henry's suspicions would soon be appeased.

Torres had used Google Maps to locate his position last weekend when he'd witnessed the plane crash. By marking the plane's wreckage site, a common map in the newspapers this past week, and then connecting the two dots, he'd easily figured out which jagged peak had touched the aircraft's left wing prior to the crash. That's what he believed he'd seen anyway. It was possible the *toloache* had altered his perception.

But by accepting as a given that the missing weapon had been knocked loose during, or because of, that earlier contact, Henry had easily formulated a reasonable search area surrounding that jagged peak. The wash they hunted with ultraviolet lanterns had been dead center of Henry's marked plot, and likely the only chance of recovery, since removal by the six-wheeled, boom lift tow truck required flat entry and exit. Henry thought finding the lost weapon any place but on this sandy mountain plateau would make theft impossible. Certainly for tonight, probably for good.

The pale bluish light made travel slow, but Henry believed government satellites could not detect the ultraviolet light. They could see flashlights from space, he said, but not these ultraviolet shadows. Torres wondered if the Great Spirit would provide for him again. First the Ordonez boys to be sacrificed, the vision of Nataska, the plane and the basket delivered to his door. Of course he had been chosen. But would the Great Spirit continue to meet his every need?

They searched an area twelve miles from the plane's crash site, and more than two miles from any government hunting party to date. Torres knew what he had seen, but could the government experts be so wrong, searching the Carrizo Badlands when he looked inside the Anza-Borrego's?

"What are the chances we'll find the weapon intact?" Torres said.

"Slim to none. We're almost at the end of our prime search area."

"Even if it landed on one of these sand hills?"

"At two hundred miles an hour, I don't think it matters what the missile landed on."

Their ultraviolet lights bloomed against the dunes and the rocks, bouncing shadows that glowed shades of blue and pink as the big truck rumbled forward. The visual stimulation resembled that of a powerful *toloache*, and Torres wondered briefly if he had eaten too much elephant tree bark over the years, if these strange colors were in fact hallucinations that would always be with him.

"If there is no hope that the missile could be un-damaged," Torres said, "why did you agree to help me search?"

Henry's hand shot out and slapped Torres in the chest.

Torres pressed back against the truck seat. Henry's love of physical violence was well known in their special circle. But, no—Henry wanted him only to stop talking and look up ahead on the left: Something pulsed and changed shape, billowing huge and then shrinking, like a giant purple jellyfish.

The huge creature glowed otherworldly in Torres's ultraviolet lantern, the bulk of its bulging shape tucked under a twenty-foot outcropping of flat rock near the bank of the arroyo. The glowing purple mass had pulled itself inside the tunnel-shaped rock pile, visible only to Henry and Torres in the arroyo.

"Holy crap," Henry said.

"What is it?"

"We had no chance to find the experiment unbroken unless it carried automatically deploying parachutes."

Torres stared at the rolling, changing shape inside the rock cave. Night wind from the opposite direction kept the white parachutes partially inflated, and when the silky sheets billowed and heaved in the wind, the ultraviolet light from Torres's lantern did indeed create the image of a giant purple jellyfish.

***

Henry showed him both pieces of a broken cruise missile that had been dragged beneath the hollowed-out outcropping. Although more time would be required to load two segments with the boom lift, two smaller units were easier to conceal. One section would slide snugly inside the F550's bed while the other hung suspended by the boom. Tarps and stretch tie-downs, which Henry had thought to bring, would conceal the cargo.

"Is this gift from the Great Spirit familiar to you?" Torres said.

"Sure," Henry said. "You have found us a cruise missile, an old AGM, or air-to-ground version, but with a booster, which it should not have. It's definitely an experiment. And most wonderfully, the missile contains a truly gigantic payload of new military explosives. We could blow up a five-story building."

Torres smiled back at Henry's grin. His new friend from the Indigenous Peoples Liberation Army was scary—the combination of size, strength, and hate—but if his claims of knowledge and special forces experience were real, not boast, Henry's interest in his missile and Lake Cahuilla project was yet another gift from the spirits. Like Torres, Henry's mother also had been part Hopi, and the two men had encountered one another at the IPLA's secret first meeting a year earlier, then became friendly after discovering their mutual heritage. Three months ago, when Henry had been released from prison, the IPLA group had pressured Torres to find Henry a job at Woodward Construction.

Henry tossed him a set of keys. "You turn the truck around and I will attach a chain around our prize. We should leave as quickly as possible."

They were on their way home an hour before sunrise.

TEN

Maggie spent the last of her cash at the liquor store, so she added the bank to her list of errands. Being single and responsible meant taking care of yourself and your money. She'd learned to save by putting aside cash every paycheck for her BeBionic, and she'd continued the practice ever since.

Her errands finished, Maggie parked her Air Force car under her apartment. She needed to find the freaking missile, figure where the hell it was. That turkey was *not* in the debris field of the B-52 crash and it was *not* in the surrounding Southern California desert. She felt like she'd eyeballed every square mile. According to the app she'd bought in conjunction with the topography charts, she'd personally searched over two hundred square miles. Was that even possible?

Maggie carried her new chair, a fat wallet, and the bottle of Irish whiskey into her apartment. She exchanged her stiff Air Force uniform and stiffer bra for a pair of well-worn, relaxed-fit jeans and an extra-large Dodgers T-shirt. She hadn't been to a professional baseball game in three years, not since her father bought tickets and suggested she meet him in Los Angeles. He'd taken her once a week the summer she was nine and Mom had been sick. Maggie still loved the game, rooted for the LA Dodgers and Gina's little league team, Gina being the daughter of Franny, an El Centro friend.

Maggie poured herself a tall drink with lots of ice instead of water so she wouldn't have to traipse back inside the apartment for a while. She carried her new folding chair and the tumbler of Bushmills outside like she was going on a picnic. A solitary picnic on the patch of grass by the poisonous bush and a smelly dumpster.

Halfway through the drink, when she first felt the alcohol's muscle-relaxing effects, she realized the booze meant she was out of ideas on her lost missile. She and her staff chased what evidence and sources they could— she had one good lead—but Maggie wanted new ideas, new directions in which to point her mind. She immediately began an internal debate. Should she? Or shouldn't she? She'd have to play the game very cool, or he'd think she was falling for his charms.

Was she?

She opened her BlackBerry and called Jordan. Dust filtered her view of the sky. The air tasted slightly of fertilizer.

"Hey, Maggie!"

She liked the warm surprise in Jordan's voice, the fact he'd left Colonel out when addressing her. "You said you had an idea or two about my missing experiment," she said, "and I need a good one for sure, Jordan Scott. That missile disappeared like it flew off to Guatemala."

Maggie placed her glass of Bushmills on the grass.

Jeez. Her tongue sounded loosey goosey. Maybe she needed a few deep breaths. Or maybe calling Jordan had been the worst idea she'd ever had. What had she been thinking?

Torres watched in fascination. By Googling simple words and examining the various images available, Henry showed him his gift from the Great Spirit was an out-of-service Boeing AGM-86C, or subsonic, air-to-ground cruise missile.

Henry lifted the canvas tarp from what looked like a broken, over-sized cigar tube, the silver-colored missile in two pieces, the shape unadorned with fins or wings. Henry printed a description and suggested Torres read how the missile changed after launch, how the tail, small slanted wings and rear-mounted air intake deployed. In the picture accompanying the story, the air intake reminded Torres of the headrest in a Formula One racing car.

"Most of the air-to-ground missiles I saw were nukes," Henry said. "But there are no nuclear markings on this one. Let's see what all these explosives are for."

In case someone later described their tow truck to authorities, Henry had driven Torres at the Woodward Construction equipment lot to pick up a new truck and a covered trailer. While they traveled, Torres had rented three utilitarian garages with offices, all near the interstate. The workspaces came with heavy-duty electrical wiring, overhead lighting, and air pressure hookups for professional tools. The adjacent office space included a bathroom with shower, a desk, a couch, a side table, and two lamps. Torres used his father's private Woodward Construction credit card number in payment.

Torres leaned against the first garage's workbench. The solid, waist-high platform stretched across the back wall of the room, the counter space covered with Henry's tools and electronic equipment. They'd been inside working most of the afternoon.

Henry used an electric screwdriver and a circular saw to open various sections of the damaged missile. With images from the Internet as his guide, Henry explored a series of interior wiring harnesses and the front payload compartment. For a man built like a giant, with hands as big as dinner plates, Henry possessed a remarkably deft touch.

"You are sure this missile is not a nuclear device?" Torres said.

"Definitely. These missiles have several purposes and all the images are online."

"What do you mean? What is *this one* designed to do? Is not a bomb just a bomb?"

"Do you remember when America tried to kill Saddam Hussein in the 1990s? They dropped those big special bombs all over the country—giant warheads that supposedly penetrated four or five floors of solid concrete."

Torres's pulse climbed. "We have been gifted a bunker-buster?"

"Exactly," Henry said. "And an experimental one as well. The payload looks twice as big as the pictures on the Internet, plus the delaying devices have been tripled. See how the main payload is kept from exploding on initial impact?"

Henry moved so Torres could more easily see.

Torres frowned. "Delaying devices? You mean those large coiled springs?"

"That's it. The charge is set behind them so the explosion is delayed."

Torres shifted his gaze to Henry's computer. On screen was a simple diagram that generally matched the interior of their recovered missile. Different sections and pieces of the computer diagram were labeled guidance, payload, fuel and storage.

"Wouldn't such a weapon carry a locating device?" Torres said.

Henry nodded. His black eyes shone with excitement as he stared at the weapon. "Yes, but I removed the transponder when we lifted the missile onto the truck last night. It wasn't working, but I smashed it anyway."

"What are you removing now?" Torres said.

"The missile casing was badly damaged, but the insides—the inertial navigation and global positioning systems, guidance, and payload—everything seems one hundred percent okay. I can use new sheet metal to patch up the outside."

"But what are you removing from it?"

"I'm taking out the TERCOM system—terrain contour matching. If we are to successfully use this missile as a weapon, we'll have to reprogram the missile's computers so we can control flight from our own laptop."

Torres's heart thumped against his ribs. A flying bunker-buster that they could direct? Torres had no idea how this weapon might yet be utilized, but he had absolutely no doubt the Great Spirit had placed the cruise missile in his hands for a very specific reason. An enormous gift of power. To deny its importance would be blasphemous.

"Are you certain you can control the missile with your laptop?" Torres said. "This is a momentous thing for us to consider."

"Give me a few days, we'll fly this missile like a toy airplane," Henry said. "There's one thing. It's an air-to-ground missile, built to be dropped from the wing of a bomber. We'll need a special way to launch it. Unlike the AGMs I saw, though, this one has a booster rocket, so I should be able to build something that will let it rise fast and high enough to fly."

"You are certain?"

"The Great Spirit wouldn't let us down, right?"

Torres stared at his new friend. Was he teasing?

"What if someone was hiking in those mountains when your cruise missile drifted by," Jordan said. "There they were, minding their own business, drinking beer and shooting lizards or beer cans or something, and then here comes a cruise missile, floating down from the sky, hanging by those parachutes you mentioned."

"That's a big coincidence in the Fish Creek Mountains," Maggie said. "Nobody goes there."

"Yeah, but not impossible," Jordan said. "There are occasional hikers."

The Air Force had spotted half a dozen people over the past week, Maggie knew. Every single one had been interviewed and none reported seeing anything like a cruise missile. Her team had one good lead: A six-wheel tow truck had been photographed from space, the truck leaving a desert road in the Borrego Badlands yesterday, its rear bed and an obviously heavy cargo hidden by a tarp.

"And if your experimental weapon is not at the B-52 crash site," Jordan said, "or lying around on open ground where your search teams would have found it, where the heck is it? Every day it gets more likely that someone hauled your weapon out of the wilderness."

"The missile weighs over seven thousand pounds," Maggie said. "It's twenty feet long. You don't just throw that turkey in your trunk and drive home."

"No, but you'd only need the boom lift on a common, six-wheel tow truck and a covered, twenty-two-foot boat trailer to haul it anywhere undetected."

Maggie knew all this days ago. She and her staff had been scouring the Coachella and Imperial valleys for trucks and trailers. "You've been researching cruise missiles?" she asked.

"Of course. It's my job."

"What did your research tell you about why some

average Joe hiker would even *want* a cruise missile?"

"To ransom for money," Jordan said. "Or blow something up. That's what every red-blooded American male wants to do these days. Go boom on something. Didn't you see that FBI report last year, how so many American teenagers tried to sign up with the Mideast terrorists? Video games are the current theory."

"Sounds like horse crap to me, but I have something for you—if it's off the record, okay?"

"You mean I can't use it?"

"No, I mean use the info but don't use my name."

"Fine. That's called unattributed. So what do you have for me?"

"I'm already looking for covered trailers and tow trucks," Maggie said. "We thought of this days ago, but the terrain is so rugged, getting a six-wheel truck in there to pick up the missile and haul it out seems like an impossible tax—task."

"You having a cocktail?"

"None of your business."

"Sounds good is all."

"It's after work," Maggie said. She liked Jordan. He'd proven trustworthy about these on- and off-the-record things. "And I'm going to get fired any day if I don't find that weapon."

"Wish I was there to have a drink with you," he said.

She held her breath. She nearly said she wished he were there, too, but managed to hold her tongue. Gosh this whiskey had everything running loose. Even her heart raced. What was going on with her? The booze?

She'd always been able to drink most men beyond their limit. Under the table, the old men liked to say.

"I mean, I could use a drink, too," Jordan said. "Some Indian chief called my great grandfather a murderer."

"You're kidding. In what context?" Maggie reached for her Bushmills and ice. Good thing Jordan Scott wasn't there with her tonight. She might jump him. Oh, what was happening, or getting into her, as Mom used to say? She didn't know whether to laugh or cry.

"My grandmother gave me an old woven Indian basket last week," Jordan said. "She said the basket had been stolen over a century ago by my great grandfather. I gave the basket back, and the Cahuilla chief who accepted it said no chief or shaman would ever gift such a sacred thing to a white man."

"The basket belonged to a chief or shaman? That's a cool story. I'd love to hear the rest of it...someday."

"There's more, a lot more," Jordan said. "But it doesn't help you find that missile, I agree. Tell me how you're looking for tow trucks and covered trailers? Did you set up checkpoints right away? Use satellites, or what?"

"I can't discuss that," she said.

"But obviously it hasn't turned up."

"Not yet. That I will confirm."

"Thanks. Well, here's my other idea. There are sixteen places in the Coachella and Imperial counties where you can rent boat trailers, but only four that offer a covered trailer long enough to hide a cruise missile inside. That's where I'll be searching tomorrow."

"Good luck, ace. Let me know if you turn up my missile."

"Are you dismissing me, Colonel, because before I go, I wanted to ask you to meet me for dinner tomorrow night. We can compare notes."

"Notes on what?"

"On the case. Your missile."

"I'll think about it," she said. "Call me tomorrow afternoon."

"Deal."

"Remember the information that I'm searching for tow trucks and covered trailers is not attributable to me, okay?"

"Military sources, yes, ma'am."

All the Bushmills didn't help Maggie's stomach that night, for sure. Neither did the disappointment over having smoked eleven cigarettes that day, nor the shameless way she'd flirted with Jordan Scott. How embarrassing. What was she, back in high school? But Maggie guessed the real reason she flipped and churned in her bed all night wasn't the booze, Jordan, or cigarettes. No, the reason was because she'd misplaced an extremely deadly weapon and someone had probably swiped it. Although her experiment would be virtually impossible for some stranger to use against a major American target, the experimental bunker-buster contained enough military explosives to level a school, church, or municipal court house all by its lonesome. The media had it right. All of Southern California was in danger. The weapon she'd built—or the explosives inside—could kill thousands if well placed.

And if by some stupid, unlucky chance her bunker-buster missile ended up in the hands of an electronic handyman, a guy or gang who could reprogram guidance systems and who knew what to do with a powerful penetrating warhead, well, there were one or two targets in the western United States that, if hit, could devastate the country.

Maggie rolled out of bed the next morning with no sleep, a hangover, a sick stomach, and that old feeling of being less than. Less than *what*, she wasn't exactly certain, maybe less than who she should have been. Less than everyone with four limbs, for sure.

ELEVEN

Before Maggie punched the blinking light and picked up a phone call from Billy Payton, she locked the door to her El Centro office and opened a window in preparation for smoking her third cigarette since breakfast. She'd be right back to a pack-a-day if she didn't watch herself. Hell, she might be back there in another three minutes if Billy Payton offered bad news. This past week had been a hell storm.

She tapped the phone light with her BeBionic, currently in the active index position, meaning she could point and wiggle her forefinger. Push buttons. "Hey, Billy."

"You're out, Maggie. The FBI is taking over your search and starting an official investigation."

"Well, hello to you, too, Billy. Shit!" Maggie returned her BeBionic to the tripod mode so she could hold and light that third smoke.

"Sorry," he said, "but I wanted to get that over with. You know it wasn't my decision."

"Well, it's our missile," Maggie said. "And we're the ones who are best equipped, motivated, and experienced in this locality to find it. I can see those FBI agents in their suits and wingtips trooping around the desert. You need to convince the FBI—"

"Maggie, the decision is made. Like they told Tom in *The Godfather*, you're out. The FBI says we screwed up and Homeland Security agrees. Whoever found that missile—it has to be gone by now—could be driving those explosives past the White House in a vegetable truck this afternoon. They're running the investigation from Washington. It's national."

"Horse crap!" Maggie drew deeply on her Marlboro and blew the smoke in a single, hard stream at the ceiling. She didn't know why horse crap was worse than other crap but it was. Totally. Her smoke spread along the overhead tiles like a San Francisco fog. "The missile is still here in the Imperial Valley," she said. "I'm certain of it."

"Why? Because you think the construction company is involved?"

"Do you think it's a coincidence Woodward Construction owned the F550 carrying the right-sized covered cargo out of those mountains?"

"The FBI thinks maybe it is. The company showed us a scheduled job on their manifest. Picked up a boat from Lake Hinshaw."

"Sounds like horse crap."

"The FBI's checking everybody that works at Woodward anyway, but they have a lead in Los Angeles, another in—"

"Whatever's going to happen is going to happen right here," she said.

"Women's intuition?"

The hair on Maggie's neck bristled. The fingers of her real hand turned white squeezing the telephone. "Of course not. And that's a horse crap comment, Billy. Taking our missile had to be a spur-of-the-moment decision, not a planned terror attack. There's—"

"It doesn't matter, Maggie. The search belongs to the Feds."

Her BeBionic hand pulled the Marlboro Silver to her lips. The sarcastic prick. Men could be such jerks. Even her friend Billy fell into the trap. Intuition, her ass. The bastards could never pass up an opportunity to make themselves feel superior to women. Maggie had been taught this truism early in life—by her father. She blew more smoke into the center of her office.

"Listen to me, Billy. Please? I'm not saying I have all the answers. But Woody Woodward wouldn't be refusing interviews, hiding behind lawyers if he didn't know something. Is Homeland Security going to shake that bastard's tree?"

"You don't know he was hiding. It's a big company. He's a busy man. But to answer your question, yes, they finally did rattle his cage enough to be interviewed. His attorneys are bringing him in soon for questioning."

"I'm still doing the interview, right?"

"Maggie, you're *out*. The FBI wouldn't even tell me where the interview will be conducted."

She stubbed out her cigarette half-smoked in the little Vegas lounge ashtray she kept in the top drawer of her desk. She rubbed the aching socket below her elbow, the mechanical device that connected her prosthetic arm and her BeBionic hand. Screw the FBI.

"Well, hell. All right," she said. "Thank you for calling personally to tell me, Billy. Maybe I'll take that vacation I was planning. A little change sounds nice right now. Can you believe all this rain?"

She smiled listening to three full seconds of silence. Billy was probably choking on his own spit. It had been two decades since she'd rolled over for him like that.

"That doesn't sound like the Bullseye Black I know," he said.

"I'm improving with age."

"Maggie?"

"What?"

"Are you up to something? If the FBI says we're out, we're out. You don't want to make this mess even bigger for yourself—or me."

Maggie's finger shot to, but didn't press, the call-cancel button. She exhaled, then closed her eyes. Truth was, she'd been expecting this conversation for a while. "No, really. I should take a few days to visit my father in Vegas. Nothing sinister planned on this end. Really. I appreciate all your support, Billy. I'll—"

"Maggie?"

"—I'll call you when I get back. So, can I hop on your Chinook to get up there? The pilot told me you've been making Friday runs to Vegas."

"Carrasco has a big mouth. But sure, you're in. Hell, if you want, call your father, have him get permission, my man will drop you off right at Hoover."

* * *

After the two hundred and twenty-mile flight to Hoover Dam, Maggie sighed with joy hopping off Billy Payton's Chinook, the same one they'd used for search and rescue. If a male ground crew member had grabbed her, tried to help her off the aircraft, Maggie might have growled like a dog. Or bitten him. Lieutenant Colonel Margaret Rebecca Black had never ever been so damned mad.

Men were crap. Horse crap!

"Colonel Black?"

She marched in a light drizzle toward the voice she assumed was her ride to Pop's offices, Maggie cursing under her breath with each step. She'd been tossed from her own recovery investigation, her CO Billy Payton was in hot water with the Department of Defense for backing her so long, and a know-nothing FBI Special Agent named Chip Daley was in charge of Maggie's career, maybe her freedom if the stolen weapon blew up and killed someone. What if terrorists had bought the lost weapon from the lucky local who'd stumbled on the package, terrorists who now planned to attack a school? Or smart terrorists who knew to attack something much bigger.

Maggie kicked at a puddle of water. Her dismissal was infuriating. They never would have done that to man. Cut her completely out. But more important than her feelings, or even her career, was the undeniable and semi-frightening fact: No one took her seriously about one of the potential attacks she feared.

What's to blow up in the desert, people kept saying. Plenty.

"Colonel Black?"

"Here I am."

"My name's Earl. Mr. Black sent me to pick you up."

Maggie gave Earl the once-over. Dark, stained boots and worn overalls covered a tall, sturdy frame. All that, dirty knuckles and the fact he hadn't thought to bring an umbrella suggested grease monkey. She said, "What are my other options?"

"Excuse me?"

"Oh, never mind, Earl. I'm sorry. I appreciate the lift. You're sweet to come out in this rain for me. Thank you."

Maggie scolded herself for rude behavior as she followed the six-footer to a door-less Jeep, both of them getting wetter by the second. The rain fell heavier in the Las Vegas-Hoover Dam area than it had in El Centro. At least the Jeep had a roof.

The half-mile drive from the Arizona-side landing area required numerous sharp turns and five minutes. Hoover Dam's nineteen turbines produced over two thousand megawatts of electric power, and the profusion of high-voltage power lines in the rocky desert was a significant obstacle for low-flying aircraft. All roads there twisted like snakes. The Jeep's headlights illuminated barren hardpan along the roadside, scenery not unlike the low desert near El Centro, though the soil was darker here. Rusty. Earl's two-seater smelled of motor oil and Juicy Fruit gum. Her butt bounced hard on the worn seat.

The road across the dam, Highway 93, had been closed to the general public for years, but Earl zipped through the guarded roadblock with a familiar nod to the armed Hoover Dam Police, as per Maggie's earlier request of her important father. Halfway across the dam, at the apex of Hoover's arch, a construction crew worked on something. Maggie asked Earl to stop the Jeep a minute.

"We're not supposed to stop out here," he said.

"Ten seconds. Pop always talks about the backside view."

She didn't wait for an answer, but hopped outside. Rain splashed her khakis as she jogged to the dam's back edge and peered down the sloping inner curve. It was like looking down from the tip of a seventy-story pyramid, the sloped cement structure growing sharply thicker as it descended to the floor of Black Canyon. Rain blew up the dam's rear face and sprayed hard against her cheeks, forcing Maggie back from the edge.

The cell phone attached to her belt rang as she hopped back inside the Jeep. The call came from Billy Payton. She shook her shoulders like a dog, spilling water on Earl and his Jeep. "Hey, Billy. Thanks for the chopper ride. Did they have any luck on the search today?"

"I have no clue. Anybody connected to Maggie Black is having trouble using the toilet. You want to know what happened on the search, call your friend Major

Bob. Daley's managed to keep me out of the loop today, but I'll fix things by tomorrow. I have friends at Homeland."

"Thanks for the warning, Billy. I'll talk to you later."

Driving to the Hoover Dam offices, Maggie wondered again what she'd do if she ever left the Air Force. Building experimental weapons had never been her dream, but there weren't many choices after her crash in Germany and the loss of her hand. She loved aircraft, she loved flying, and she didn't want to stop being part of America's Air Force, a career that gave Maggie pride and a sense of helping others. There were angry people all over this world who wanted to kill Americans. If Maggie could be part of the team to fight that, to protect the United States, that's where she'd always want to be. But what if they didn't want her?

She'd better find that experimental weapon.

At a Vegas steak house that night with her father, Sean Black, a senior engineer for the U.S. Bureau of Land Management, Maggie decided to risk upsetting him with a question. She needed the information for her mental health, and Pop was a perfect source. He'd worked at Hoover Dam since her first year at the Academy.

"So what's up?" he said. "I can tell there's planned interrogation on your mind. Anything to do with your lost cruise missile?"

She smiled. "I had a day off and a free helicopter ride, thought I'd come see how you're doing. You know, see how your last few months of gainful employment are shaking out. We haven't talked much since Christmas. You having a retirement party?"

Maggie knew he was, even if her father didn't. She was a key, financial-supporting member of the planning committee.

"Oh, sure I'll probably go out for dinner with a few of the guys," he said.

"And the work's good?"

"Fun, actually. We've been busy around here with the record rain and snow runoff. Twenty-five years of worsening drought, and then bam, a fall and two winters of rain and snow like never before. Climate change is here."

"Really?"

"It's good right now," her father said. "The BLM has some Colorado River water to actually manage. Every dam is filling up and the Western states are fighting over the stuff like sharks in blood. Heck, there might be some water left for Mexico—if they ask nicely."

"I can't believe how big Lake Mead has gotten," she said. "Wasn't it just two or three summers ago it was at an all-time low?"

"Scary how fast things changed. The lake hasn't been this full since the 1980s. We're actually approaching capacity."

"So this means you have plenty to do?"

"Tons. The job's busy. Plus, my back's much better. I played golf last weekend."

"Wonderful. I like that you have something to do

besides clean the generators." Maggie sipped her *pinot grigio*. "So, Pop. I wanted to ask you about the security up here."

"Security? I'm not involved in top-level stuff. That's a hush-hush topic at Hoover Dam, I can tell you. But why do you want to know? Is that tonight's interrogation topic?"

"Let's say I was reading a report—"

"No. Let's tell your father the truth. Your experiment is still missing and it poses a threat to Hoover Dam. Is that it?"

"Hoover Dam has nothing to worry about," she said. "I know it's more than two football fields thick, but—"

"What the hell is missing, Maggie?"

"It's classified. I can't say."

He frowned, eyebrows crawling together. She'd seen that glare all her life and her reaction was always the same. Tenseness gripped her, head to foot.

"Great," he said. His voice mocked her. "You can't tell me how your experimental military weapon might be used on Hoover, the place where I work?"

"I never said Hoover was a target."

"Maggie, you asked me about the dam's security."

"Okay, but I'm not worried. Honest. It's not even a hunch. You're the one who taught me to ask, what's the worst that could happen? I'm being extra cautious. I'd like to be reassured that if some jerk tries to drive an explosive warhead across the dam, you guys are going—"

"Jeez, Maggie, it's not a nuke, is it?"

"No, I promise."

"But it could be used on a dam?"

"Gravity dams like Hoover? Only theoretically."

She tried to appear skeptical, but command and control, strategic fortifications and key infrastructure, including large gravity dams, were definitely potential uses of her experimental bunker-buster weapon. Maggie had drafted the report on possible targets when she'd come to work on the project with Billy. But there's no way she could tell her father. The information was classified. Top secret.

Sean cleared his throat. "Okay. Let me tell you what I know. One, the public can't drive on top of the dam anymore, not since the Highway 93 Bypass Bridge was finished in 2010. Eighteen-wheel trucks were banned from crossing over the dam in the days immediately following September 11, 2001. So were buses with luggage, double-stacked trailers and any vehicle with cargo that couldn't be inspected."

"Everything gets inspected?"

"Nothing public goes right over the dam anymore, so it's not necessary. Even BLM vehicles aren't supposed to stop on the bridge. Pedestrians are prohibited at night. I don't see how anybody could get explosives up there."

"Then why is security such a hush-hush topic?" she said.

"The BLM doesn't like speculation about attacks on Hoover, that's all. Goes back to one of the old *Superman* movies, I think from the 1970s. The BLM doesn't want people talking about what *could* happen if the dam ever burst."

"What do you mean?"

"On any day in the spring and summer, there are a couple of hundred thousand people living and playing on the Colorado River. The cities between Hoover and Yuma, Arizona—Laughlin, Bullhead City, Lake Havasu, Parker, Blyth—could potentially disappear if Hoover suddenly collapsed like it did in that Superman movie. All that water, all at once, what do you suppose would happen? Nine trillion gallons of water rushing out of the Grand Canyon toward Yuma?"

"Did you say nine *trillion?*"

"Enough water to cover New York state a foot deep."

TWELVE

In a dream that night, Maggie once again reclaimed the title of Whole Person, a woman with all her parts, all her charms. But while she usually flew an F-15, soaring between white clouds in a powder blue sky, tonight she piloted a B-52.

Groaning, twisting, flightless.

Falling toward earth.

Maggie woke up sweating, barely remembering what had frightened her. But as always, a familiar heartache tormented her. She was *not* complete as she'd been in the dream, working the controls with both natural hands. She'd lost one. She would always be different.

Maggie's cell phone buzzed the next morning while boarding Billy's Chinook back to El Centro. The call came from Jordan Scott, who quickly proved he had excellent sources, people with better current knowledge of the FBI's lost-weapon investigation than Maggie. People like Special Bastard in Charge, Chip Daley?

"I can't stop you from publishing that," Maggie said, "but I'll find my lost weapon faster if you don't print

Woodward Construction's name right now."

"I thought you were off the case," Jordan said.

"You heard that, too?"

"You told me the other night you were going to be fired any day. But you'd had a few, so maybe you've forgotten."

"I remember." Maggie cleared her throat. "Listen, can we make a deal of some kind?"

"Like what?"

"I could tell you all sorts of things about the weapon and the investigation once I get my experiment back. An exclusive, behind-the-scenes look at military planning, maybe, or how we use the satellites for *all* kinds of things. Got a little dirt on that one. Can you keep a secret until I have my bunker-buster back and any bad guys are in custody? It shouldn't be more than a day or two."

"Bunker-buster? Bad guys? You sure know how to raise my interest."

Was that a double-entendre? Was he flirting? "So we have an agreement?"

"You have my interest in more ways than one, Maggie Black. I will only agree, however, if we seal the deal at dinner."

Maggie was right. He *had* been flirting. "Sorry, Don Juan. I'm in Las Vegas."

"Okay. Doesn't have to be today. I should drive home to San Diego tonight, see Grandma tomorrow. But you must say yes to dinner sometime, or I'm printing everything in tomorrow's newspaper."

"That's blackmail."

"Whatever it takes to break bread with Colonel Maggie Black. Now if we're agreed, tell me about this bunker-buster. It's experimental?"

She couldn't think of anything sexual connected to breaking bread. "You don't need to check with your editor?"

"About having dinner with you?"

"Funny. About our deal."

"Nope, I don't need to check. No mention of Woodward Construction for twenty-four hours."

"I said after I find the missile." Maggie leaned against the Chinook, wind whipping her light brown hair. From inside the cabin, two full-bird Air Force colonels and a half-bird like her stared with grim expressions, the chopper and ten other passengers waiting on Maggie Black maybe thirty more seconds.

"Twenty-four hours only on the news hold," Jordan said. "Dinner together by the Fourth of July."

"Forty-eight hours hold. And I agree to dinner—but no fireworks."

"Ha ha. Deal."

"Okay, what's missing is an outdated air-to-ground cruise missile," Maggie said. "The weapon is old—"

"You already told me all this."

"—but the AGM was the size my team needed for our experiment, a very powerful bunker-buster. You're too young to remember when the term bunker-buster was all over the television and in the newspapers. Back in the 1990s—"

"The U.S. was trying to kill Saddam Hussein. I've read about it."

"Let's say the United States President might have use for such a weapon again someday, and I've been running a program to create a bigger and better one."

"How much bigger and better?"

"None of your business. At least for now. But what I *will* tell you—to show you the bargain with me is worth keeping—the Ford truck they discovered at Woodward Construction showed traces of a special Air Force paint matching my cruise missile. The FBI made the forensic link this morning."

Jordan whistled. "Sounds like the investigation's over."

"You can't arrest a corporation," Maggie said. "Although Special Agent Daley might try. Imagine the wonderful publicity he'd get."

"No kidding. Corporate greed with horns. Thanks, Maggie. I'd better go write my story. I'll talk to you tomorrow."

"Please don't use the name of the company."

"Why do you care if you're off the case?"

"I didn't say I was off the case."

"Okay, I'll try to wait a day, but *The New York Times* has a tight hold on Special Agent Daley's scrotum—please pardon the expression."

She grunted.

"And if the *Times* publishes Woodward's name online tonight, I'll have to use the name in my story tomorrow, too. So, you understand."

"Then I'd get nothing for giving you that info?"

He coughed. "We'll figure something out."

The flight home took an hour and fifteen minutes, Maggie worrying about her experiment blowing up and killing people the whole ride. What else could she think about? She remembered U.S. Defense Secretary Les Aspin on the television news saying female military pilots would now be assigned to combat roles. That was 1993. Maggie had been fifteen, a year after her Uncle Dennis had introduced her to flying, and she knew from the second she'd watched Aspen, that's what she wanted to do. Be a combat pilot. The next three years of high school became planning for the Air Force Academy in Colorado. The way she'd seen it back then, that's how she wanted to help people. It wasn't a warrior thing, Maggie not thinking of herself using swords and guns, chopping, shooting, slaughtering the enemy. It was about airplanes, cool machines with electronic weapons, creating a twenty-first century warrior, a woman trained to defeat in combat the enemies of the United States. At fifteen years old, she pictured herself as Sigourney Weaver in *Alien*—the warrior inside a machine, using technology, moxie, and hydraulic power to thrash evil.

Twenty-three years later, she identified more with that old movie's broken robot.

Torres listened intently to the mechanical voice on the phone. For the first time he could remember, his father sounded frightened. Agitated and fearful. What could a man with the wealth and power of Woody Woodward be afraid of?

"Do you have any idea where your friend Henry and that equipment disappeared to?" his father said. "There's a truck tractor, a flat-bed trailer, and a tripod drill missing. Plus two boxes of construction explosives."

Jerry was a top foreman. That Torres's thefts already had been discovered was a surprise and raised an alarm. Good thing he'd left work for the safety of their newest rented garage. His gifts from the Great Spirit, including Henry and the stolen equipment had been transferred and safely hidden. But if Henry's identity became known to the authorities, his own name and address would likely soon follow.

"Henry isn't a friend," Torres said. "He's your employee, and he's on a maintenance project in Phoenix as far as I know, those supermarket cogeneration units we installed last year. I told him to take whatever was required, but he had no need for *any* kind of explosives."

"He's not in Phoenix," Woodward said. "The feds already checked, okay? Right now, I need you to find Henry and examine your equipment records, make a list of anything missing, plus do a crate-by-crate count of our registered explosives. The ATF will be here in two days for an extensive inventory. If Henry stole any explosives—one fucking stick of that nitro-dynamite—he's going to jail. Maybe you and me, too."

Torres's heart drummed. His father's words and the early pinpointing of Henry suggested the Great Spirit's plan might be in jeopardy. He should have been more cautious. Woody Woodward was a serious impediment.

"I'm sure it's all there," Torres said. "I'll complete an inventory and bring the tally by your house no later than tomorrow night...father."

"Don't call me that." Woodward clicked off.

His father's anger made Torres smile. Being Woodward's bastard son had many advantages, an easy chuckle but one. He motioned for Henry to return to their workplace's table and the topographical map he'd spread out. When he earned his skilled friend's attention, Torres tapped the same Highway 8 turnoff he'd shown Chief Reynaldo.

"Here is the place we will strike."

THIRTEEN

Torres squinted through the slashing rain and tire spray, a layer of water barely disturbed by the truck cab's windshield wipers. Up ahead, the wide line of red lights eastbound on Highway 8 twisted sharply to the left. He'd talked Reynaldo into driving the flatbed so Torres could navigate, and this turn was the marker he'd been expecting. He gathered his courage with a silent prayer.

Though the highway was busy, the fifty-mile stretch of California desert between El Centro and the Colorado River at Yuma was virtually uninhabited. A handful of off-ramps became dirt roads that died in abandoned farming or mining projects. A few turnoffs led south to service roads for the All-American Canal.

"Pull off at the next exit," Torres said.

Reynaldo switched to the off-ramp lane and followed the sweeping asphalt to a stop sign. Less than a hundred yards from the highway, a five-foot dirt levee and chain fence appeared in their headlights. The All-American Canal. Twenty-four hours a day, seven days a week, the manmade channel drained Colorado River water for Imperial Valley farms.

On the canal's parallel access road, tucked against the

fence-like thicket of tall river reeds, a green and white SUV roared into the beams of their truck's headlights. Big block letters on the four-wheel-drive vehicle read U.S. BORDER PROTECTION AGENCY.

Torres grabbed the door handle. "Watch both sides of the access road for a second SUV. The border agents work in pairs, one man per vehicle."

Reynaldo's forehead bunched, but Torres scrambled out before his friend could speak. Rain splashed his face. His boots sloshed in mud as he strode toward the U.S. government vehicle. From inside his green and white SUV, the federal agent raked Torres' face and hands with the brightest flashlight beam Torres have ever seen. His eyes shut in reaction.

"You fellas lost?" the agent said.

Torres couldn't see him. "No, sir, we're right where we're supposed to be."

A fine layer of sweat spread across Torres's upper lip. His body seemed to glow under the flashlight's intense beam. Seconds passed before the uniformed border patrol officer shifted the light from Torres to the truck's rain-drenched windshield.

"You. Driver. Step out of the truck."

Reynaldo jumped down onto the mud and wet gravel. The border agent's flashlight traveled the length of Reynaldo's frame, then switched back to Torres and the flatbed trailer. The officer let himself be silhouetted in the truck's headlights for the first time. He was thick-shouldered, perhaps twenty-five years old. He walked slowly, his light including Torres's drilling equipment in its beam.

"We have a hole to drill for the U.S. Geological Service," Torres said. He turned his back on the agent and walked to the trailer.

The agent stalked him. "Bullshit."

A semiautomatic pistol filled the leather holster on the right side of the young agent's belt, and Torres held his breath when the agent unfastened the holster's security strap. The agent's fingers tapped the weapon's exposed grip.

"We were supposed to be here this afternoon," Torres said, "but we got tied up on another job, and then we had a flat tire. Our boss said this hole has to be finished before—"

"Nobody's drilling any holes around here," the agent said.

"We were told the Geological Service called your supervisor."

"Like I said, nobody's drilling any holes around here. That levee protects the All-American Canal, and on the other side of that is the Mexican border. You two are in an extremely high-security area, and you need to leave. Now."

"Officer, please. I have all the proper paper work."

"Bullshit. Now get out of here."

Torres turned and leaned against the flatbed trailer. The space between his shoulder blades felt like an icy bullseye. His shirt was soaked with rain. His knees trembled slightly. He hoped the agent couldn't see. Thunder cracked in the distance.

"Hey," the agent said. He stood two yards away. "Get back in your truck, pal, or you and your friend are going to spend the night in jail."

"Looks like a giant corkscrew, doesn't it?" Torres said. He nodded to the hand-guided, tripod drill, currently folded and strapped tightly to the flatbed. The drill did in fact resemble a super-size wine opener, and the verbal diversion worked, if barely. Torres gained the extra half-second he needed, reaching beneath a thick, wench-tightened belt used to secure the drill to the trailer. Earlier that day, Torres had discovered a few inches of space near the wench.

"Keep your hands where I can see them," the agent said.

"Just look at this paperwork, Officer," Torres said. "I'm telling you, we're supposed to be here."

Torres spun. Instead of papers, Torres had snagged a semiautomatic pistol, a Beretta, this one loaded with nine rounds and equipped with a noise suppressor—the gun, the bullets, and all accessories supplied by Henry. The border agent yanked at his holstered weapon, but Torres didn't hesitate. He squeezed the trigger twice, hitting the young man with both bullets. The agent hit his head against the edge of the trailer as he fell.

Torres checked him. The young man no longer breathed. Torres's heart skipped, the sorrow briefly physical because he knew it was wrong to kill. But as his mood changed with the young boys near the sacred elephant trees, the feelings of sadness and guilt disappeared.

Revenge against the white man was a great battle that disregarded individuals. Native Americans could never recover from the white man's genocide.

A second border patrol SUV skidded onto the scene from the opposite direction, brakes squealing. Torres crouched and scurried to the front of the Woodward truck. He listened, then crept along the cab's chrome grill. He stayed low, kept going until he found a spot where he could see the newly arrived vehicle from cover.

The second SUV's door stood ajar, the cab light on, the agent outside with his weapon drawn and his head and shoulders blocking light from the cab. He stepped toward the shadows, but too late. A muffled rifle shot from the nearby river reeds felled him.

Henry's plan had worked well. Torres ran to the second SUV and shot the driver again in the temple. This second murder offended Torres's spirit more than the first. He could not say why, but his stomach squirmed as if he had eaten raw datura root. He had to admit the truth. At that moment, Torres did not feel like a warrior on a path with heart.

Henry the sniper emerged from the river reeds.

The blast offered Torres a breath of victory. Even half a mile away, the explosion disturbed the ground and nudged the rolling truck. An orange ball of fire soared a hundred feet above the All-American Canal. An angry and frustrated Reynaldo had refused to help, so Torres and Henry needed fifteen extra minutes to unload the truck, drill a hole, and plant the explosive charges. They were still picking up speed on Highway 8 when the nitro-dynamite went off.

Reynaldo wrestled against his restraints. "You two are madmen."

Henry drove. The motorcycle he'd used earlier to follow them rested on the flatbed trailer with the drilling equipment, tied down even better than Reynaldo.

"Why am I crazy?" Torres said.

The chief occupied the passenger's seat. Torres sat behind him in the jump seat, his Beretta ready. Henry had suggested they kill the chief and leave his corpse with the border agents, but Torres had explained the body would lead quickly to himself.

"You killed two young men for nothing," Reynaldo said. "Nothing."

While Torres knew he would someday be caught, he hoped the time had not yet arrived. He needed to be alive and free long enough to accomplish the Great Spirit's mission, and there were still many preparations.

"It was not an easy or righteous thing to do, I agree. But is the survival of your people's heritage and history worth a few lives? You, our chief, allow our Cahuilla brothers and sisters to disappear unchecked into the white man's world of alcohol and material gain."

"You exaggerate," Reynaldo said.

Torres wanted to shoot him right there. "Those two border agents gave their lives to our struggle, yes, but so did thousands of our people die for the white man's greed. What we have accomplished tonight will close the

All-American Canal for weeks. By tomorrow night, we should be able to work the magic of Chaco Cruz's basket at the proper location. If we access that channel from the Arizona side—"

"Stop. I do not care," Reynaldo said.

"Are those emergency lights behind us?" Henry said.

Torres checked traffic through the rear window. Security was tight along the border. Other green and white Border Protection vehicles would have arrived on the explosion scene by then. But Torres saw nothing following them. "No. They're road work signs."

"You'll have to kill me," Reynaldo said. "I won't help you any longer, and if you let me go, the border authorities will know your name and address within an hour."

Henry nodded. "That's what I told him hours ago."

Torres thought it strange Reynaldo would call for his own destruction, but apparently there was much about his old friend he would never understand.

"As you wish," Torres said. "Where would you like to die?"

As the sun hinted a new day, Torres directed Henry to a nearly invisible dirt trail near the base of Carrizo Mountain. In one of the most rugged and desolate regions in all the California deserts, they drove as far as they could up a thirty-five-story pile of rocks, then dragged Reynaldo the rest of the way, their destination a remote and backyard-sized oasis known to Native Americans and a few brave hikers. Reynaldo had chosen not to participate, so Torres had appointed the place of his chief's execution.

Rain water collected somewhere inside the mountain and fed the grove of palms and bunches of tall grasses year-round from a paper-thin crack in a sheer face of granite. A small pool of water collected at the base of the trickle, feeding the palms.

Torres drank from the special water and prayed for guidance, though he knew the Great Spirit's answer already. Nothing was more important than refilling Lake Cahuilla, and that included Torres's friend and chief.

Torres had Reynaldo set upon a task, but his former friend and doomed chief recognized his fate by the shape of the hole he'd been ordered to dig. After considerable struggle, and to save time, Henry accomplished most of the excavation with Torres providing frequent rest.

Torres was in a hurry to return to El Centro and produce a fabricated inventory of Woodward's construction explosives for his father. Also, he needed to make certain he could meet inside his father's secluded ranch house.

Tonight was the maid's night off.

FOURTEEN

At her kitchen table with a second mug of morning coffee in hand, Maggie kept reading while she waited for Jordan to answer her phone call. *The New York Times* and Jordan's *San Diego Sun-Times* had both published the name of Woodward Construction in their stories that morning.

"Maggie?"

She had him on speaker. His voice sounded tinny. "Hi, Jordan. Where are you?"

"San Diego."

"Are you coming back to El Centro?"

"This afternoon. After I see my grandmother. You saw *The New York Times* used Woodward's name, so I had to as well?"

"Yeah, I saw. Is your grandmother sick?"

"She had a stroke two years ago. She lives in an assisted care facility in Chula Vista. I like to visit twice a week."

"You're a nice grandson."

"She's all I have."

Maggie considered that statement. No parents, no siblings, no children? No ex-wives? "Well, when you get back, I want a sit-down. I need to hear everything you know about Woodward Construction. There was information in your story I didn't know."

"There's a ton on Google," Jordan said. "What's your angle?"

"Angle?"

"Well, why Woody, why right now?" he said.

"Because the world is closing in on Mr. Woodward. I won't be there to hear his response when the FBI poses him questions. Off the record, I know the ATF has a warrant to seize his inventory of construction explosives tomorrow. They're sending a dozen agents. Woodward thinks he's being audited."

"Well, that's nice to hear," Jordan said. "Maybe I'll drop by. I figured Woodward for a big political contributor who couldn't be pushed."

"I don't know about his contributions, but he is rich, and he can afford smart, expensive lawyers. He's been hiding over a week."

"So, I have an idea," Jordan said.

"Oh boy."

"Hey. Be nice. My idea is that you and I have dinner together when I return to that beautiful desert of yours. We can discuss the target, Mr. Woody Woodward. Then you and I will visit him, ask Woodward face-to-face what he's telling the FBI tomorrow."

"Are you kidding?"

"No. We go to his house and knock on his door. That's what reporters do. You'd be surprised how many people answer the bell and talk to you. They think they're smarter, or something, like they can avoid revealing themselves."

Maggie grunted.

"Come with me when I knock on Woody Woodward's door tonight?" he said. "After dinner."

"Really?"

"Sure. Why not?"

Maggie sipped her coffee. "I don't know. I'll think of something."

Maggie stared at Jordan as if he were crazy. Wait, he *was* crazy, suggesting they break into Woodward's totally dark mansion. They'd knocked, no answer, waited and knocked again, no answer. No exterior lights on, none showing inside either. Woodward's estate was as quiet and gloomy as a funeral home.

"Come on," he said. "Let's go through that side gate."

Jordan had been late getting back to El Centro. He'd wanted to drive straight to the big house he claimed belonged to Woody Woodward. Now Jordan wanted Maggie to get thrown in jail with him. To say the least, she had concerns.

"Are you freaking nuts?" she said.

"Woodward is wealthy," Jordan said, "the kind of guy who, like you said, has expensive lawyers and expensive security. Where is all that money? There should be lights, cameras, motion sensors, at least a pit bull or two. Even if he's out of town, does it seem right he'd leave the estate unlighted and unprotected?"

"No, you're right," Maggie said. "These are exactly the conditions under which the El Centro Police Department would expect criminals to break in."

Jordan waved at the massive home. "Look at all this emptiness. No people, no pets, no cameras, no lights. Woodward's one of the richest men in Imperial County, and this is *the* most expensive single-family home within forty miles. Something's wrong."

Maggie glanced at the wet street, rain splashing. "Woodward probably knows who stole my weapon, but what you're suggesting is too aggressive for me, Jordan. I'm a lieutenant colonel in the United States Air Force. I am *not* committing burglary."

"Breaking and entering, I think, unless you planned on taking silverware."

She slapped his shoulder.

"But it's not a crime to help someone in trouble," Jordan said. "And I think I heard a call for help inside."

"You did *not*!"

"I think I did. More importantly, I'm not calling my editor Sam Carson and telling him I have no story for tomorrow."

"I'll wait in the car and listen for the sirens," Maggie said. "And when the police come, I'm giving them your name, so don't try to run away."

Jordan smiled, those blue eyes as bright as his teeth. "I'm swearing this was *your* idea, Colonel Black."

Maggie showed him a tall middle finger, then zipped up her brown leather pilot's jacket and headed for the car. Jordan was nuts. She wasn't breaking the law on some flimsy excuse, but she figured hanging around made sense, not only to see what Jordan discovered, but to protect him if the police showed. She could warn them about his presence.

She slipped behind the wheel of her Air Force sedan. Another thing she liked about Jordan, he hadn't minded when she'd wanted to take her car and drive. A little quirk she had. Wherever she traveled—land, air, or sea—Maggie needed to pilot.

Jordan ran through Woodward's open, driveway gate and looked for shelter. A perimeter of twenty-foot cypress trees failed to block the wind or slashing rain. His clothes were soaked. But a previously invisible point of light caught his eye, an electric bulb above what might be the home's kitchen entrance. He jogged toward the glow.

He'd been right. This was the kitchen entrance. He checked the door. Locked. He slipped off his water-logged shirt, wrapped it around his left elbow and smashed the glass with a quick, sharp blow. Most of the broken window crashed on the kitchen floor inside, but a jagged six-inch piece landed beside Jordan's sneaker. He maneuvered his hand and let himself in. If he had to, he'd tell the cops he heard a scream. He and Maggie had come to talk to Woodward, found the lights off, and Jordan had heard a muted cry for help.

So muted, Maggie hadn't heard it.

Inside the kitchen, his sneakers crunched on the broken glass. A tiny red light over the restaurant-sized stove filled the tile and stainless steel room with vague, rusty shadows. Pizza smells drifted in the air—tomato sauce, garlic, maybe pepperoni or sausage.

"Mr. Woodward?" Jordan said.

Nothing. To his right, he ducked down a short hallway into a tropical forest. Woodward's sun room, or greenhouse. The rectangular space burst with palm fronds, hanging vines, orchid blooms, and seedlings under glass lids. A steamy organic smell filled his nose. The humidity popped beads of sweat on Jordan's forehead.

His phone buzzed. A text. Maggie. Her message was a question mark.

He called her. "Are the cops here?" he said.

"No. I wanted to see if you were all right. I thought I heard glass breaking."

"That was me. I'm fine."

"You broke a window to get in?"

"Yes. Now let me find someone. Nobody's answering."

"Keep me on the line," Maggie said.

"No. I want my hands free. I'll call you back in a second. *Mr. Woodward?*"

The jungle trail through Woodward's greenhouse of palms and tree ferns ended at a sunken formal dining room the size of a three-car garage. He flipped a light switch. China-filled hutches and sideboards stuffed with liquor bottles lined one entire wall. Persian rugs covered the hardwood floor. The crystal chandelier had to weigh as much as Jordan's Ford.

"Mr. Woodward?"

Again nothing. Jordan eased through a portal on the far side of the dining room. The sound of running water froze him. Maybe Woodward frolicked in the shower. That would explain why he hadn't answered the doorbell. But showers didn't explain the big estate being dark and unguarded.

Or did it? Having a party when the help was off?

"Mr. Woodward? It's Jordan Scott of the *San Diego Sun-Times*. Are you all right? Why are there no lights on?"

The sound of the shower pulled him into the master bedroom. Matching walk-in closets, matching dressers. A bed big enough for mating thoroughbreds. Blue jeans and a white cowboy shirt lay rumpled on the unmade bedding. So did a half-eaten slice of pizza and several chewed crusts.

Jordan walked past the bed and a wall closet on his way to the bathroom and the sound of splashing water. He felt like an intruder. Hell, he *was* an intruder. Woodward probably had the right to shoot him.

"Mr. Woodward? If you're okay, I need to talk to you. It's very important."

His phone rang. Maggie.

"Is he in there?" she said.

"I don't know yet. I'm still looking."

"I think you should get out of there, Jordan. Before

something bad happens. What if he thinks you're a burglar?"

"I was thinking that myself." Maybe he'd let his ambition and curiosity pull him in a bad direction. Maybe Maggie was right. He should get out now, head back to the motel. "Hang on," he said.

No. No way was he turning around now. A breaking national news story might wait on the other side of this slightly ajar bathroom door. The water in the shower still ran. Maybe Woodward and the weapon thief were one and the same person.

"What are you doing?" Maggie said.

"Hang on one second."

Jordan nudged open the door. The solid wood swung easily at first, then stuck. Something low and heavy blocked the opening. Something with thick hairy legs. Jordan's throat went dry. He groaned.

"What?" Maggie said.

He stuck his head inside the steamy bathroom. A man with white hair and the wrinkled skin of a sixty-five or seventy-year-old lay stretched out naked on a grass-green tile floor, belly up, one arm and both legs extended. A drying creek of dark blood trailed off the old man's forehead to the floor and traveled two feet to the shower. Jordan shuddered. The hole in the man's head looked bullet-sized. His blank unfocused eyes held a wide, unknowing gaze that talked to Jordan about everybody's death, even his own. Jordan snapped a picture with his phone.

"Jordan?" Maggie said.

He withdrew from the bathroom and flipped on a bedroom wall switch. Two lamps charged the sleeping space with soft light. His stomach gurgled.

"Jordan?" Maggie's voice had risen two notches.

He sent her the photo. "Is this Woodward?"

"Oh, my God. I'm not sure, but I think so."

Rumpled blue jeans called to him from the bed. He found a hand-carved leather wallet in the left back pocket. A driver's license read Oliver Winston Woodward. The age and picture matched the dead man.

"Call the police," he said to Maggie. "Woodward's been—"

"It's nice to meet you, Jordan."

Jordan jumped. A man in a crazy Halloween mask had snuck up behind him in Woodward's bedroom. The disguise had bright colored horns and an alligator mouth with giant, sharp teeth. Maybe some kind of Indian kachina likeness. Jordan's heart drummed against his chest.

"Who was that?" Maggie said.

Jordan bolted through the bedroom's far doorway, but a second man waited in the hall; a strong man who grabbed Jordan's shoulders and used Jordan's own momentum to spin him one hundred and eighty degrees. He wrapped Jordan's neck in the crook of a massive elbow. The pressure cut off Jordan's oxygen.

"Jordan? What's hap—" Maggie said.

The man in the Halloween mask snatched Jordan's telephone.

Jordan stabbed over his shoulder with his fingers,

trying to find the eyes of the man who kept him from breathing. But he made no contact. Each effort cost him strength and tightened the man's grip on Jordan's neck. One by one his muscles went limp, paralyzed in the bigger man's python embrace. Jordan sensed himself losing consciousness.

FIFTEEN

Maggie cursed when Jordan's phone cut out. There was at least one other man inside Woodward's dark house, a man who'd caught Jordan by surprise, a man who'd refused to let Jordan speak or use his telephone. A man who'd made Jordan call out for the police. She called 9-1-1, gave them Woodward's address, Jordan's name as Woodward's guest, and described a burglary in progress.

"Your name please," the operator asked.

"Colonel Maggie Black, U.S. Air Force. And tell the El Centro Police I'm going inside, too. I'm wearing—"

"No, wait! Colonel, please. You need to stay on the phone with me."

"I'm wearing a brown leather aviator jacket and blue jeans."

Maggie cut the connection and scrambled out of the car. Her pulse thudded. Lightning flashed above the clouds. She jogged through the heaviest downpour of the night to the driveway gate Jordan had disappeared through ten minutes earlier. Thunder cracked. By the time she reached the gate, her flats and jeans from the knee down were soaked.

What the hell was she doing? She wanted to find her

missing experiment, yeah, but this felt like she was trying to protect Jordan. The turkey. She'd told him breaking in was a bad idea. Now maybe he'd gotten himself killed.

She caught her breath, then ran toward a porch light at the side of the sprawling ranch house. Glass had been broken. The door was open. This must have been Jordan's entrance. She hesitated, then nudged the door all the way open and crept inside. A noise froze her. In another part of the house, a heavy object scraped or rubbed across the floor. The dragging sounds made a steady trail toward the front of the house.

Was it Jordan, dead or unconscious?

A wooden rack of knives caught her attention on the kitchen counter. But Maggie decided against arming herself. This wasn't her house. Maggie was the intruder. She tip-toed to where the noise seemed to be going, Maggie shifting from the kitchen to a parlor-sized sitting area nearer the street. In the thick unfamiliar shadows, she tripped over a winged-back chair, but caught herself before falling. Her adrenaline pumped.

The dragging stopped. Maggie halted as well. She waited ten, twenty, thirty seconds. Nothing. Then a loud truck pulled up at the curb in front. The dragging noise started again.

Maggie crept to a window overlooking the cul-de-sac street. A six-wheel tow truck slowly turned into Woodward's driveway. The Ford F550—she knew her common tow trucks well after this past week—carried a ten-thousand-pound boom lift. The boom's steel triangle silhouetted black against the lighter horizon. The diesel engine pinged noisily.

The tow truck turned through the same driveway gate Maggie had used, and she focused on the dragging noise. Whatever traveled across the floor of Woodward's massive ranch home now moved in a direct line toward Maggie.

She withdrew as quietly as she could, tip-toeing back into the kitchen. She crouched behind the kitchen's marble-topped center island. She checked her watch. It had been seven minutes since she'd called 9-1-1. Felt like an hour. Her heart raced.

The tow truck backed near the kitchen and flipped on a spotlight atop its triangular boom lift. The high-wattage lamp was normally used to illuminate nighttime traffic accidents, and Woodward's kitchen lit up like an open-heart surgery suite. Maggie crunched herself smaller, her face and chest hugging the center island. A scratching noise made Maggie glance over her shoulder.

A man's bulk moved at her. Thick and tall like a professional football player, the man's black hair was cut in the shape of an up-side-down cereal bowl. His face showed Native American features—the high cheek bones and a majestic nose—but the ingredients were oddly asymmetrical. Three of his front teeth were broken.

His elbow cracked the side of Maggie's head. The near-instant blackness reminded Maggie of when she'd been conked on the school playground by a baseball bat.

* * *

Maggie woke up thirsty on the floor of Woodward's kitchen. Her head throbbed and her vision wasn't right, although at first she couldn't identify why. Blurry in one eye maybe? What a punch. Kneeling above her was an emergency medical technician, a young woman with broad shoulders, two gold teeth, and gentle hands.

"My name's Charlie," the EMT said. "You're going to be just fine."

She said her name a few more times, then asked Maggie to call her Charlie. Asked Maggie what year it was. Blue shirted cops and plain clothes agents milled about the bright noisy room. Radios crackled. She smelled gun oil. Maggie didn't recognize any faces, and she didn't see a single Air Force uniform.

"How you feeling, young lady?" Charlie said.

"I could use some water. Do you know if they found anybody else in the house? I came inside after my friend. A young man. Jordan."

Charlie cracked open the top of a water bottle, handed the container to Maggie. "You shush now, young lady. You probably have a concussion from the looks of that contusion on your temple."

"What happened?" Maggie said. "Where's my friend?"

Maggie's gaze followed Charlie's instinctive glance. A stretcher rattled and rolled out through the kitchen door. Two EMTs attended to the patient onboard with cavalier nonchalance...oh, no wonder.

The person on the stretcher lay inside a plastic body bag.

Maggie groaned.

Maggie slipped inside the Defense Department limousine. She joined Billy Payton, the two occupying a breed of government limo Maggie had never been inside—long and luxurious and covered with more radio antennae than the Cal Tech science department.

She'd learned with relief the body she'd seen headed out of Woodward's kitchen had been Woody Woodward, not Jordan, but little else about the night had worked out in her favor, including this summons from Billy.

The extra-wide door snapped shut behind her. She couldn't resist leaning back into the well-cushioned leather, easing her sore spine. The last four hours had been grueling—hostile interrogations by the El Centro Police Department, the Imperial Country Homicide Unit, and even the FBI's Special Bastard in Charge of her lost experiment, Chip Daley. "Great work," Daley had said. "You lose a deadly experiment, then kill the only guy who could lead us to it."

Maggie stared at Billy. "*Who* wants to talk to me?"

"The Assistant Secretary of Defense is going to call." Billy pointed to an old-fashioned, cradle and barbell telephone. The antique rested inside a mahogany, rear-seat console that separated Maggie from her old wing commander. "And like you get called Colonel, this assistant secretary gets called Mr. Secretary by the likes of us."

"Of course. But what does he need to talk to me about?"

Billy stared at her, his eyes droopy and dejected—more than she'd seen in years, not since she'd told him they were through dating over twenty years ago. "What did you think, Maggie? Maybe breaking into a witness's house and getting the man killed is going to bring you a promotion?"

"I didn't get anyone killed. Whoever murdered Woodward had to—"

Billy held up his hand. "Maggie! What the hell were you thinking? Coming to Woody Woodward's house the night before he was to be interviewed by the FBI? Breaking inside the house? A private residence with Woodward's dead body inside? I cannot understand how you could make decisions like that."

Maggie rubbed her prosthetic hand. "I was with the reporter, Jordan Scott. He said he was coming here with me or without me, so—"

"You broke into the house together?"

"No! I did not break in, and I told the reporter not to as well. But I followed him inside when I heard trouble. We were on the phone together when someone attacked him. Whoever it was had to be Woodward's murderer. I saw him when he tried to kill me."

"I heard the description you gave the local police. Daley says the man sounds like someone they've been trying to find at Woodward Construction."

"Really?"

"Yes. A very dangerous man. A foreign national."

"Sounds like Daley's getting somewhere," Maggie said. "Did he hear anything about Jordan?"

"No. He didn't say anything except the reporter wasn't in the house, where you thought. Maybe the man you saw took him, although they sure won't get much ransom from that San Diego rag he works for, the news business being what it is."

"I don't think they want money," Maggie said.

"You're certain there were two?"

"Yes. One dragging the body, another driving the truck. Not sure which one hit me, but he was no ordinary criminal. The black clothes. The gun belt. Very quiet and efficient. They had the right kind of tow truck. They were at Woodward's. I believe these are the guys who have our missile and experiment, and I'm afraid they have big plans."

"Why do you say that?"

Maggie shrugged. "Because of how they've acted and the guy who hit me—the kind of man he was. Pretty sure he's a trained soldier, maybe special forces the way he snuck up on me."

"That's scary."

"No kidding," Maggie said.

"Why were you with Jordan Scott? Was he interviewing you? You shouldn't be talking to the press."

"He found out about Woodward on his own, so I made a deal with him to keep the news out of the paper until tomorrow—until the interview was done. It didn't work out because *The New York Times* had Woodward's name anyway."

"But why come here with him?"

"Why not? I'm not part of the investigation anymore. I wasn't going to hear any of Woodward's story unless I came here with Jordan. He was going to knock on the door and talk to Woodward. Honestly, I figured we'd be thrown off the front steps. I had no clue he'd break into the house, find Woodward's dead body. I had to make up my response as events happened."

Billy gave her a friendly pat on the shoulder. "How's your head?"

"Hurts like hell."

The antique cradle and barbell telephone lit up.

"Let's hope the pain doesn't get worse," Billy said. "It's possible the assistant secretary will ask for your resignation."

SIXTEEN

Asdrubal Torres filled his mother's bowl with a *toloache,* this one sweetened with honey to hide the bitter taste of elephant tree bark and datura root. He wanted the white man Jordan Scott to drink a mouthful.

Datura had been killing teenage experimenters in the West since the 1960s, maybe longer, and since Torres assumed Jordan had no experience with either powerful drug, even a taste of the *toloache* gambled with his life. But too bad. As soon as Torres heard the voice on the phone call out the name Jordan, Torres guessed the brash young home invader was the same Jordan Scott who had returned Chaco Cruz's basket. Reynaldo had mentioned his name, and since the spirits had shown themselves over and over to be spectacular providers, why not one more time with the man who could answer Torres' questions about the basket's use.

Imagine the things Jordan could encourage the basket to reveal: Not only how Scott's great grandfather had obtained the woven treasure, but perhaps the steps the great *puul* Chaco Cruz had taken to gather the water spirit and redirect the Colorado River. This information might be available if Jordan's ancestor had been involved in the basket's theft.

The basket would remember.

If Jordan's great grandfather had ever touched this powerful *puul's* basket, a piece of the man's spirit would remain. And if he had killed the famous Cahuilla shaman, soiled the basket with his own blood, then Scott's great grandfather had been a man of great power himself, and every physical action, every emotion belonging to him that night might still remain within the basket's weave. As a direct descendant, Jordan Scott could help Torres tap the imprinted information.

Torres sighed in wonder. Exact memories could be available.

There was reason to hope Jordan could handle the power of any vision as well as the toxic ingredients, and though the secrets Torres sought were worth a hundred young men like this one, Torres believed the reporter would survive. Perhaps Jordan Scott would someday write stories about the return of Chaco Cruz's water basket and the recreation of ancient Lake Cahuilla.

"Drink some of this tea," Torres said. "It is medicine that will make you feel invigorated. Your injured neck looks sore."

"Aren't you having any?"

Torres took back his mother's handmade bowl and tasted the *toloache*. "Drink. You will be healed. I give you my solemn word as a warrior."

Jordan sipped the *toloache*. After licking his lips, he drank more.

Torres said a silent prayer. Minutes passed before he reopened his eyes and spoke. "You and I are about to make an incredible journey, perhaps back in time. We must observe and record as much as we can. Your vision could be different than mine, so try to remember as many details as you can."

The young man stared at Torres. Eyes wide. Blank muscles in his face. Perhaps he'd realized on what kind of a journey he had embarked.

"You drugged me?"

"The *toloache* is key to a special door we must open."

"I feel woozy. Why did you drug me?"

"The basket, your great grandfather and the *toloache* will show us exactly what happened in 1907. Did you not tell Chief Reynaldo you could not believe your great grandfather murdered Chaco Cruz? For me, the crucial issue is to understand, not only how your ancestor acquired Chaco Cruz's basket, but exactly where. And what was Chaco doing with his basket at the time. Why were they near the ocean? I must see for myself how he invoked the spirit of the water."

"You can't go back in time and you can't recreate Lake Cahuilla," Jordan said. "I heard what you and that other guy said. That's crazy talk."

"Perhaps, but I believe you can pass on to me your ancestor's knowledge imprinted in the basket. I will see if your tale is true and if the basket wants me to know. Are you ready for our journey?"

"My journey feels like sleep."

Torres smiled. "Hold the basket as I do, Jordan Scott.

Hold the basket with both of your hands."

Spring, 1907.

Barton Scott crawled on his stomach up the windward side of a Mexican sand dune, his Winchester repeater wrapped in soft leather and cradled in his elbows. Safe to say, this would be his best chance. Thick clouds offered little moonlight for visual tracking, let alone a clear shot from high ground.

At the crest, staring down the dune's slip face, Barton recoiled as three inches of sand gave way beneath his fingertips. He held his breath as a small river of ancient rock and shell cascaded down thirty-five feet of sheer cliff and became a pile only twenty feet from the three Indians he'd been tracking. He remembered the outrageous instructions he had received, first from his railroad supervisor and then from the old man who never left his railcar, Mr. Barrington: "Find them and kill them, Scott."

"I'm no killer."

"You are now, son, or you can get on your horse and ride back to San Diego. And I'm not saying it that way to be the leather-necked prick I am reputed to be. I am saying it because you, sir, are the only tracker we have left. If you cannot find these Indian medicine men, stop them from doing whatever it is they're doing, that damn Colorado River will flood one-eighth of California."

"The railroad thinks the flood is shaman's magic, do they?"

"How else would you explain what's happened? Sudden flows and surges at precisely the wrong moment? Submerged tree trunks rising up from nowhere and dislodging the brand-new gate? The Swede accidentally blowing himself up with the temporary dam? Not to mention the two men we've lost looking for these Indians. In fact, Scott, it's hard to believe what has happened is *not* witchcraft in my fucking book. My wife's Presbyterian preacher in Yuma says it's the Devil himself."

In the end, it was his friends and coworkers who'd convinced Barton Scott to try, not the railroad tycoon Barrington. All their jobs were at stake, they told him, each and every man, some rather sternly. Safe to say, Barton would be headed back to San Diego one way or another if he didn't track and stop these Indians and their magic.

Stretched out in the cool sand, Barton carefully unwrapped his Winchester 1894, a gift from his father. The old man had traveled to the World's Fair in Chicago, seen the new rifle introduced. When he'd returned to San Diego, the lever-action repeater had been a gift for Barton's fourteenth birthday.

Barton had watched these three Indians fill their woven basket with Colorado River water. They had collected the water at a bend in the river just above the Mexican Cut, the same place where the railroad's irrigation dam had burst; where water still flowed north into California. The Indians then had dragged the water-loaded basket on a crude sled through the sand, advancing in a direct line toward the new lake being formed by the flood. It was truly amazing to Barton that woven sticks could even hold water. How could their actions possibly have caused the project's strange accidents? Magic, indeed.

Bloody foolish, is what this was.

He licked his finger to test the wind. Or perhaps he was stalling. He smiled at himself. Barton Scott was an English-born horseman turned cowboy; an educated surveyor who'd by necessity become a tracker and gunman. He'd been hired away from his San Luis Rey River ranch to help lay new railroad track after the flood, but the Colorado River had been flowing into Southern California for two and half years. Nobody knew where to safely put the new track.

He sighted his Winchester on the chief Indian, the one who never took his hands off the big basket. Such a reverent touch the silver-haired old gentleman kept on those woven sticks and grasses. As if he were holding his grandchild. And no easy target, either, sitting below the slipface of this tall sand dune. A cloudy sky.

Spotting Barton, the chief jumped from his squat and hopped backward, providing Barton with a perfect target. Hawk-eyed son-of-a-gun detecting him up here, the chief was. The two Indians at his side split off, running in opposite directions along the bottom of the slipface. The long-trunked men sprinted across the sand like web-footed lizards.

Diversions. Barton stayed his sight on the chief with the basket, or at least the Indian who looked like a chief.

Painted up rather nicely with those large golden eagle feathers on his clothes. Those feathers were rare. At this range, no more than fifty feet, his Winchester's .45 caliber rifle slug would punch a hole through that fellow. What a bloody mess. The proud old man didn't seem to care much, either, standing there with his arms spread, murmuring what Barton assumed was a prayer.

Barton's finger touched the cool trigger. Could this poor old Indian and his basket really be responsible for the flood? Did he really deserve to die? Barton lowered the rifle and crawled backward off the dune. Damned if he was going bushwhack three men because some crazy, San Francisco railroad prince believed in hocus-pocus. Why not just dump their sacred water and take the chief's magic basket? Looked like that would put a crimp in *their* style, maybe finish this foolishness, send these Indians home. The huge water-tight basket would make a nice souvenir, too.

Barton needed two minutes to work down and across the dune's slack, find a place where he could operate on the same level as the sled and the giant woven basket. Trouble was, the chief Indian still guarded his midnight caravan, plus both of his tough-looking pals had returned.

Barton lifted his Winchester. These gents wouldn't understand English, but his tone and rifle prop should help translate. "You boys ought to be leaving before I change my mind about shooting somebody tonight."

Nobody moved.

After four or five heartbeats, Barton figured these

Indians wouldn't respond any better to Spanish. Safe to say it was the gun that needed to speak. He aimed and fired a round through the chief Indian's eagle feathers, the gold-tipped beauties fixed to the side of his head.

The muzzle flash and explosion thundered across the quiet dunes, but faded quickly in all the emptiness. Worse, none of the three Indians blinked a bloody eyelash, even the chief who'd had his hair parted. Tough sons-of-guns.

With a show, Barton chambered a new round in the Winchester, the *clickity-clack* of the big repeater's lever-action ringing out like farm machinery. Now what the hell was he going to do? If he wanted that basket, he was beginning to think—

All three Indians yanked knives from their belts and ran at him, the action swift, fluid, and simultaneous, everything happening, everybody coming at once. They screamed at the peak of their voices, too, hair-raising yelps that grabbed at Barton's nerves.

His reactions were instinctive and quick. He fired, reloaded and fired the Winchester again in rapid succession. Two of the charging Indians fell dead.

But before he could reload a second time, the chief drove his shoulder low against the rifle barrel and swept his knife underneath Barton's blocking hand. He caught the Indian's wrist, but the knife blade pushed within an inch of Barton's throat.

He had dropped his prized rifle to catch the chief's wrist, and the two men wrestled in the sand. The Indian was strong, his muscles long and hard like wire. Barton needed both hands to keep the knife blade from slicing the side of his neck.

Barton turned the chief onto his backside, the two of them locked together by arms, legs and the desperate battle to survive. The Indian's knife held within inches of Barton's neck no matter where they rolled, or who was on top. Moonlight glinted in the Indian's polished black eyes, and there was a moment when Barton wondered if Mrs. Barrington's preacher in Yuma had been right, that Barton wrestled with the Devil himself. The chief even smelled like a dead goat.

The chief acquired a top position once more and screamed, higher pitched than previous, perhaps sensing Barton's fear. But in the split-second the Indian slightly lifted his nose to howl, Barton wedged an elbow onto his own breast, locking the Indian's blade well away from Barton's throat.

And freeing Barton's right hand.

The chief saw Barton's fingers on the tiny Remington too late. The two-shot pistol he kept in his waistcoat, a .41 caliber Remington, blew off a teacup-size chunk of the chief's forehead.

Blood splashed in Barton's eyes. He rolled the dead chief's body off his chest, sat up and gasped for air. With each breath, the world felt fresher and newer to him. As if he were alive and breathing for the first time.

Torres awoke from his vision in awe of what he had seen: Chaco Cruz had been "priming" Lake Cahuilla—

carrying Colorado River water from the Mexican Cut across the Imperial Sand Dunes to the newly created Salton Sea. The ocean waves he'd imagined inside the basket's weavings had in fact been tall sand dunes.

By repeating the transfer over and over, carrying the river water in his magic basket, Chaco Cruz had captured and maintained the water spirit as an ally despite the railroad's two-year effort to stop him. Again and again, the spirit of the water defeated the white man's attempts at control.

Torres could do the same.

Checking Jordan Scott, Torres noticed an abundance of sweat and a violent quivering of the reporter's facial muscles, symptoms that suggested an overdose of datura root. How disappointing it would be to lose the reporter before discussing what his great grandfather had done to the great Cahuilla shaman and the two braves.

SEVENTEEN

Tough to throw a Jamaican party in the Southern California desert, even with Bob Marley music rattling the glasses, but Maggie's friend Franny the bartender tried hard in her wraparound Gucci shades, green bowling shirt, and an accent like Al Pacino in *Scarface*. Maggie was smiling before she sat down—much needed relief from the worrying she'd been doing about her missing weapon and Jordan. Plus, her brain still throbbed from that elbow punch the previous night. A sturdy shot of Bushmills and a joke from Franny always helped a headache. Maggie kept her cell phone close.

Franny had been a friend since the first day Maggie arrived in El Centro, Maggie staying a week in the new hotel by Highway 8 before getting an apartment. Franny had been bartender in the tiny hotel lounge and still was, but that day had been Franny's first on the bartender job, and like Maggie, her first day in El Centro. Maggie had walked up to Franny's bar six years ago for a Bushmills before bed. Now she came in once or twice a week to shoot the bull, or as might be the case tonight, tell Franny about a problem, see if she offered insight. They both liked to laugh, but neither one knew exactly why they'd become close. Maggie sometimes looked after Franny's ten-year-old daughter.

Franny leaned across the slick wooden bar, her hand tapping the beat of the radio playing "I Shot the Sheriff."

"Nobody chop the ax like Marley, mon," she said.

Maggie grinned. "That's a Cuban accent, Franny. And Marley's good, but have you ever listened to Mark Knopfler?"

"Oh, mon, you can't mean that country rock boy, play with all the fingers, all the time?"

Maggie laughed. "The best rock guitar player, ever."

Growing up, Maggie had treasured things that swept her away from the freeway life in Burbank—vacations, school trips, books, movies, and good music. Flying came later to top them all, but her first real crush had been a band, U2. She'd been nine when their hits "With You or Without You" and "I Still Haven't Found What I'm Looking For" were popular. Just weeks before her mom died, when Maggie was ten, her mother had introduced her to the recordings of Chuck Berry, B.B. King, Bo Diddly, and the early Rolling Stones. Maggie loved the way her feet wouldn't stand still, how the rhythm and blues made her dance. Those tasty, gutsy guitar solos were the best—music that took her to another world. For her taste, in today's world Knopfler was king.

"I've heard every name you can think of," Franny said. She mixed cosmos for two patrons. Her hands moved like she was potting house plants. "Hendrix,

Clapton, B.B. King, John Mayer. Last week, some woman from Vancouver was in here telling me the best axe man was—get ready—Gordon Lightfoot."

Maggie checked her phone and placed it on the counter. "I thought Gordon Lightfoot was the new Canadian prime minister."

Laughing, Franny served the cosmos to a couple of young women in business suits. She still grinned when she came back. "Ready for another Irish?"

One Bushmills helped her headache and left Maggie mentally sharp. She knew her limits. "No more, thanks. I need to remain ready."

"You're still looking for that…thing you lost?"

Maggie nodded. "And the man I met."

Franny's hand stopped wiping the bar. "A new man?"

"That missing reporter on the news. The one who was kidnapped."

"You're kidding? Oh, my God. Who do you think kidnapped him?"

Maggie leaned close to her friend. "It's an ongoing investigation, so keep this to yourself, but the men who took Jordan might be the same ones who have my—thing."

Franny's eyes sparkled. "Does Jordan know about your *thing* yet?"

They both laughed.

"No," Maggie said, "and I haven't handled his thing either."

They laughed again. The cosmos women glanced at them.

"Wait a minute," Franny said. "Let's define our terms. He's a new man, but you're not dating yet?"

"We haven't had time for a meal. He's writing stories about my...lost thing."

They giggled.

"But you like him, huh?"

Maggie sipped her whiskey. "Kind of, but he's too young."

Two couples came into the bar laughing, and Franny left Maggie with her thoughts. Her friend was always good for laughs, but what Maggie really needed that night was a shot of reinforcement. That old feeling of being a loser had gripped her an hour ago when she'd watched a news report about her lost missile and the kidnapped reporter.

She'd thought of herself that way for the first time at ten years old, following the death of her mother. She felt so unlucky. Other kids didn't lose their moms. Becoming a combat aircraft fighter had banished that emotion seemingly forever. But her crash fourteen years later brought the negativity all back, and then some—a bout of depression. She hadn't seen a shrink, but rather read up on the disease during rehab after she'd lost her arm. She'd easily diagnosed her self-anger. Getting better hadn't been as easy, but she'd done it, and until these past two weeks, had managed the problem well.

Maggie's physical recovery had started with surgery and rehab back in the United States. An Australian pilot named Robbie helped with the mental aspects of her recovery. Maggie had been first fitted with a purely cosmetic hand—no functionality at all. Her second device, a body harness allowing her upper body muscles to open and close a hook, turned out to be uncomfortable as hell and not capable of anything delicate. After a particularly romantic weekend that summer, Robbie had showed her a British website displaying early versions of the BeBionic with individually motorized fingers. Maggie had started a special savings account to buy one the same day. She'd also begun to heal more quickly, finally accepting the amputation and other minor physical injuries associated with the Spangdahlem crash. Robbie had been restorative in several ways.

Her phone chime inexplicably made Maggie think the call was from Jordan. No. Of course not. The poor man was probably dead. The call came from her father.

"Hey, Pop."

"Hi, Maggie," Sean Black said. "Any luck finding your lost experiment?"

"Not yet, no. How are you doing?"

"I'm working twenty hours a day. The spillways aren't operating right. Plus, I can hardly sleep, worrying about your lost missile."

"You're being silly, Pop. There's no substantiated threat to Hoover."

"If there were no threat, you wouldn't have asked me about security the other day."

Maggie needed to change the subject. "I heard Lake Mead is full. Is that true?"

"Almost. It's been more than thirty years."

"Wow."

By providing fresh water and electricity to Los Angeles, San Diego, Phoenix, Las Vegas, Tucson, and a thousand smaller communities since the mid-1930s, Hoover Dam had almost single-handedly converted the nation's Southwest deserts into a green habitat, a new home for thirty million Americans. And every single one took drinking water for granted.

"Two prima donna electricians from Los Angeles arrived this morning to fix the spillway wiring, if that's the problem," her father said. "Hopefully, they'll at least get the manual override switches operational. Maybe you know a psychic who could tell me how the spillways could malfunction the first time we might actually need them."

Her father had worked at Hoover Dam twenty-one years next March.

"Sorry, I have no psychics on my contact list," Maggie said. "Let me know if you find a good one. I'd like to know how a lightning storm from nowhere downed my plane and crew."

"I'll sleep a lot better when you find that weapon."

"We shouldn't talk about that," Maggie said. "I'm not on my Air Force phone."

Her father's guttural noise and the following silence told Maggie he might have figured out what had happened. Sean Black had given Maggie a lot of disciplinarian crap growing up, but genetically, he'd also bestowed her with a good supply of brains.

"Uh, oh," he said.

"What?"

"Are you off the case? Did they turn over your problem to those alphabet knuckleheads in Washington? That's why you came up here the other day, isn't it?"

Maggie's fingers paled squeezing the phone.

"Don't start smoking those damn cigarettes again," her father said.

EIGHTEEN

Fascinated by what Jordan's great grandfather had shown him, Torres knew he would not sleep. He remained awake in the rented garage all night to watch over the Great Spirit's gifts, and to puzzle over his last award, Jordan Scott. Why did he worry about the young man's health?

Near dawn, Torres forced Jordan to drink water. He mopped the reporter's perspiring forehead with a cool, damp cloth and soaked up the sweat pooling against his collarbones. Torres soon noticed improvement, and within minutes, Jordan surprised him by opening his eyes and speaking clearly.

"Can I have more water?" he said.

Torres pointed to a four-foot refrigerator near the workbench on which Jordan had been stretched. "You are no longer bound. There are soft drinks and bottled water in the refrigerator. Help yourself."

Torres was pleased to see the reporter roll off the table, stagger to the refrigerator, and open the appliance door. His movements were those of a drugged and sleepy man, not a failing one. Perhaps there were stories Jordan could write for the world to read.

"Did you see what your great grandfather did to my ancestors?" Torres said.

Jordan blinked. "I dreamed about him aiming a rifle at three Indians from the top of a sand dune, down the slipface. But he didn't shoot them when he had a perfect chance."

Torres pointed to his second gift, the basket, the one that cost the life of his stubborn friend Reynaldo. "The blood of my ancestors is on that basket. So, too, is your great grandfather's. He was the last killer the railroad sent. And he was successful. He tracked our great shaman Chaco Cruz and murdered him."

"I saw no murder. I saw self-defense. He could have bushwhacked them—I remember he used that word—but he ran down the sand dunes to talk to them instead."

"Yet he killed Chaco Cruz and two of the *puul's* apprentices."

"They attacked him. He thought if he threatened them with the rifle, they would run away, that he could take the basket without killing them."

"Your great grandfather expected our *puul* to give up his magic without a fight?"

"To my great grandfather, it was just a basket. Why would anyone die for a basket?"

Torres could only stare. White men understood nothing.

* * *

Jordan didn't figure Torres's logic. He'd seen the same things in his technicolor dream. But Jordan's great grandfather hadn't acted badly. Not by 1907 standards, anyway. He hadn't planned on killing anyone. He'd refused until the three Indians ran at him with knives. Of course, his great grandfather had been stealing, so the self-defense angle wouldn't hold up in today's courts.

But arguing about events they'd dreamed happened more than a century earlier seemed stupid to Jordan. He couldn't say for sure what happened. Was Barton Scott a vision or a dream? He knew he'd been under the spell of a powerful hallucinatory drug. Images and sounds had distorted in false ways.

None of that mattered, he realized. Jordan needed to get out of there. That's what mattered. The big room he and Torres occupied looked like professional garage space, and newly constructed, too, the light gray paint on the walls fresh and clean, the cement floor devoid of dirt or grease. Three-quarters of one wall consisted of a push-up garage door that Jordan guessed led to an alley or street. A standard, walk-through door stood next to the bigger one, and special latches with padlocks on both secured him inside.

Jordan squinted at an odd shape against the far wall. Another vision? Was this an after-effect of Torres' *toloache?* What else could look like a giant aluminum cigar tube strapped onto a boat trailer?

"Your great grandfather had no idea what the *puul* and his apprentices were doing with the basket," Torres said. "Yet he interfered and murdered strangers for his own purpose. The railroad's purpose—money and profit."

Jordan tried to focus. It wasn't easy with the cruise missile parked nearby, the *toloache* leaving him woozy and uncertain. Just then Torres's voice had carried a strange echo.

"Chief Reynaldo told me Chaco Cruz used the basket to divert the Colorado River, but surely he didn't carry the water one basket at a time," Jordan said. "Why would anyone lug around Colorado River water?"

"To awaken the water spirits," Torres said. "To suggest a change in course for the great red river, a change that has repeated itself over and over for millions of years—since before the beginning of human time. A change the river knows well how to make."

Jordan pointed at the missile. "Where does the flying bomb come into it?"

Torres blinked. Jordan wondered if his captor had forgotten the cruise missile rested in clear view. Jordan hadn't forgotten. What a story. His fingertips practically tickled when he thought about writing the opening sentence on his laptop. He hoped he lived to tell the tale.

"Of course you would recognize the conventional air launched cruise missile," Torres said. "You've been writing stories about my gift from the Great Spirit."

"Your gift?"

"I saw where it landed. The basket was a gift, as are you, Jordan Scott. Now I know how Chaco Cruz used his magic."

"What are you going to do with the missile?"

"The weapon will make the Colorado surge free as it did in 1905."

Jordan shook his head. "Since they built Hoover Dam, I think the flow of the Colorado River is pretty much under control. You'd have trouble changing the river's course if you had a hundred cruise missiles."

"Perhaps," Torres said. "But let me show you something. Perhaps you will write a story someday."

"You're going to let me go?"

"Probably. But why not write stories here?"

Jordan nodded, trying to show Torres he might consider it. Jordan would use his natural curiosity, lie his ass off to feign interest in Torres' plan. He knew the man was crazy and violent. He had to get out of there. No matter what Torres said, eventually they would kill him.

Torres used a felt-tip marker to draw a straight vertical line on the smooth, plastic tabletop. At the top of the line, Torres drew a half-circle, as if the vertical line balanced an empty bowl. At the bottom of the line, Torres drew an upside-down V. The image appeared as an armless stickman with an open basket for a head.

"Imagine the basket is Lake Mead," Torres said. "The body of water behind Hoover Dam?"

"Yeah, I know."

"It holds nine trillion gallons."

"Trillion with a T?"

"Yes. And this vertical line, or the stickman's spine, is two hundred miles of Colorado River—from Hoover Dam to Yuma. These two legs at the bottom represent the dual and alternating ancient paths of the Colorado River from that point."

"Say that again."

"As its raging water carved the Grand Canyon, the Colorado River carried silt to the Gulf of California—the ocean. Gradually, the silt separated the Gulf of California into two parts. Sometimes the river flowed north of that silt divide, sometimes south."

"So?"

"So when the Colorado flowed south, the water emptied into the ocean. But when the river turned north of the silt—" Torres used Henry's marker to slice off one of the stickman's legs, "—the water flowed north into Southern California and filled a giant freshwater lake. Lake Cahuilla."

"I understand how nature did it," Jordan said. "The river runs right across the San Andreas Fault. Massive earthquakes must have been regular events, at least in geological time. But the process must have taken centuries for the river to fill the fresh water lake. You and your friend don't have time for that."

Torres slashed a line through his stickman's head. "This time, Lake Cahuilla will fill more quickly. The white man's weapon of war will bring the water down this river all at once."

Jordan stared. He could not hide his astonishment.

"You believe I am joking?" Torres said.

"I didn't say you were joking."

"I see your heart. You believe I talk but cannot act. Tell me, Jordan Scott, did you read of the murdered border guards last week? The explosion at the All-American Canal?"

"*You* killed those border guards? Why?"

"Because for at least a few days, while the canal is being repaired, great quantities of Colorado River water will be diverted south of Yuma. The river's ancient, northwestern course has been almost completely reconstructed."

NINETEEN

The next day Maggie called FBI Special Agent Chip Daley's office. Had he followed up on her description of the bowl-haired attacker? She stuck her apartment's house phone between her ear and shoulder while she poured a cup of coffee.

"He's very busy," Daley's gatekeeper said. "I can have the special agent call you back as soon as he gets a chance. Perhaps later today."

"A man's life is at stake," Maggie said. "How about giving me his cell phone number?"

"I'm sorry, Colonel. I'm not allowed to release that, especially over the telephone. I'm sure you can understand."

Maggie's temper flickered. Daley was chasing a lead she gave him. Maggie sniffed and shut that bad boy emotion down. Anger made her impulsive, stupid. She had to be careful.

"Thank you," Maggie said. "I'll call back when I need another load of crap."

She used her cell to hit Billy Payton's number.

"Can you give me that FBI turkey's cell phone number?" Maggie said. "You know, Chip what's his name?"

Billy chuckled. "Hang on."

"Thanks."

"Here it is. I'll text it to you."

"You're a pal."

"Anytime. In fact, I could send my chopper down this afternoon if you wanted to fly up and have dinner with me tonight. I could have my chef make us—"

"Oh, take a hike, Romeo. You had your chance twenty years ago. Thanks again for the number." Maggie hauled a chair up to her kitchen table, sat down to finish her coffee. Billy's wife, a romance novel author, must be out of town. Until today, the horny, ice-cream loving bastard hadn't tried the booty call on Maggie in three years.

Did she sound vulnerable? Was she?

She touched the first three digits of Daley's cell number, then stopped. Why go through all the baloney with the Special Bastard in Charge? Even if the FBI had already discovered the broken-tooth man's name, Maggie couldn't trust Daley to be truthful. He knew she hated his guts for replacing her, keeping her off the investigation.

She poured another cup of java. She needed to wake up. She'd been wasting time. Two or three men must have been inside Woodward's house when Jordan broke in. If they'd kidnapped Jordan, they had to be considered strong suspects in the death of Woody Woodward, too. *And* the disappearance of her experimental weapon.

She didn't need Daley.

Maggie Googled Woodward Construction in El

Centro, found a number on their website and punched the number on her cell phone. A middle-aged woman answered in a sing song voice. After identifying herself as United States Air Force Lieutenant Colonel Margaret Black, she asked for Woody Woodward's private secretary.

"I don't know if you heard or not, but Mr. Woodward was murdered yesterday," the woman said.

"Yes, ma'am, I am aware of that," Maggie said. "I'm Colonel Black, the one who called the police from Mr. Woodward's home. And it's very important I talk to his—"

"Wait. You're Colonel Black, the lady on TV?"

"That's me."

"You were at Mr. Woodward's house while he was murdered?"

"Not *while* he was murdered, I assure you. But yes, I was investigating something else there. That's what I'm doing now, investigating."

"The FBI thinks the murderer's here at the company. Isn't that scary? They're coming here in an hour with sketches."

Maggie liked this lady, this uncoerced volunteer of wonderful information. And like Jordan the reporter had showed her, once you had a source going, push it. "I'll bet you can help me," Maggie said. "I want to speak with someone who knows your employees, someone who knows what they look like. I saw the man the FBI is looking for."

"I'd like to help, but I think I've been stupid. I'm not

supposed to talk about Mr. Woodward. The lawyers said we should refer calls to them."

"Listen, I don't think you understand, Ms.—what did you say your name was?"

"I didn't say, and be careful with your tone. I don't like being bullied."

Maggie stared at the phone and sighed. A bully? Well, maybe. "I'm sorry," she said. "You're right. I apologize for trying to strong-arm you. But a very nice young reporter was kidnapped by those people and he needs our help. I'm afraid what—"

"Jordan Smith, right?"

"Jordan Scott. He's the nicest young man. So kind to his grandmother in the nursing home. Visiting her three times a week for years. These bad people could have done such horrible things to Jordan by now, I hate to think. If only I knew the name of the man who hit me in the head."

"What did your attacker look like?"

Maggie held the phone away and grinned. "He's big, very physical. I'm sure he wouldn't work inside an office."

"Yes, but everybody comes in here on payday."

Maggie laughed. "He's big, like a professional football player. Dark skin, Hispanic maybe. Black hair cut like a bowl."

"That's Andy's friend, Henry. Henry Melancon. And I can tell you it will surprise no one at Woodward Construction that Mr. Melancon is mixed up in more trouble."

"*More* trouble?"

"Andy forced Mr. Woodward to give this Henry a job, right out of prison, only he didn't know which prison and then Mr. Woodward's private investigator couldn't find out anything either. The man is totally frightening, and so are the people he drives around with."

"Who's this Andy person?" Maggie said.

"Mr. Woodward's son. Asdrubal Torres."

TWENTY

Jordan decided Henry was *seriously* sketchy. Jordan's father would have said Henry gave off "bad vibrations," but that downplayed the size of Henry's shoulders, chest, and arms. It dismissed his short neck smashed onto those powerful, broad shoulders, and excluded the way he carried himself in light, desert camouflage. Henry didn't walk. He advanced. Henry didn't carry things. He transported them. The guy was ex-military. A trained-killer and proud of it. Sketchy.

From the crew seat of Henry's truck, Jordan wondered if Henry and Torres weren't minutes away from killing him. He'd been forced into the truck's cramped backseat. They wouldn't say where they were headed. Jordan's hands were wrapped in duct tape. A tight blindfold pressured his skull.

He forced himself to breathe as slowly and deeply as he could, overdosing his blood with oxygen, preparing his body to run or fight. The two-to-one odds made physical resistance difficult, even though Jordan was an athletic six-footer. The last thing Jordan wanted to do was wrestle Henry. Clearly, his best chance at survival was to run.

Maybe he'd wanted his lost-weapon story too much. Maybe he should acquire more experience before letting everything ride on his twenty-nine-year-old instincts. Breaking into Woodward's had been a bad idea, and Jordan liked to ruminate on his mistakes, learn from them. He hated making the same one twice.

Torres asked Henry to stop the truck so he could urinate. Henry slowed without hesitation, as if he'd anticipated the order. A hand removed Jordan's blindfold. Torres. Jordan gazed out the truck's smoked windows. He had no idea where they were; parked on a dirt trail in a vast expanse of empty desert, a treeless and brush-free landscape of brown and gray hills, the rock surfaces sliced and furrowed by centuries of wind and water. Except for themselves and the truck, nothing manmade was visible. When Henry opened the driver's door, only a hiss of wind touched his ears.

Torres waved at Jordan. "Relieve yourself while you can."

Henry motioned for Jordan to jump down. The big man with bad teeth stared at him with a dull, lifeless gaze—like a bird or a fish. Henry's upper arms were as big around as Jordan's legs.

Jordan hopped to the ground, easily holding his balance with his hands bound behind him, but making himself look awkward, stumbling. Bright afternoon sun warmed his head and neck. The air tasted of dust. What a lonely, desolate spot Henry had picked to stop. If they were going to kill him, this would be a great location.

This might be the moment. Jordan's gut twisted like a rubber band.

He tried to walk toward the truck's grill, but Henry blocked him. Loose at his sides, Henry's mitts were as big as apple pies. The hands, Henry's size and those muscles were all intimidating, but what really scared Jordan was Henry's "go ahead and hit me" grin. The toughest kid in Jordan's high school had been Tommy O'Hara, a skinny, five-foot-five carrot-top with that same, go-ahead-and-hit-me smile. It didn't matter how big any new boy was, or how many times and how hard the new kid hit Tommy O'Hara. Tommy's dad was in jail, his mom was a drunk, and the two older O'Hara brothers had beaten Tommy every day growing up. Tommy's nerves no longer registered pain. You couldn't hurt him, and when he fought, he battled for his life. He kept hitting and kicking until his opponent quit. For Jordan, there was only one plan when you faced a guy like that, the only plan Jordan had been working on, the only plan a rational man could have with his hands tied behind his back. Run.

"You going to cut this tape on my hands?" Jordan said. "Or do you want to work my zipper, pull my dick out?"

"Turn around," Henry said.

On the far side of the truck, Torres opened his door. Jordan smelled what was coming. This whole stop-exit-pee thing had been an act. No one needed to go, and no freaking way was Henry going to untie Jordan's hands. Henry and Torres were going to kill him. That was the agenda. Kill him and hide his body somewhere in these barren rock hills.

Jordan retreated a step, giving himself extra space, then turned his back on Henry as ordered. Leisurely, trying to make Henry think Jordan had gone along with the command, offering his taped hands for untying, trying to make Henry think he had no intention of taking a quick hike.

Jordan ran.

Henry lunged during Jordan's first step, but the big man was a split-second late, maybe surprised. His steely fingers raked Jordan's backside below the belt, briefly snagging a hip pocket. But Jordan shook him off.

Two long strides ahead, Jordan sprinted for an outcropping of red rock hills, his legs pumping hard, running fast, the pounding of Henry's feet right behind him. The big man with the bowl-shaped haircut ran like a rhino, his heavy combat boots tearing and crashing at the rocks and sand.

Having his hands taped kept Jordan off balance and prevented him from achieving maximum speed. But he exaggerated his shoulder movements as counterweight to his feet and legs, and paid strict attention to the placement of his feet. Jordan ran with the thoughtful and careful motions of a man being chased by the hounds of death. To fall was to be eaten alive.

In less than a hundred yards, Henry's heavy stride faded. As Jordan reached a small crest on the same trail they'd driven, he risked a change in balance to glance back over his shoulder. Henry had ceased running. The big man stood crouched on the dirt trail, his plate-size hands on his knees more than twenty yards back. A football field away, Torres leaned against his truck and watched.

Another hour, darkness would offer Jordan the cover to easily hide in the red rocks by the road. That would be his plan—run, hide, and wait them out. A moonscape surrounded him as he worked higher up the barren mountain of rocks. Large birds circled high above the trail ahead. Were those vultures?

Around a bend near the top, where he could see in all directions, Jordan stopped to catch his breath. Torres and Henry had given up, their truck kicking up dust on the way back down the sloping road. They probably figured he'd die out here alone with no water and with no idea where he was or how to live off the land. Maybe they were right, but Jordan felt tougher than that. Henry was big, but the muscled sucker couldn't keep up with Jordan in a race. And Jordan could see a pool of water straight below him.

Near the water, a shifting blotch of color captured his gaze, some kind of furry animal. Beside the water was a stand of wild desert palms and a steep mountain gully. What was that? Should he risk going down there with his wrists taped together? Of course. He wasn't thirsty now but he'd need water soon.

He slid on his butt and the soles of his shoes, his restricted hands poking and clutching at shapes in the ground behind him as a feeble brake. As best he could, he aimed toward the furry animal that had caught his eye, the beast hunched, mouth working the ground, eating something.

A twist of the animal's head profiled sharp pointed ears and the natural, tri-color camouflage came into focus. Jordan recognized a coyote. In Southern California, almost everyone knew coyotes. They were everywhere—skinny, dog-like scavengers that had adapted to suburban living better than overweight humans.

Jordan skidded closer. His heartrate jumped. The coyote licked and nibbled a human head. What had Jordan stumbled across, a lost hiker? The head of a dead crew member from the crashed B-52?

From twenty yards away, the coyote looked at Jordan in a different manner. Ears back. Shoulders low. Threatening. Doubt gnawed at Jordan's gut. His city-boy instincts hadn't understood the primitive nature of his journey at first. Now they did. Some of the white rocks in the dry wash he knew were really pieces of broken bone. They glared in the late afternoon sunshine, and he remembered a news story last year about lost hikers in the Carrizo Badlands; a car breaking down, people stupidly wandering off to find water. The park rangers had discovered their three bodies one week later. That would happen to him if he tripped and broke his leg in this wilderness. That might happen anyway with taped hands.

He ended his slide inside the wash and against a boulder the size of a pickup truck. Nature had half-buried the rock into the mountainside, creating a flat place for water to collect and a stand of palm trees to grow. The boulder had a semi-sharp edge.

While he rubbed the tape on his wrists against the broken rock, the coyote snarled. Not at Jordan, but at the human head. The animal's attack posture was complete—ears back, fangs bared, the low growl coming from deep inside the coyote's gut. Jordan was no wildlife expert, but he'd never heard of an animal arguing with its dinner.

Unless the dinner were still alive.

The tape broke, freeing his hands. He ran at the coyote, screamed and flapped his arms. Size meant a lot in nature, he knew, and the doglike creature disappeared into the thicket of palm trees. Jordan crouched beside the head.

The mouth opened and closed.

Jordan gasped. This wasn't a human head. This was a human, buried in the ground up to its neck. Ants, flies and beetles covered the eyes, nose and mouth.

Jordan worked first to clear the air passages, brushing the wounded face with a green palm leaf, then finally using his fingers to pick bugs from the nose and mouth. Jordan saw an Adam's apple at ground level. This was a man. After Jordan removed a black beetle from his throat, the poor guy's breathing became a loud whistle.

Digging him out required hours, although Jordan first collected water from the shallow oasis pool in a palm leaf and washed away the insects. Jordan also first poured water onto his lips until the man had drunk enough. Jordan washed the single wound that was his raw face again during the digging process and once more before tugging him out.

"I suppose you do not recognize me," the man whispered. "But I remember your voice clearly—Jordan Scott."

The voice was faint, a crackly murmur, but understandable. Jordan leaned in closer and stared at the long hair. "Chief Reynaldo?"

"Last night was the worst," the chief said. "All kinds of tiny creatures come to eat. But it is good that you do in fact recognize me. Perhaps my wounds are not as bad as I imagined. Besides being blind, of course. Have you called nine-one-one yet?"

"I don't have a phone. I'm running away from the guys who had your basket. Torres and Henry. Did they do this to you?"

"Yes, but no matter. Check my back pocket," Reynaldo said. "They buried my iPhone with me."

TWENTY-ONE

Maggie enjoyed the way Billy Payton glared at the Special Bastard in Charge. So far, Chip Daley had held up well under the general's most withering scowl, but Maggie doubted the FBI agent could remain unruffled. She knew that look. Billy was pissed. The three of them huddled in a private room near El Centro Regional Hospital's Emergency Room. Maggie held a fresh Starbucks. Untouched. The lid on.

"You haven't found either Torres or Melancon," Billy said, "so I don't give a rat's ass what you think, Daley— not about Colonel Black's interrogative skills, not about who's in charge of the interview, not about the evil reporter."

Daley said, "I—"

Billy cut him off. "Don't open your mouth until I'm finished. What I *do* give a rat's ass about is finding that weapon before it kills somebody. The FBI is supposedly the best at finding people. Why don't you go find Torres and Melancon? This reporter Jordan Scott could know a lot about our two suspects and the missile's location, but he didn't call you, he called Colonel Black. She should not only be back on the investigation, she should run this interview. Do you understand?"

"She has no experience," Daley said.

"Do I have to call Washington and have you re-placed? Bet I have higher-placed friends in the DOD than you."

Daley lifted his chin. "Give Washington your best shot, General. But Homeland Security says the FBI is in charge of this hunt, and that means I'm doing this inter-rogation."

Maggie hated guys like Daley. Or maybe she hated Daley.

"As a courtesy to the Air Force," Daley said, "and to you personally, I will let Colonel Black sit in."

Billy glanced at Maggie. She accepted Daley's terms by signaling with an eyebrow. Maggie was thrilled to be included in the FBI interview. Sort of.

Maggie followed Special Agent Daley into a claustro-phobic cubicle with gray curtains for walls, white tile floors and a bright blue cupboard topped with jars of bandages and cotton balls. She offered the untouched coffee to Jordan. "So, you've seen my missile?"

Daley glared. "I'll ask the questions."

Jordan held his blue eyes on Maggie like spotlights. "It had to be your missile. Twenty feet long. Looked like a giant silver cigar tube with an Air Force insignia on the side. I recognized the old AGM. I looked them up last week."

Maggie nodded.

"Where were you when you saw the missile?" Daley asked.

"I don't know what city, but we were in a professional work space, maybe one of those rent-a-garage places that began springing up a decade ago. This one was recently built, too. Clean floor. New paint. Even the workbenches and office furniture looked right out of the crate. The lamp still had plastic on the shade."

"But you don't know what part of town," Daley said.

"No."

"Over by the highway maybe? Did you see anything recognizable—a shopping center, any landmarks?"

"No. I was blindfolded. I saw nothing that wasn't inside the workspace."

Woodward Construction's talkative secretary had given up the payroll information on the two men to Maggie and the FBI, but the listed residences had been fake.

"Did Torres and Henry Melancon understand what the weapon was?" Maggie said.

Daley scowled at her again.

"Yes," Jordan said. "I saw Henry working off diagrams on the Internet. The heading said bunker-busters. Parts were marked and labeled. Guidance, propulsion, and charges are three headings I remember."

"You're not serious?" Daley said.

"I sure am," Jordan said. "Henry checked sets of photos on the Internet against phone camera shots he'd taken. The missile was sitting right there. Henry said he even had a choice of websites. He said *Jane's* was where Henry confirmed they'd stumbled onto an experimental design. There was nothing like the insides of Maggie's missile anywhere."

Maggie chest tightened. She was too young for a heart attack, wasn't she? "Did they say what they planned to do with the weapon?"

Daley didn't glare at her this time. Maybe he liked her line of questioning. Or maybe he'd gotten the same ugly flash of doom as Maggie.

"Torres told me he wants to recreate ancient Lake Cahuilla," Jordan said. "He said most of Coachella and Imperial valleys—the most inhabited parts—are below sea level. That's true, incidentally. He believes he can redirect the flow of the Colorado River and flood the valley again."

Maggie did not like the sound of that. Her sixth sense turned into a stomach ache. "Did he mention Hoover Dam?"

"More like I did. I reminded him Hoover Dam didn't exist in 1905 when the flood created the Salton Sea, but Torres said the Colorado River had been changing course for millions of years, did I think it was impossible for that to happen again?"

The confirmation of her worst fear, that Hoover Dam was a possible target, spiked Maggie's pulse. "What else did he say specifically about Hoover?"

"Torres drew a stickman on his workbench," Jordan said. He tried to illustrate in the air. "The stickman had no arms, only two legs and half a head—like a basket. He said the head was Lake Mead, and he planned to make all that water come barreling down the stickman's right leg and flood the Salton Trough again like it did a century ago."

"That's what he said *exactly*?" Daley said.

"Exactly?" Jordan closed his eyes. "Imagine this basket-shaped container is Lake Mead—the body of water behind Hoover Dam. It holds nine trillion gallons."

Maggie pulled a chair close and sat down. The stomach ache and worry about her father and Hoover Dam made her head spin. "Was it your impression Torres and his friend could repair and reprogram my experiment?"

Daley groaned. "How would he know?"

Maggie's jaw tightened. "You spent time with these men, Jordan. Are they the kind of people who could actually see a project like this through—that is, rebuild and launch my cruise missile?"

"Torres is nuts," Jordan said. "A crazy man, wearing that kachina mask, kidnapping me, trying to kill his friend Chief Reynaldo. Now he's gotten hold of your experimental missile and a psychopathic handyman named Henry, a monster who works electronics and can murder you with his bare hands. I wouldn't underestimate the dedication or talent of either one."

Daley sneered. "Dedicated to what?"

"The white man's destruction. And they *want it bad*."

Jordan had directed his gaze at Maggie exactly when he'd spoken the words *want it bad*. He kept that blue-eyed stare on her, too. Oh my. A new emotion in that gaze of his, a raw desire that caught Maggie's breath.

"And you know how that is, Colonel Black, right?" Jordan said. His voice had become huskier, the eyes somehow bluer. "When you want something bad?"

Oh my. "Bad-*ly*," Maggie said.

Maggie and Jordan hadn't spoken for fifteen or twenty minutes, not since making love the second time. The alarm clock by Maggie's bed said two minutes after midnight. Where had the time gone? They must have fallen asleep, although the hours seemed to have passed worrying about Torres and her lost experiment. A street light kept her apartment from total darkness. The wet tires of cars hissed by on El Centro's main drag.

Next to her, Jordan breathed like he was awake, too. Air hissed softly between his teeth. Her curiosity and concern about Torres's motivations and possible actions pestered her into risking a question. Something bothered her. "You awake?"

"Yeah." He touched her thigh. "Got something on your mind?"

"Not what you think." She grinned, though she doubted he could see her face. "Why was Asdrubal Torres dressed up like a kachina doll when he grabbed you at Woodward's? I don't understand the mask's connection with my experimental weapon and Torres's plan to recreate Lake Cahuilla."

"I don't know if there is a connection," Jordan said. "Maybe they only share space in Torres's drug-scarred mind. But so you understand, kachina—that's plural, too—are spirits, not dolls."

He snuggled closer, his body warming her. He'd been a gentle, caring lover. Not afraid to laugh.

"They can be symbolized by a doll for educational purposes," he said, "or for sale to tourists. But most commonly and traditionally, the spirits or kachina are portrayed by men dressed in costume and masks, dancing at ceremonies."

Jordan's hand brushed her breast. They were both naked, cuddled together under clean sheets. In an unusual piece of good timing, she'd changed them yesterday. Her bed smelled like blooming lilac. And their sex. She kissed his shoulder. "Okay, but why did Torres wear a kachina mask in Woodward's house? And you said he talked about the cruise missile and your grandmother's basket as gifts from the spirits. There has to be a connection."

"I can't be sure. I looked through online Native American gift catalogs today and found that face, that specific kachina with the bright horns, long mouth, and teeth. He also carries a saw. He's Nataska, the Hopi's Black Ogre, the Punisher of Wicked Children. It'll be part of my next newspaper story, the copy I should have started writing tonight. Hopi parents still use Nataska to keep their children in line, like a boogie man. I'd guess Torres wore it to kill his father, like a punisher."

"But why a Hopi spirit?" she said. "The tribes around here are Cahuilla? Torres is Cahuilla, the Lakeside band."

He leaned closer, his breath warm and moist against her neck. She shivered.

"Daley told me Torres's grandmother was Hopi," Jordan said. His hand traveled to more exotic locales.

"He did?" Maggie said. "What else did that rascally FBI agent tell you?"

Jordan pressed himself against her. Oh my. The man certainly had a lot of…energy.

"He said third time's the charm."

Maggie dreamed she waited on top of Hoover Dam for an exploding bullet the size of a Cadillac limousine. In one hand she held a pair of Night Optics D-321B binoculars, in the other, her Air Force-issued M9 Beretta.

The cruise missile's elongated blue flame became a fiery halo around a black dot as her experimental weapon lined up perfectly with Maggie and the center of the dam. Like Dr. Frankenstein's fabled experiment, her bunker-buster monster had returned home to destroy its maker.

Maggie feared death, but this was her job, a warrior's job, to fight the enemy until she could fight no more, protecting America, righting the wrong she'd created by losing the weapon. She had to try stopping this son-of-a-bitch missile with whatever energy and resources she had.

Bringing down a five-hundred-mile-an-hour rocket with a nine-millimeter slug bordered on the preposterous, but if all Maggie had was a rock to throw, she'd still be here, on the dam fighting back. Why? Because if her three-stage, bunker-buster worked as well as she and her engineers had planned, tens of thousands of people might die that day, and Colonel Maggie Black would forever be remembered as The Woman Who Destroyed Hoover Dam.

TWENTY-TWO

Maggie woke up in a sweat, her mind racing. How much concrete could her experimental missile punch through? The original bunker-buster bombs were proven to penetrate thirty feet of solid cement. The newer Bomb Royal Ordnance Augmented CHarges, or BROACH warheads, had penetrated targets twice that deep. Maggie's engineering team had predicted their warhead would punch through ninety, possibly one hundred feet of cement. How thick was the pyramid-shaped Hoover Dam at the waterline? Maybe the real question was, how far down the dam's cement slope would Torres target the missile? Would he know enough not to aim too low—where hundreds of feet of solid cement would absorb even the bunker-buster's massive, penetrating charge?

A noise in her bathroom brought Maggie back from her dreamlike notions. Jordan? She'd forgotten she'd invited a man to spend the night in her bed, the memory lapse more about her concern over Hoover than a reflection of Jordan's romantic abilities. He'd been a satisfying and imaginative lover. A sweetie, too. If she wasn't so worried about her lost experiment, she might have been enjoying her first romantic crush in years.

Maggie rolled out of bed, slipped into her robe, and headed for the kitchen to make coffee. She hoped the ace reporter didn't take too long in the bathroom. Would he laugh or be pissed off if she called him Jimmy Olsen?

Jordan came out of the bathroom bare-chested. He stood in the hall between the bedroom and kitchen to stare at her. What the hell was he looking at?

"Is everything all right?" he said. "I heard some banging and crashing."

"I'm fine. You?"

"I'm great." He smiled at her.

He held a clean towel from her bathroom cupboard wrapped around his waist. Water dripped from his dark hair onto his bare shoulders. He had a solid if not muscular body. Nice. She'd been over every inch of it with her hands last night, but in the dark of her bedroom, she hadn't collected this eyeful.

"Coffee's coming and there might be an egg or two in the refrigerator." She tried to sound cheery. "Maybe some Jimmy Dean sausage. Are you hungry?"

"I'm extremely hungry, actually. I was thinking we should go out for breakfast. Go have a nice conversation in public."

He let the towel drop, stood there grinning and naked. "Or we could stay right here."

She hoped she wasn't blushing as badly as she thought she might be, her face so hot. Wow. She'd been caught off guard by the sight of him, embarrassed, not only by Jordan's nakedness, but maybe by last night. The man hadn't needed to manufacture much of a courtship. She hadn't put up any resistance. Jordan had aroused strong passion in her, and frankly still did, but did he have to act so bold about it? Did he think she was going to jump on him before breakfast?

"No need to go out for a conversation," she said. "I think we can say what has to be said right here. You and I both know what happened last night was probably a mistake—fun as hell—but not good judgment. Any personal relationship between us is a total conflict of interest, a risk to both our careers."

He picked up the towel from her hall floor. His face had set into a frown.

"At least I know it's a conflict for me," she said, "and I bet sleeping with sources is not on your editor's list of preferred activities."

He nodded. "Of course—"

"But the big thing, Jordan—gosh you're a nice guy— the big thing is, I'm ten years older."

"I don't care about that."

"I didn't care about it last night either, but you shouldn't be wasting time with someone my age. Honestly, it would end up embarrassing."

Forget the frown. A black storm clouded Jordan's face.

"You're embarrassed to be with me?" he said.

His blue eyes burned. Oh, no.

"That's not what I meant. Come on. I meant *you'd* be embarrassed by my age, eventually. I meant being an older woman with a younger man is, well, it could draw unwanted attention, make me feel, or make you feel…oh I don't know what I meant. Someday, somebody's going to think I'm your mother, that's what I meant. The relationship can be difficult. Look at the trouble I'm already in."

"I would never be embarrassed in your company," Jordan said. "Proud is more like it."

He grabbed his clothes from the sitting room, where he'd first kissed her last night, then disappeared into her bedroom, Maggie assumed to dress. Hell. She followed him across the hall and spoke to the semi-closed door. "Listen, Jordan, I didn't mean what—"

"You don't need to say anything more." His filtered voice sounded calm and measured. "I understand what you're saying, and I have a whole bunch of copy to write. I'll be out of here in two minutes. Maybe we'll talk later."

"Oh, Jordan, please don't go off angry. You've misunderstood me, or I'm not expressing myself correctly. That's all, okay? I'm not embarrassed to be with you at all. I like you."

"Don't worry about it."

"I don't want you to leave," she said. "I promised Billy—General Payton—I'd bring you to a briefing this morning at my NAF office."

Maggie scratched her head. That hadn't come out exactly right.

* * *

The silence in Maggie's El Centro NAF office had lasted a full minute, the whole time Billy's fleshy forehead lined with furrows, his lips pinched in a bulldog pout. Maggie knew all of Billy's tells. The General had decided Maggie was full of crap.

"Why don't we take a break?" she said. Maggie opened the bottom drawer of her gray metal desk. The guides squeaked. "Let's have a shot of Bushmills, talk about the Dodgers."

"Can't." Billy nodded toward Maggie's rain-streaked, office window. "My car is waiting, and Homeland Security expects me to show up sober. Please explain this once more, Maggie. I need to understand this theory before my meeting—not that the FBI will listen."

What the hell was so hard to understand? Maggie thought she'd made things pretty clear. "What do you want me to go over again? The stickman Jordan said Torres drew on his workbench? How he said if he could cut off the head—Lake Mead—he could send all that water into the Salton Trough like the river did a century ago?"

"You're saying this guy who wears the kachina mask wants to recreate an ancient lake that once covered today's Coachella and Imperial valleys, right?"

"Forget the kachina mask," Maggie said. "Forget the ancient lake. Torres is crazy. But huge portions of those valleys are sitting hundreds of feet below sea level, so he *thinks* he can get Lake Cahuilla going again by using our super bunker-buster on Hoover Dam, bringing down all that water at once. Nine trillion gallons."

Jordan gazed out the window with a stony face. He'd been a pain in the ass since he'd put his clothes on. The movies made it seem like you could have sex with a guy because he was nice looking or you were in the mood for a happy roll, but that's not the way it was with Maggie. She didn't have to be in love, but she had to think she might be falling—comfortable enough to get naked. For Maggie that normally required a certain amount of friendship. Or a great deal of passion. With Jordan, clearly it had been the latter. Wasn't it? She wasn't sure anymore.

"Okay, this is where you keep losing me," Billy said, "and the FBI as well. I hate saying you're full of shit, Maggie—you know I do—but that experimental bunker-buster you built can't punch through Hoover Dam. Yes, gravity dams were one of the weapon's potential targets, but it can't work on Hoover. The dam is over six hundred feet thick."

"Six hundred and sixty at the bottom," Maggie said. "But only forty-five feet thick at the roadway on top. Less than ninety feet at the capacity waterline, which last I heard, the lake was fast approaching. Our experimental bunker-buster was designed to destroy hardened targets through ninety feet of solid concrete. Maybe more."

Billy's eyelids became cracks in his fleshy face. "Hoover is a giant pyramid. It wouldn't matter if you knocked off the tip."

"Obviously, you didn't read our target research—the report I wrote," Maggie said. "The report you signed off on?"

"I'm sure I did."

"Yeah? Did you read the part about our bunker-buster creating a breach?"

"Breach?" Billy said.

Maggie opened the desk drawer where she kept her cigarettes, but decided against lighting one. Billy was in charge of only half a dozen projects. You'd think he'd be fully informed on them, although her list of potential targets had been eighteen pages.

"A hole or rupture in the dam is a breach," Maggie said. "You do that below the waterline, the weight of all that water rushing through would cut down a mountain."

"Jesus," Billy said. "What would happen?"

"If Hoover collapsed?" Maggie said. "The flow of water would be nightmarish, easily over-topping the smaller dams below. Davis, Parker, all the rest. Every one of them would fail. It happened in China during a typhoon in 1975. A hundred and seventy thousand people drowned."

A green light caught Maggie's eye, a call she'd been waiting for. She clicked the FaceTime icon on her laptop, and swiveled the computer so its built-in camera could see her. She clicked a switch on her desk phone. "Pop, are you there?"

"Sure am." Her father's voice squawked over the auxiliary speakers on Maggie's desk. "But not for long, okay? I have work to do."

She shifted the computer once more so Billy and Sean

Black could see each other. Jordan, Mr. Stone Face, sat in a corner.

"Pop, the TV news reported Lake Mead was nearing a record high," Maggie said. "They claimed all the rain was causing you additional problems. Can you explain to my commanding officer? There's a reporter in the room, too, but you're off the record. This meeting for him is background only."

She glanced at him. He nodded. Sort of.

"I wish it were only the rain giving me headaches," her father said. "Every snow field in the Rockies has been disappearing like butter in a fry pan. The high elevations are enjoying sunshine, while it's raining all over Nevada and the Southwestern deserts. Every dam above Glenn Canyon has been full for a week, and now Glenn Canyon—that's the dam above Hoover—reached capacity yesterday, had to start dumping. Our own Lake Mead hasn't reached its current depth of one thousand, two hundred and twenty feet since 1983."

"We need the water, though, right?" Maggie said. "Isn't that good?"

"Not when Hoover is at capacity and we can't dump water. That's the problem I need to go work on."

"What? What do you mean, you can't dump water?" she said.

"Quickly, okay. Hoover Dam is protected against over-topping by spillways on each side, long tunnels dug through the rock canyon walls, bypassing the dam. Put simply, if Lake Mead gets too full, we open these spillways and water gets directed around the dam and down river through these giant underground tunnels.”

“Like a bathtub overflow,” Maggie said.

“Pretty much,” her father said. “Except the spillways can take water from various levels of the tub, not just the bottom or top. My problem is that each spillway’s entrance is covered by four, five-million-pound steel gates. We test them all the time. There’s never been a problem. Only now we need the spillways, the gates won’t work.”

“How long until the dam tops over?” Maggie said.

“Don’t even say that,” her father said. “It’s not going to top over. It can’t. Don’t even joke about it. Some dams can do that, not Hoover. The canyon walls would erode—oh, Jesus Christ, Maggie, I don’t even want to talk about what might happen. In fact, I’m not allowed to discuss it.”

“You’re kidding?”

“No.”

“Okay,” Maggie said. “Let me ask you this then: How thick is Hoover Dam at the current, above-maximum waterline?”

“Thick?” her father said. “You mean how far across?”

“The cement. How thick is the dam’s structure at the current extra-high waterline?”

“You’re scaring the crap out of me, Maggie. Between eighty-eight and eighty-nine feet right now.”

Billy whistled. Jordan looked up from his notebook. Maggie held her breath.

"Maggie, are you sure that lost weapon is not a nuke?" her father said.

"It's not a nuke, Pop. You have to trust me."

When Maggie's father hung up, Jordan was quick to speak. "I understand what you're saying, Maggie, but like General Payton and the FBI, I'm skeptical. I've read expert articles that said even a nuclear blast wouldn't destroy Hoover Dam. It's six million tons of solid concrete, built in blocks like the pyramids in Egypt. They're still around."

Jordan's cell phone chirped.

Billy took advantage. "How could Torres even launch an air-to-ground missile?"

"Oh, he could launch my AGM easily enough," Maggie said. "Remember we had the booster added to test an extreme low-altitude launch, so a homemade ramp, even a hill or a sloped trailer would do the trick. Scarier, if this guy knows what he's doing—and it sure sounds like his friend Henry might—Torres could install his own secure guidance codes we couldn't intercept, even after launch."

"Okay, so maybe he gets our weapon in the air. Maybe," Billy said. "But come on, Maggie. Knock the dam down? Really?"

"That experimental weapon carries our latest global positioning system, a unit that could strike within inches of its target. Our three-stage, experimental bunker-buster was expected to punch through ninety to one hundred feet of solid cement. You heard my father say Lake Mead was eighty-eight feet away from where that missile could strike. Our missile could produce a breach."

Jordan glanced up from his cell phone. "The FBI supposedly has a location for Torres. They're on their way to Yuma with an El Centro TV station following them. I'm out of here."

TWENTY-THREE

Torres ran his fingertips over the simple workmanship, the smooth hardness of the wood, the carefully planned angles and the silver-colored bolts and nuts that held Henry's project together. "I cannot believe how solidly you have constructed our launching device," Torres said. "And in such a short period of time."

"It's a motorcycle ramp," Henry said. "That television daredevil who jumps over canyons and alligator pits builds one like ours for every event. His company produced all the specs on his website. All I had to do was leave out the flat sheeting on top."

Torres nodded his approval. Henry's structure featured strong cross-support beams in the shape of an X that formed a cradle for the cruise missile. "It is a magnificent piece of work."

"Now that it is ready, we should not wait," Henry said. "We should do what we are going to do. I thought I killed that bitch at your father's house but her head must be harder than a bowling ball. Now everybody knows what we look like."

"You believe it is time to begin?"

"Even without descriptions, we used to show up for

work at Woodward Construction and now we don't. The FBI knows or will know today who we are."

Torres had always expected to be caught, but not until the missile was in the air, on its way to recreating the new Lake Cahuilla. As long as he and Henry stayed away from Woodward Construction, their former apartments and the first, rented garage in El Centro, they should be safe a while longer.

"Well, we are ready," Torres said. "There is no reason to hesitate. Did you make the hotel reservations in Yuma?"

"Yes. I took a corner suite with a view of our former spaces. We can wait for them to arrive before we set off the explosions."

"The charges are set?"

"Of course."

"And the cell phone we took from Jordan Scott?"

Henry handed him Jordan's old iPhone. "Here it is. I programmed a number from his contact list for you to use. It's a number he'll be certain to answer."

Torres nodded. "Excellent. Then let us load the missile onto our truck."

Henry had built the launch ramp on top of a thirty-foot-long flatbed trailer. The trailer had removable wooden sides and a back gate, all of which had been taken off and stacked neatly against the garage wall. Henry's ramp occupied most of the flatbed's surface, the device sloping upward at a forty-degree angle toward the rear.

After the missile had been loaded, he and Henry

would reinstall the sides, rear gate, and canvas cover that rolled back and forth along the top edge of the siding. For transport to its launch site, their loaded and ready-to-fire, bunker-buster-equipped cruise missile would be invisible to the world.

"What will happen when the missile fires?" Torres said. "Won't the truck burn?"

"The truck will stay in one piece long enough for the missile to launch."

"But we'll need another vehicle to get home from the launch site?"

"Yes. The ramp and missile take up a lot of space. There's my M107 rifle case, too. But there would still be room on the flatbed for a motorcycle. Or we could tow something."

Torres had another idea. "How about your friends near the border?"

"Maybe. I will ask. But we need to pack up and remove ourselves from this place. The FBI is not one hundred percent ignorant."

Protected within the dark, covered trailer and beside his gifts, hurtling toward the completion of the Great Spirit's plan, Torres meditated on what he assumed would be his final battle on earth. Soon another explosion would make the final correction for the Colorado River, and then he would launch his mighty arrow to bring back Lake Cahuilla.

He spread his mother's blanket on the trailer's

vibrating floorboards and carefully arranged his handmade Nataska mask, Chaco Cruz's magical water basket, a candle, and the hunting knife he'd used to kill the Ordonez boys. Each had its place of honor. Then, with both hands, he slipped the Black Ogre's likeness over his face. A current of strength raced through him, as if Nataska's spirit flowed directly to his heart. There was comfort in the darkness, a cover for his inner feelings, his soul. This was natural. All living things should have a black kachina, a killing spirit to use when fighting for their survival.

When Torres considered Life, he saw that everything in this world both ate and was eaten. Nature sought out every one for slaughter, and staying alive for any length of time meant protecting one's ability to wage war, to struggle for one's life.

And while the white man and half the world would criticize him, see him as a villain, Torres knew he fought for his people, his culture, and himself. He fought for all the forgotten people everywhere in this harsh world.

With the desperation of an embittered, helpless man, he lit the candle. He cared not if the fire engulfed his world.

TWENTY-FOUR

Jordan prepared to leave the NAF facility, using Uber to arrange a ride. Maggie had to stop him. But how? What could she bribe him with?

Billy had been easy, the general quickly agreeing to dump his useless meeting with Homeland Security and come with her, but Jordan was determined to head for Yuma on his own. She couldn't let that happen. She needed the reporter with her when *she* went to Yuma. Tens of thousands of lives were at stake, possibly a quarter of a million.

The reporter had spent two days with Torres and his friend Henry, the guy who had elbowed her with the deadly training of a martial artist. One inch forward on her temple, the elbow might easily have killed her, her doctor had said. Jordan knew more about him than anyone available, more even than Jordan himself probably remembered. She couldn't let him go off on his own, but her stressed brain came up with nothing.

"Don't go, Jordan, please? I need you stay with me until I figure out where this launch is going to be."

"I have a job, Colonel."

Oh, so Colonel now, was it? Even Billy had raised his

eyebrows. But finally, an idea struck. "How about if I let you see my copy of the FBI's preliminary report on Henry?" Maggie pulled the papers from her drawer. "You come to Yuma with me and Billy, you can read the whole thing, take all the notes you want."

"You're bribing me?" Jordan said.

"Sure am. You can work while we travel. But no copies."

"Deal," he said.

Maggie had already experienced how hard Henry hit, so she'd taken for granted the man was a bad ass. She'd had no idea how bad until she'd read the FBI report she'd handed to Jordan.

Henry Melancon's fingerprints matched those of one Enrique Colon, a deserter from FES, *Fuerzas Especiales,* the Mexican Navy's special forces. Trained in unconventional warfare, counter-terrorism, and special reconnaissance, Henry—Enrique in Spanish—had been an electronics engineer before joining. He'd spent two years working for the police undercover with drug lords, hiding their communications from the *Federales* and building submarines, all the time running a U.S.-led surveillance program against the cartels themselves, although he'd apparently fed *every*body lousy information and taken a salary from both sides. He'd deserted the FES shortly after his commanding officer accused him of the corruption. There had been strong evidence of his guilt, and the same CO was murdered minutes before Henry had disappeared.

What was a man like that doing in Southern California, working at a construction company? She'd found a possible answer on page two: Mexico's *Fuerzas Especiales* sometimes trained with U.S. Navy SEALS at the Naval Special Warfare Center on Coronado Island in San Diego Bay. Henry had been confronted by his CO and then deserted on such a training assignment. Though informants told the FBI Henry spent much of the next few years in Mexico, the author of the FBI report thought Henry likely had strong contacts and a base in Southern California as well.

Billy coughed. "Shouldn't we be headed for Yuma, see what the FBI turned up at that garage?"

"Torres isn't going to be waiting for us at some address," Maggie said. "I want to go there, see what's in the garage, sure, but we need to figure where these two turkeys want to launch my weapon. Torres will want to fire it from some strategic spot."

"What are you talking about?" Billy said.

"Strategic to him. A historical or sacred location that fits with his magic basket's history, Cahuilla traditions," Maggie said. "The same place Chaco what's-his-name wove his basket maybe. I don't know. That's what we need to figure out."

"Torres thinks he needs the help of the water spirits," Jordan said. "I heard him say that. But we should go to Yuma. That missile of yours is ready to launch, Maggie. Torres must have known he couldn't hide forever. I'm betting the FBI wouldn't know the address of that Yuma garage unless he's ready to go."

"But where would he launch from?" Maggie said. "Why run to Yuma if he's going to launch in El Centro?"

"I don't know where he wants to launch from," Jordan said. "But something closer to the Colorado River than we are now sounds more likely."

"Why? Where did your great grandfather take that basket from those Indians?" Maggie said. "Where did the Indians come from? Where were they going? One of those places must mean something to Torres."

Jordan shrugged. "In that vision, or dream, I remember my grandfather said he'd followed the Indians from a spot on the river called the Mexican Cut. That's where they started carrying Colorado River water."

"But where were they going?" Maggie said.

"They were crossing huge sand dunes, I remember. Uh...I think he said in the direction of the new lake being formed by the flood."

Billy lifted himself to his feet. "Let's figure the rest of this out on the way to Yuma, okay? My Chinook won't be available for several hours. We have to drive, so let's get started, blab on the way. We need to stop that missile before Torres launches it."

Smiling, Jordan reached out to Maggie. "Can I see that FBI report on Melancon now? Before you destroy it."

Maggie glanced down, noticed her real hand had crumpled the Melancon report like useless trash. So what? Something Jordan just said held the key to understanding Torres's plans. Maggie was sure of it.

But what?

Jordan watched Maggie and General Payton cover themselves with plastic rain ponchos, then trot through the rain to a huddle of police and plainclothes cops on the Yuma municipal sidewalk. FBI Special Agent Chip Daley waved his hands as if making introductions.

Jordan had agreed to wait in Maggie's Air Force car on the promise she'd get him an exclusive look inside Torres' rented spaces later, but maybe he'd made a mistake. He should be badgering Daley, a source who'd already proved himself talkative.

His smart phone beeped, a preset sound for text messages. He slipped the phone from his pocket and checked the screen. What the hell? The text message came from the assisted living facility in Chula Vista where his grandmother lived. But the message sure wasn't from his grandmother.

Arriving Thunderbird Hotel tonight. Room 147. Full story if u meet me, come alone. Safety guaranteed. Torres.

Could this really be from Torres? He'd taken Jordan's old phone at Woodward's that night, so he could have taken Grandma's number from it. The message sure sounded like Torres. What other explanation was there?

Jordan glanced across the street. Wasn't that the hotel right there? The Thunderbird? The brightly lighted entrance and street-side parking area bulged with expensive cars and SUVs. Half a dozen limos stretched along the curb.

"Hey, Peterson," Jordan said, "is that a new hotel across the street? It wasn't here last time I was in Yuma."

"Yeah, the Thunderbird," Maggie's driver said. "It's the first new golf resort around here in years."

Jordan silently cracked open his passenger's door. "Where would they get water for a golf course? Water has to be way too expensive in the desert."

"We're right alongside an old channel of the Colorado River," Peterson said. "Not that you'd want to drink the stuff that trickles up through the pumps, but it probably doesn't kill grass. Hey! Where are you going?"

Jordan had pushed outside. Wind and water crashed against his face, the rain startling in its intensity. The gutter carried a six-inch-deep torrent of water, twigs and a soda can. He stretched a leg across the water, use the door as support, and hopped to the sidewalk.

Peterson shouted through the hastily opened window. "Colonel Black expects you to stay in the car...sir."

Rain soaked his head and shoulders but Jordan was focused on the hotel. The Thunderbird. Room 147. Was it a trap? Torres and Henry had imprisoned him before and then tried to kill him. Assuming they'd planned to bury him in the desert alongside Chief Reynaldo. But Torres had said he might want his deeds recorded. The dude was as nutty as a bag of almond cookies. So the text message he'd received could be on the level, the guy wanting Jordan beside him to witness things, to write down events. Even if it *was* a trap, could Jordan stay here wondering? Look at all the FBI agents in the neighborhood. All he had to do was go see if Torres was really there, then call Maggie.

Jordan stuck his head back inside the car.

"Please get back in," Peterson said.

Rain pounded Jordan's back. "Do you have a cell phone on you?"

"Sure."

"What's the number?"

"760-555-7876. Why?"

Jordan saved the number in his new iPhone. "I have to check something at that hotel. I might call you for help."

"That sounds like a bad idea, sir. Colonel Black will be unhappy. I know it."

"Wait until you give her the punch line."

"What do you mean?"

"Tell her to bring weapons. I just got a text from Torres, the man she's looking for. He says he's right across the street at the Thunderbird, room one-forty-seven."

Jordan checked the highway as he walked past the car grill, then sprinted across the four-lane road, his shoes splashing in puddles and streams of rainwater. Wind lashed his face and neck. A car honked at him. By the time he'd dodged and leaped between the median's five-foot oleander bushes, scrambled to the other side, there wasn't a square inch of dry clothing on him.

***

Regally ignoring his trail of dripping water, Jordan nodded with a smile to the hotel doorman and entered the Thunderbird's grand lobby under the shield of Grandma Scott's first rule of social etiquette: Always walk in like you own the joint.

Well-dressed ladies and gentlemen snuck quick polite glances as he crossed the lobby. Must be some kind of political function going on. Soft jazz. Tuxedos and big jewels. On the far side of the glass and marble entrance area, down a short oak-paneled hallway, Jordan found the elevator. Room 147 was one flight up.

He rose two steps at a time and peeked down the hall from the second-floor landing. Brass numbers posted in the softly lighted hallway indicated rooms 140 to 180 on his left. Laughter drifted up the stairway from the lobby party downstairs. He dialed the number Peterson had given him. "It's me. Jordan Scott."

"Where are you?" Peterson said.

"In the Thunderbird Hotel across the street. Like I said. So you remember the room number I gave you?"

"One-forty-seven. But your orders were same as mine, to stay in the car."

"I don't take orders from the colonel," Jordan said. "But tell her to hurry over when she gets back?"

"That message had to be a trap," Peterson said.

Jordan hung up. Probably was a trap, but all he needed to do was keep lookout until the cavalry arrived. He'd changed his mind about knocking, seeing who was there. Even sitting here watching was risky, but Torres, Henry, and the lost missile could be the biggest story of his life. He'd have job offers from all over the country. He'd received two inquiries already following the piece yesterday about his own kidnapping. One asked him to fly for an interview in London.

The hallway was quiet so he strolled leisurely past room 147, reaching the elevators, then doubling back. This pass, he slowed and stopped to hold his ear near the door. Canned laughter filtered through the thin wood, those goofy television guffaws the studios used to favor on daytime game shows. That probably meant someone was in there. Footsteps? He should get back to the stairway landing, wait for—

The laughter in 147 boomed when the door snapped open.

Jordan gasped as powerful claws seized his neck. He'd forgotten how long Henry's arms were, how big those hands.

TWENTY-FIVE

Maggie ducked too quickly into the back of her Air Force car, snagging her see-through poncho on the door latch. After Peterson told her about Jordan's disappearance, where he'd gone and why, she'd ripped the plastic falling into the back seat, then slashed a watermelon-sized hole in the fabric unhooking herself. "He said *what*?"

"He's still at the hotel if you want to talk to him," Peterson said. "He just called."

"What?"

Peterson offered Maggie his phone. "He's waiting for you to come save him."

"Damn." Maggie dialed Jordan's number but there was no answer.

She handed the phone back to Peterson. "Get hotel security on the line, see if you can get them to check the room. Say you're working with the Yuma Police Department."

Maggie would have called herself but she needed time to think. In Torres's business rental and garage they'd found a library of Native American literature, semiautomatic weapons, and packaging for the explosives stolen from Woodward Construction. They'd also discovered dozens of maps of the Colorado River system, including the dams, canals, bridges and tributaries. Plus, the thing the FBI's Daley was most excited about, the address of a third rented garage space in El Centro. Daley figured the lost missile was there waiting for him.

Maggie was torn. Did Jordan really need her help capturing Asdrubal Torres and Henry Melancon right across the street? Could those two creeps be so stupid as to actually give their location to a newspaper reporter? Up until now they'd been smart. If Daley and the FBI headed back across California to capture her lost weapon, she should follow.

She stared at Billy. "Let's go check the hotel."

"Maggie? Are you sure?"

"I don't believe our weapon is across the street," she said, "but Jordan's not dumb and he believes Torres is there. My gut says we listen to Jordan."

"Jordan getting some text invitation smells like total bull crap to me," Billy said. "Think about it. If Torres were really across the street, then *every*thing here was a trap—for us as well as Jordan. Torres could have blown us all sky—"

Three explosions of orange fire billowed into the air directly behind the Thunderbird Hotel, deep, hollow concussions that rattled the Air Force car windows and punched Maggie's chest.

Peterson's fresh-scrubbed face lit up as the flames expanded, soaring hundreds of feet into the rainy sky.

The first thing Maggie worried about was Jordan, not

her missile. That surprised her as much as the explosions.

Jordan fought his restraints to see outside. Orange circles of fire ballooned into the night sky. Three linked but separate waves of compressed air had rattled the windows of room 147, flashing the electric lights off and on.

"Stand up, *gringo*," Henry said. He sliced the tape around Jordan's ankles. "Nataska wants you to burn up inside the trailer as our missile is launched, but do not make trouble coming downstairs with me. If you say anything or try to run, I will cut your throat here and now."

Jordan stared at Henry's nine-inch, serrated blade with as much anger as fear. Part of him wanted to kick Henry in the balls, see what happened. Not a good idea with your hands still taped. Mr. Impulsive. Like dropping the towel on Maggie before she'd had her first cup of coffee in the morning. What a dope he'd been.

And speaking of Maggie, where the hell was she? Where was his hero Air Force girlfriend and the FBI? Could they still be inside Torres's rented garage after those three explosions? Impossible. Everyone with a gun and a badge who'd heard them had to be headed in the direction of those booms.

"Start walking," Henry said.

* * *

The clueless FBI finally let her pass. Maggie strode past burning cars and shouting firemen to cross the Thunderbird Hotel's two-acre, rear parking area. The rain had stopped, but a sea of flashing lights threw red and blue reflections on every slick surface. EMT stretchers clattered over wires and water hoses.

Maggie hoped Jordan hadn't been hurt. She'd sent Billy and Peterson to room 147, but the hotel's central, main wing—including room 147—hadn't been damaged except for broken windows. But to Maggie, the explosions strongly suggested Torres was close, that the text Jordan received had been real and a trap. Torres and the deserter Henry had captured Jordan a second time and no doubt planned to kill him.

She focused on her upcoming confrontation. Maggie wouldn't scream at Special Agent Chip Daley, but she wanted to. Minutes after the explosions, Daley had established his own FBI-operated perimeter and turned off the one cell phone Maggie knew about. Maggie—and later Billy and Peterson, too—had been barred from the crime scene for nearly an hour. Besides following up with the Thunderbird's security people, Billy had searched the room himself. One-forty-seven had been very recently occupied, and its corner bedroom possessed a clear view of Maggie's Air Force car parked across the street.

Maggie pushed closer to Daley. An acrid sulfur smell nibbled at her nose. Tired, ticked off, and in a hurry, Maggie half-tripped over a six-inch canvas fire hose. She caught herself by grabbing Daley's pudgy shoulder with her black-gloved BeBionic. Already in the thumb-opposed position, her prosthetic device locked on to a chunk of his flesh.

Daley howled. "Hey."

"Sorry," Maggie said. She twitched her muscle and the BeBionic let him go. "What the hell exploded?"

Daley pulled back like Maggie's hair had turned to flaming snakes. His hand rubbed his shoulder. "Shit. You have batteries in that thing?"

"Of course. A flame thrower, too. I'm the bionic Air Force Colonel. Please tell me what exploded, Special Agent."

"It wasn't your missing weapon," Daley said. "My expert thinks the explosion was nitro-based dynamite—the same construction stuff used on the All-American Canal. Probably the same stuff we found wrappers for in Torres's office."

"Have you heard from the El Centro people you sent to Torres's other garage?"

"There was no missile, no Torres. But lots of evidence. He used the garage to build a launch ramp, maybe on top of the missing flatbed truck trailer. We're checking security video in the surrounding blocks."

Maggie sighed. "He's going to launch my weapon at Hoover Dam, Special Agent, and I'm afraid tonight is the night."

"How do you know *that*?"

She waved at the flames and scene around them. "This."

"What do you mean?"

"That's the Colorado River back there, isn't it?"

"Who knows? Who cares?"

"So these explosions diverted a major channel of the Colorado toward the Mexican Cut," Maggie said, "the place where the railroad accidentally set the river loose last century."

"What are you, a hydraulic engineer? A historian? Maybe you're a fortune teller, because there isn't enough water running through your so-called *major* channel to fill a swimming pool."

"Not yet."

"If Torres's plan is to recreate Lake Cahuilla, it might happen faster carrying water in that magic basket."

She edged closer, forcing him back on his heels. "You should listen to me, Special Agent. If Torres manages to slam my experimental bunker-buster high on the inside curve of Hoover Dam—high, but below the waterline— this hotel two hundred miles away could be gone in twenty-four hours."

"That's crap."

"The changes Torres made in the Colorado River— closing the All-American Canal and shutting this eastern- most channel—these alterations will be fixed in a day or two. That's why I know he's going to launch my weapon tonight."

Daley laughed. "You are *completely* full of shit, Colonel. And none of this matters anyway. You know why? Because if a bat shit crazy person like you helped design this experimental weapon, I personally guarantee it's a dud. It wouldn't bring down a white-tail rabbit, let alone Hoover Dam."

Acid raced through Maggie's blood. She wanted to take Daley's skinny ass to the ground with a basic Shotokan greeting—a quick, strong push to the chest and simultaneous foot-sweep. She sighed. The little weasel would probably file assault charges. Maggie didn't become a lieutenant colonel and a top combat pilot by losing her cool. Hell, you couldn't be *any* kind of pilot without a belly full of cool.

TWENTY-SIX

Sweat spilled along Jordan's ribcage, a third trip from armpit to waist since the trailer had picked up speed. The eighteen-wheeler's uneven ride poked Jordan's spine and ramped the tension throughout his back. The rolling prison reeked of diesel exhaust and rocket fuel.

What a dummy he'd been, going to the hotel. Karma-wise, he figured he deserved whatever happened, although he wasn't going to die without a fight. He squeezed his fingers into fists, hoping anger would aid his survival. There was something personal about his fury, too, a condition Jordan hadn't expected: Everything Henry had done and might do would hurt Jordan's new friend, Maggie.

Sleeping with Maggie had easily been the warmest, most loving sexual experience he'd ever known, knowledge that had placed Jordan in a euphoric cloud, a state of mind her morning-after rejection had failed to disperse. Logically, he knew better than to declare his love. He'd better wait at least another day to bring up marriage.

The thought of Maggie made him smile, even while the trailer's rattling hard surface pinched his spine and punched his skinny ass. He'd have to remember that—the Maggie technique—if things went from bad to gruesome with these two crazy bastards. Obviously, they were capable of anything. When they'd tossed him in the enclosed trailer earlier, Jordan had easily recognized the sturdy launching ramp cradling a cruise missile. Maggie apparently had been right all along, meaning her experimental bunker-buster now targeted Hoover Dam.

That's when the size of the moment hit him. The night's struggle and his need for courage weren't only about his survival, or even Maggie's. The stakes had grown by hundreds of thousands of lives, and there was a good chance the battle all came down to Jordan. He might be the only person left alive with an opportunity to stop Asdrubal Torres.

Maggie pulled Billy across the four-lane highway where FBI agents continued to examine Torres's space and catalogue the amazing stuff inside. She wanted to check one of those maps again. Earlier, she'd studied a detailed chart of the Colorado River, but since then, both Jordan and Daley had commented about the basket, and their words had tickled something in her memory—something that had been right in front of her.

She changed the grip on her BeBionic and pointed to the map an inch or two south of Yuma. "Look at this, Billy."

"What?"

"The Mexican Cut. We're less than ten miles from the Mexican Cut."

"Is that like a prime rib? I could use a meal."

"Knock it off. The Mexican Cut is where the railroad screwed the pooch, accidentally letting the Colorado escape an irrigation experiment back in 1905. They created the Salton Sea." Maggie's black gloved, artificial forefinger touched the spot. "The river broke out right here, traveled west through what's now Mexico, then turned north into California."

Billy shook his head. "I don't understand what you're saying."

"Stay with me. By closing the All-American Canal, up here, and altering the flow right here tonight with those explosions, Torres has directed the Colorado back toward the Salton Sea—at least the largest flow. And until they fix those two interruptions in the normal flow—a day or two—Torres has a chance to begin the recreation of Lake Cahuilla."

"You mean if he brings down Hoover Dam," Billy said. "And *if* Hoover brings down all the other dams. I count seven between Hoover and this last one, Morelos."

"Which we are not going to let happen," Maggie said.

"Which could never happen," Billy said. "But even if it could, how does that tell us where Torres is going to launch our bunker-buster?"

Maggie left her forefinger on the same spot. "Remember what Jordan told us, how his great grand-father took the basket from Indians carrying water through the sand dunes? Here's the Salton Sea. Here's the Mexican Cut, which the great grandfather also mentioned. And here, drawn with a black ink marker—Torres has to be the one who marked this map—is a fresh dotted line between the two, a line that runs right through the Imperial Sand Dunes."

Billy stared. "You're saying the map fits Jordan's hallucination?"

"Did I just say that? I guess yes, it's true. Why? Because Torres believes it. What better place for him to summon the spirit of the water but the place he knew history used before to break the river north."

Billy grunted. He pointed at the Salton Sea. "Why not at *this* end of the magic dotted line?"

"Look where you're pointing. Thousands of people live near the Salton Sea. Torres and his Navy SEAL-trained pal Henry would be seen setting up to launch."

"How about the sand dunes?" Billy said.

"You can't drive a flatbed truck into the sand dunes," she said. "No, next to the Mexican Cut is where he wants to launch our experimental weapon. This Mexican Cut is where there's no one around, but there's a highway and decent farm roads right up against the river channel."

"I don't know, Maggie. But the explosions tonight tell me *plenty's* going on I'm unaware of. You think you understand, I trust you. Let's go for it."

"Come on," she said. "Peterson can drive us to the Mexican Cut in twenty minutes."

"My Chinook's landing next door, right now," Billy

said. "We can get there in five minutes if we take the chopper. Plus, it has some serious flood lights."

"Shouldn't we have weapons?"

"I have side arms in the chopper. But our plan should be to locate Torres and our missing cruise missile, then call in the FBI and local police."

Jordan knew his limitations, knew to wait for an opening, some odd moment or event that would give him a reasonable chance. Against Henry, he figured that pretty much meant a weapon. The man was too powerful and too well-trained for Jordan to defeat in hand-to-hand battle. Mexican Special Forces might be a cut below American Navy SEALs, but compared to Jordan's training—zero—Henry was Superman. Besides a lot of luck, Jordan would need a rock or a knife, something dangerous.

A bazooka would be nice.

First, of course, Jordan had to get free. Instinctively, he strained again at the bindings around his wrists. Duct tape held his hands together like glue. Unbreakable. He needed a knife, although even if he had a blade in his pocket, how would he remove it with his hands tied behind him?

The truck's powerful diesel engine whined into a lower gear, boosting the engine revolutions and slowing the vehicle. Jordan's head buzzed with the high-pitched noise. The floorboards rattled. An oily, metallic taste of high-octane, jet aircraft fuel watered his eyes. If the cruise missile's fuel tanks had been loaded—and the stench suggested they had been—launch time must be close.

The truck made a hard turn, leaving the smooth asphalt for a dirt road, vibrating Jordan like an overloaded washing machine and rolling him onto his side. Righting himself, he used the trailer's bouncing motion to inch up flatter against the interior wall, pushing with his heels. He wanted to sit straighter, be more comfortable by pressing his lower back against the boards, not just his shoulders.

The big rig slowed. Old brakes squealed the vehicle to a hurried stop. The laws of physics spread Jordan flat against the plywood. Ouch. Something sharp bit his forearm. A splinter or a nail. He tucked his butt up even tighter to the wall to search for the sharp point again with his forearms, rubbing the restraining tape across the wood.

A nail might tear the duct tape. If the point were long enough.

Henry called from outside the trailer, and Torres lit his lantern. The preparations had been rehearsed, the pull-cords, tie-downs, and hooks, all unleashed and stored in a specific and logical order. The canvas top rolled back in a minimum of time.

Opening the canvas top drew cool night air into the box on wheels and revealed a patchy, possibly clearing sky. A handful of stars blinked through holes in the clouds. The city lights of Somerton, Arizona scratched the horizon.

Thanks to Henry's remarkable help, Torres could visualize success. The cruise missile pointed toward the sky, and was indeed capable of bringing his people a new Lake Cahuilla. Water would lap again at the feet of their desert mountains. For Torres, an even lovelier scene would exist two hundred feet below the new lake's surface, decaying in the murky water—the white man's liquor stores, pornography shops, and hamburger stands. His chest ached with hope. The time of his redemption had arrived. He had only to launch the missile.

Henry lowered the trailer's first side panel to the gravel roadway, creating an opening into the box. He used his flashlight to find Torres. "Hand me down that gun case," Henry said.

The hard leather gun case rested at Torres's feet. The weapon inside must be extremely heavy. "Why do you need your rifle? Let's take these other side panels off and launch our missile."

Henry refocused his flashlight between the ramp's wooden foundations, creating long narrow shadows. Through the forest of wooden beams, the light found and halted on Jordan Scott, his back against the truck cab, hands behind his back. Jordan's eyes glistened.

"Because that man's friends might come looking for him," Henry said. "We need to be ready if they do. Now hand me down that gun case, Mr. Black Ogre."

Torres handed Henry his weapon and jumped down

beside him. Though gifted and encouraged by the spirits, Torres's quest became more violent by the day. Flooding the white man's cities to restore his people's natural culture was surely worthy. Yet men had died and what Torres planned next could lead to thousands of deaths. Would the number of white men and women and children killed exceed the number of Native Americans who died of small pox a hundred and fifty years ago? Would the Great Spirit's plan, as enacted by Torres, produce a greater evil than the white men who traded his people infected blankets?

The world was and still is a savage place. Revenge and retribution were common. Who was he to question the reaction of those who had suffered so long? Without a doubt, Torres acted on behalf of Nataska, the punisher of wicked children and the Great Spirit. Had they not revealed themselves to him over and over?

Torres walked nearer the river channel. He had not known his own place in this mysterious world until the night he met Nataska, the night the Great Spirit had shown him the weapon. Until then, Torres had seen no hope for his people or himself. He had never been anything but the bastard son of Woody Woodward, tortured by his father's destruction of the natural world. Now, his life would create value for all Native Americans.

Henry assembled his rifle. The long, large-bore weapon seemed more powerful and ominous than anything Henry had previously shown him.

"We could be ready to launch if you hadn't spent so

much time putting that rifle together," Torres said.

"Not true," Henry said. "Not entirely ready. You always exaggerate. Besides, we're going to need my light fifty pretty quick."

"Why? There's no one here."

"Don't you hear that chopper?"

TWENTY-SEVEN

Billy's lips moved. He was talking to her but Maggie couldn't hear. Something about the dam. The Chinook's twin, turbo-shaft engines, rotors and blades—the overall *rattle*—seemed louder than when she'd searched for her weapon or flown to Las Vegas. The vibration seemed more intense. Maybe all the empty seats made a difference. The Boeing HH-47 had carried a full load on Maggie's previous trips. This time, only she, Billy, and the pilot traveled aboard the powerful search and rescue chopper.

Or maybe the difference was emotion. This time she was edgier.

She leaned forward into the three-seat cockpit, sticking her head between Billy and the chopper pilot, a U.S. Air Force Captain named Carrasco. She knew him from a previous flight. There'd been a seat for her up front, but Maggie chose to give Billy additional room. Mr. Ice Cream Man needed the space. "Sorry, Billy. Couldn't hear you. Say again?"

"Any luck getting your father to evacuate the dam?" Billy said.

"No." She shook her head. "Honestly, I'm surprised

you're listening to me. I know you don't really believe me about Hoover possibly coming down."

He grinned. "I believe *you* believe. And I've known Maggie Black long enough to understand that means you might be right. Hell, if past experience is the only judge, you're almost certainly right. Remember that bartender in Frankfort?"

"Ha." When Maggie had trained for Billy's Iraq unit, she'd been the only woman in the squadron, one of a hundred and fifty or so female combat pilots in the entire United States military. It had taken Maggie's observations one weekend to straighten out Billy about the gender of a German mixologist.

Checking her topography app, she spoke to the pilot, "We should be getting close."

Maggie had loved flying fighters in combat—not war, not killing, but flying in the exciting and purpose-filled battle environment. The job was, to say the least, intense. Lives were on the line, including your own. And because Maggie's crash in Germany meant the end of her flying fighters, that accident had taken a piece of her heart as well as her left arm and hand.

Billy pointed down. "What's that?"

Through the windshield, Maggie saw the stationary, rectangular shadow approximately half a mile away. From a higher altitude, they'd followed the Colorado River south, gone past the Mexican Cut, then dropped much lower and doubled back. The chopper cruised north above the various farm roads and crop fields that bumped against the eastern-most channel of the river. In some places, the river ran four separate, dry, and narrow courses, and Mexico's border stood several miles to the west. Until this rectangular shadow, they hadn't spotted anything but farm machinery and a few pickup trucks.

Maggie checked her app. "That truck's in the right the spot. According to the map at Torres's place, they're parked directly parallel to the Mexican Cut."

Billy clicked an overhead switch and the Chinook's super-bright, rescue spot lights illuminated an eighteen-wheel truck and trailer parked beside a channel of newly rushing water. The river surge had yanked up weeds, bushes, and small trees and dragged them inside a milk chocolate-colored current. Even with the big lights, the helicopter's strong and steady vibrations made focusing difficult through the cockpit windshield.

"There's no top on the trailer," Carrasco said. "Something's inside, too."

"Who's that?" Billy said.

Human shadows darted near the rear of the trailer, a man scurrying for cover as the chopper dropped down at them, lights ablaze. But for Maggie, the most interesting shape rested inside the truck: Perched on a ramp aimed directly at the helicopter, so the form had been difficult to recognize, Maggie's AGM cruise missile waited to be reclaimed. The ramp beneath the cruise looked sophisticated and sturdy.

"There it is, gents," Maggie said. "Wahoo. We need to radio our position to—"

A hole the size of a fifty-cent piece appeared in the Chinook's windshield, and a bright flash popped below near the parked truck. At the same instant, an asteroid or meteor passed within inches of Maggie's right ear and left through a new, baseball-sized hole in the rear of the chopper's fuselage.

The crack of a large-caliber rifle reached them a split-second later.

Carrasco banked to the left, but one of the chopper's two beacons went dark as another shot flashed below. The sound was louder this time.

Another bullet struck the chopper. Then another. They were being hit with heavy fire, as if the bastards expected a chopper—or a tank. Maggie couldn't see where the aircraft was taking punishment, but a new whistling sound pricked her ears and the blade rattle had gotten much worse. Outside air streamed into the cock-pit.

One engine sputtered. The whole chopper shook like a dog throwing water.

"Shit," Carrasco said. His voice had jumped in pitch. Was he hit?

Carrasco waved at Billy with a bloody hand. "Get on the radio. We need a Mayday. We're losing fuel and oil pressure."

Sweat covered Jordan's neck and the hollow of his throat. Behind his back, blood dripped onto his palms and wrists, the skin raw from working to free himself against the nail. He'd made progress, the duct tape partially ripped, but he'd pushed himself to near-exhaustion since Torres had left him.

He pressed his shoulders and arms against the trailer's headboard once again. He needed to snag that nail with the tape. There wasn't more than a quarter-inch sticking out. The first pass, he missed. The second one, too. He shifted weight onto his wrists, stretching the tape. He had to be careful, stay steady, but he needed to hurry as well. He was running out of time, losing even a bad chance at stopping Torres. On his third try, he caught the point.

One stabbing pain in his wrist nearly forced him to cry out, but the last bit of over-stretched duct tape finally snapped. His hands were free and the torment eased. He filled his lungs and relaxed his muscles.

Nearby explosions punched Jordan's chest. Gunfire. Big gunfire. Whatever had been in that rifle case Torres handed down to Henry, it made a boom like cannon fire.

The Chinook lost altitude rapidly, and to Maggie's ear, at least one engine had failed. The synchronous spinning rotor blades grew rougher each turn. The chopper was going down, and of all the things she should have thought about, Maggie instead wondered what kind of weapon Henry had fired at them. Henry Melancon had trained so much on Coronado Island with the U.S. Navy SEALS, they were lucky the bastard wasn't firing a grenade launcher.

The Chinook lurched and rolled out of control, tilting

this way then that, blades slowing, the smoking chunk of machine plummeting toward a wet channel of the Colorado River. Billy shouted into a hand-held headset. "Mayday, Mayday. This is...oh Christ, Maggie! Our pilot's hit."

Billy's voice told her plenty. All those years flying with him, she'd never heard her former wing commander frightened or at a loss to describe the condition of his aircraft or the plane's position. The chopper's transponder would tell flight control where they were, get them help, but she worried about the upcoming crash. Though the chopper plunged from an altitude of less than fifty feet, the big Chinook dropped hard. Maggie believed all three of them could easily die in an explosion of burning fuel.

Checking her sidearm and seatbelt, Maggie remembered the mission over Iraq where she'd taken small arms fire as they'd turned for home. Slugs from an AK-47 had damaged her F-15C's hydraulics, and although she'd limped almost back to the German base, the controls had failed completely a few miles away. She'd parachuted into a set of telephone lines that snapped her wrist and forearm. She'd been trapped in the air, hanging from ripped flesh and broken bones over an hour.

She expected this crash to be worse.

Her Beretta M9 was loaded and ready, if she got the chance to use it. The twenty-five-thousand-pound helicopter was a split second away from dropping out of the sky, and if the crash or a fire didn't kill them, that Mexican special forces killer would no doubt travel this way to finish what he'd started. She had to somehow survive, shoot Henry and get to the truck with her experimental weapon. Her lost missile rested less than a football field away.

She felt a little unlucky, a touch of that old feeling about being a loser, but she knew at least once a day everybody thinks the world picks on them. Truthfully, everybody had troubles. Everybody's life was touched with tragedy. What's important is what a person does when the bad luck arrives. Can you fight it? Can you put up the best battle possible? Or do you roll over and give up?

If this crash didn't kill her, Maggie knew she would keep fighting to reclaim her experimental weapon. That's who she was.

The ground leapt up to crush them.

The rifle reports came one after another. Because the chopper noise was so close, Jordan imagined Henry's shoulder-fired weapon repeatedly struck a wounded, double-engine Chinook, General Payton's private helicopter that Jordan knew often carried Maggie.

He kept his freed hands behind his back and walked to the rear of the trailer. He stood within a few yards of a river channel, water rushing right-to-left about ten feet below the trailer bed. Neither Henry and Torres paid attention to him, Torres watching Henry while Henry focused through his rifle scope on the helicopter.

Jordan saw no reason to hesitate. His target was right

below. He filled his lungs, pretended the new air he breathed was courage, and broad-jumped off the back edge of the trailer. His plan was to crash a knee and his weight onto Henry's neck, maybe break it, at least knock the man out. Jordan didn't want to wrestle a trained killer who practiced with Navy SEALs.

But as soon as he was in the air, Henry side-stepped out of the way. Jordan recovered enough to land one foot on the ground before tumbling, but when he quit rolling, Henry drove his rifle butt into Jordan's stomach.

Air raced from his lungs, doubling him over in pain. Henry grinned with those broken-ass bad teeth, then slammed the gun stock into him again, this time targeting Jordan's face. He rolled away, but not enough. Pain and adrenaline exploded in his head. Blood spilled like a creek from his nose and mouth.

"You shot the chopper down," Torres said.

Jordan spit blood and a piece of tooth. He rolled on his side to glance past Henry. A hundred yards away, the chopper's twin blades tilted, then pounded water as the Chinook hard-landed inside a river channel. Gears and tearing metal shrieked. The ground shook.

Henry looked, too, and Jordan took advantage. He leaped to his feet and ran, zigging one way to avoid Henry's outstretched mitt, a desperate clutch to stop him, then zagged the other way to pass the corner of the trailer. His long strides aimed him toward the grounded chopper.

The night air stung Jordan's face. The ripped and open flesh around his nose and mouth burned. His leg muscles tried to cramp from sitting so long. But a new sense of power gripped him as well. The pain and the blood had stirred something primal. Or maybe it was Maggie. He wanted to protect her as much as he wanted a story, and that was an idea he'd never had before about anybody or anything. Weird, especially since Maggie was a trained, professional warrior. She knew a boatload more about protecting people than he did. But that wasn't going to stop him from running as fast as he could, hopefully see that Maggie was safe, or help her if she needed him.

Did that mean he loved her? Not possible after one night. Was it?

He raced toward the now-smoking chopper, his mouth wide open, panting, wondering if and when Henry would shoot him in the back. Water rushed past in the channel below, the dirt road he ran on covered with loose rocks.

Moonlight washed the farmland on his left in shades of gray. Where the hell was everybody? Where he lived in San Diego, it was impossible to stand outdoors without seeing or hearing other people. Walking on the sidewalk. Driving by in a car. Grilling food on a balcony. A television in someone's apartment. The time of day hardly mattered. Out here, in the lower Colorado River desert, where the human population rivaled that of the South Pole's science teams, distant lights and heat-loving crops were the only sign of man.

He heard a metallic click. Henry making an adjustment to his rifle? The noise put a bullseye on Jordan's back. So did the lighter-colored ground beneath his feet, the dirt good background for Henry's gunsights, offering a sharp contrast with darker crops on one side, blackish water on the other.

He broke hard right toward the water. He barreled two long strides, skidded to a halt and belly-flopped into the dirt. A split-second later, a meteor whizzed overhead, a bullet from Henry's rifle. Jordan knew when the familiar report followed. The way the air moved around Jordan, a storm following the projectile, those bullets Henry shot at him must be as big as Maggie's missile.

He'd been lucky to guess Henry's timing. Lucky with a capital L.

It wouldn't happen again.

Jordan rose and burst toward the river channel, a finishing run that needed two strides before he left his feet in a horizontal dive. His head and shoulders crashed through a riverside bush over the embankment. Jordan hoped his estimate of the ten-foot fall hadn't been off too much. Another bullet passed inches above his spine during the dive. The Navy SEAL-trained fighter had been much closer for that second shot.

Jordan saw the ground coming, but bruising pain still smacked his chest and arms. The splashdown knocked air from his lungs and slapped his forehead on a flat rock. His face throbbed like a jackhammer.

Heavy footfalls thrashed closer.

TWENTY-EIGHT

Maggie lay on her side, black smoke pushing into the Chinook's cabin. Water covered half her body and part of her face. She coughed, breathed, then tried to move. She was stuck. Something held her inside the chopper.

She unclipped her seatbelt and pushed onto her feet. Not easy with the Chinook on its side, muddy water covering everywhere she needed to stand, her head dizzy. At least she didn't have far to travel. The cockpit was right beside her. But she struggled to grip with her BeBionic, battling the smoke and slippery surfaces.

Her mechanical hand was in the wrong position. She needed a hook grip in the opposed thumb position. While she made the two separate adjustments, Maggie saw the pilot, Carrasco, was dead, half his body under water, half his head missing. Billy was belted in his copilot's chair, semi-conscious and hanging above her on the chopper's new cockpit ceiling. Fire erupted in the back of the cabin, orange flames, bright and crackling through the smoke. Sneaking their way forward.

Her BeBionic in the proper grip, Maggie hauled herself into the cockpit to reach for Billy's seatbelt latch. She pushed. Nothing. His seat belt apparatus was stuck.

She wedged her foot against the control panel and pressed again, harder, using her weight. The buckle popped open. Billy rolled out of the copilot's chair into Maggie's arms, knocking them both into the cabin water.

The helicopter trembled, shifted violently, and slipped deeper into the rushing river channel. Maggie lost her footing, gasping for air as her head went under.

Water and vegetation debris filled the cockpit.

On his belly, Jordan lifted his head to peek between the branches of a broken bush. Henry watched him from ten yards away. Stared right at him.

"I see you, *gringo*."

Jordan didn't react. Neither his heart nor his adrenaline glands could pump any faster. The way his mouth, cheeks, and skull throbbed, every resource he had must already be laboring overtime to keep him breathing.

Jordan struggled to his feet. Henry must have run fifty yards in five seconds. Worse, he'd carried that giant rifle with him. The bowl-headed monster could kill Jordan anytime he wanted.

But Henry wanted to fight man-to-man. He placed the rifle gently against a rock and motioned for Jordan to come at him. Hands up, curling his fingers.

"What are you waiting for, *puta*?"

Jordan froze. This trained killer, an expert butcher, wanted a hand-to-hand "fair" fight with a newspaperman. Like he'd read Jordan's mind, Henry laughed, and the memory of Henry's chokehold at Woodward's house played with Jordan's courage.

Not for long. Some prehistoric gene had inflamed Jordan's spirit in a way he never could have imagined. Inside his hard-pumping blood, the adrenaline rush of fight-or-flight had turned exclusively to fight. Wind scratched his broken face and pushed dust into his throat. He hadn't noticed, but he'd been breathing through his mouth. His pulse hammered from the sprint to get here, as well as Henry's presence, probably being battered with the butt of a rifle, too.

Jordan covered the distance between himself and Henry in three strides, reaching full speed as he arrived. He forced his weight low, ducking his torso low and bracing his shoulder for the moment of contact.

Henry avoided him at the last second, side-stepping to the right like a matador. As Jordan rushed past, Henry snagged him by the neck and the seat of his pants, then used Jordan's speed and momentum to spin-lift the reporter from the ground and throw him like a sack of wet laundry.

Jordan landed on his back and slid into the running water. Popping lights flashed in his head. He rolled onto his stomach and pushed up to stand. Dizziness made him stagger.

Henry hugged him. His long fingers clutched Jordan's throat. The torment inside Jordan didn't have a name. Sadness and fear he'd understood since his family died. But he'd never experienced this kind of rage before, an anger so consuming he wanted to tear Henry's organs into bloody pieces. Maybe the feeling was about survival.

Jordan yanked one arm free. Instead of wrenching at the hands around his windpipe—a major temptation because he needed air—Jordan shot a stiff forefinger at Henry's over-hanging face. Using Henry's broad nose as a guide, Jordan's locked finger flattened the soft flesh of Henry's left eyeball.

Henry leapt backward, crying out, both huge hands cupping his face. His bowl-cut hair flapped across his forehead like a hula skirt. He rolled backward, gasping.

Jordan breathed deeply. New energy gripped him. He scanned the wet ground and scooped up Henry's fearsome rifle. Cradling the heavy weapon in both arms, Jordon ran toward the downed chopper. The smoke seemed thicker than it had a minute ago.

Flames erupted around the rear blades.

Maggie filled her lungs with cool river air. She spat the breath out, sucked in another, then reached back inside the chopper to grab Billy. The guy floated like a rock. Earlier, inside the Chinook's water-filled cockpit, she'd worked open the copilot's emergency window hatch and scrambled onto the dry fuselage. Now she locked her BeBionic hand on Billy's collar and towed him up beside her. He sputtered, but didn't finish waking up until Maggie called his name and pinched his cheek.

"What the hell happened?" he said.

"We crashed. Can you stand up?"

Maggie half-walked, half-dragged her old wing commander across the fuselage to a spot farther away from the burning helicopter's rear rotor. She gripped Billy around the chest, lifted his arm over her neck and shoulders, then carried him through a patch of calm water. The muddy bank was only five yards away.

"Crash? The hell you say, Bullseye Maggie Black. If we're walking away, that was a *good* landing."

Maggie whispered. "Our pilot's not walking away and your personal air transport system will be spare parts and scrap next week. Now keep your voice down. Even better, Billy, don't talk. The man who shot us down has to be that special forces deserter, and dollars to donuts, he's on his way here."

"Why do you say that?"

Billy's body and mouth made headway toward full recovery while his brain remained as slow as a turtle. She wasn't sure how much help he'd be if it came to a fight with Henry and Torres. Could she trust Billy to take orders? He should be giving directions, of course, but even he seemed to know better.

"The Chinook didn't explode when it crashed," she said, "so I think Henry might want to make sure the job is finished. We're so close, why not? And I hope I'm right because that bastard coming here is a whole lot better than him staying at the trailer and launching our experiment. Gives me some time to stop his ass."

"Right." Billy wagged his head, trying to rouse himself. "You need to get him, Maggie."

"I need to stop the rocket launch. You stay here with the chopper, my friend. The Air Force will come looking for us soon. Stay under the embankment and behind this rock while I try to sneak down there and stop them."

"I'm not hiding here while you have a firefight with two guys."

"You're not hiding. You're on the spot. That killer is probably headed this way right now. Are you prepared to use your sidearm if Henry gets here and finds you? You'll want to be the one who shoots first, right?"

Billy nodded and checked his holstered M9. "Right."

Maggie didn't think he was in shock. Stunned a little, although he'd gotten better over the last minute. "You ready?" she said.

"Hell yes, I'm ready. Ready as this old goat will ever be." He glanced up at her. "Listen, before you leave, Maggie, uh, can you forgive me for making that pass on the phone the other night? I'm sorry. I was drunk and I know that's no excuse, but sometimes old feelings come out when you've—"

"Shut up, Billy. You're forgiven. Now wish me luck. I should go."

"Wait. What's your plan?"

She kissed his forehead. "I was checking the topography before we crashed, remember? I got a decent look at our location, including the farmland I'm about to invade through this east-west drainage ditch." She pointed behind her and up to the ridge of the gully where they rested. "There's another east-west ditch approximately a hundred, hundred fifty yards north that runs next to where they parked the truck and trailer. I can use it for cover to get close."

"Then what?"

"Shoot my way in, I guess. Disarm the missile."

Billy grunted. "Great plan, only Henry is special forces and you're a pilot. Not to mention his weapon makes your Beretta look like a slingshot. I can't believe that son-of-a-bitch brought down my private Chinook."

"Private? Like when we get out of this, you won't have to do any explaining to the chief of Edwards's air rescue squad?"

"You know what I mean. And don't change the subject. You know I respect you, Maggie Black. Shit, you are the toughest airman I've ever known. But you and your M9 Beretta are no match for a special forces marksman like Henry and whatever the hell that bastard is shooting. The rifle that downed my Chinook had to be at least a fifty caliber. And with Browning machine gun ammunition."

"I'm not worried about Henry and his big gun," Maggie said. "Like I said, that son-of-a-bitch is most likely headed here for you."

Jordan approached the downed Air Force chopper. The Chinook's tail rotor burned, and the cockpit was mostly underwater, resting sideways in the river channel. Slow-moving water piled bushes and debris against the fuselage. The copilot's emergency exit had been kicked out. Jordan bet Maggie had dragged everyone to safety.

The night air was warm. A light mist rose off the crop fields above the channel. He wondered if he should wade out to check the helicopter, but decided anybody trapped was long dead. There would be no rescue now. He tried the obvious.

"Maggie!"

He wasn't worried about calling out. He had the big ass rifle and Henry was missing a working eyeball. Mortal combat—or maybe walking away alive—had produced an unfamiliar, macho bravado inside Jordan Scott.

"Jordan," a familiar voice whispered. "Over here. It's General Payton."

The heavy rifle sapped Jordan's tired and adrenaline-stressed muscles. Thing had to weigh thirty pounds, maybe more. He shifted his hold, stacking the weapon's weight on his shoulder as he stalked the general's voice. He found Maggie's commanding officer cuddling a rock in the wet dirt beneath a four-foot cliff.

"Where's Maggie?" Jordan said.

"She's headed toward the truck, after her missile. Where do you think?" General Payton pointed. "She left five minutes ago, trying to stop the launch."

"By herself?"

"She didn't want me go with her. I figured all I'd do is get her killed, I'm so big and slow. You look like you've had some action."

"Yeah, I took a rifle butt in the face."

"Was it Henry who brought down my chopper—with *that* light fifty?"

"Henry. Yeah, this is his rifle."

"I was admiring it. A Barrett Light Fifty, or M107."

"Are you all right, general? Do you need medical attention?"

"I'm gimpy, but okay. The pilot's dead. There's nothing for you to do here, son. Take that light fifty back to where the missile is and help Maggie stop the launch. If you have to, that rifle can bring down the missile. Aim just in front of those little wings that pop out, you understand?"

"Yes, sir. You want me to leave—"

"How did you get that weapon from Henry, anyway? That son-of-a-bitch trained with Navy SEALs."

"I poked him in the eye."

TWENTY-NINE

Maggie crawled between thickly bunched rows of spiked-leafed greens, her head down, her nose close to the wet dirt. The long, tubular leaves kept her hidden, under cover, but they also stunk and made her eyes water. Leeks, shallots, or plain old onions, she couldn't be certain, although when the smell grew extra pungent, Maggie guessed garlic. The jumping wet things were toads or frogs; the slimy sticks chasing them, probably snakes. Something bigger croaked every few seconds, too, a throaty rasp.

Were the tears in her eyes really from the smell of the garlic? She tried not to doubt herself, but the feeling slipped through all her defenses. Snakes, toads, and a special forces deserter with nothing to lose were her adversaries. Who the hell did she think she was, Superwoman? Maybe that famous old cowgirl, Calamity Jane? How about Joan of Arc? Sure, Billy, I'll shoot my way in and disarm the missile. No problem. Not for Maggie Bullseye Black, a trained pilot with a few hours of small arms experience and an artificial hand.

She stopped crawling and almost burst into tears. She stifled the would-be sobs by burying her face in the sticky mud. What the hell was she doing playing combat hero? Disabled. Trained to play electronic video games in cramped spaces, not to shoot or fight people, Maggie was no match for trained killers.

She caught hold of her emotions when the negativity reached a near-laughable level. Disabled woman? She rolled onto her back and stared up at the sky. A hole in the clouds showed her perhaps the thickest patch of stars she'd ever seen from the ground. Hundreds, maybe thousands of lights above this one garlic field. Eternity. The place everybody starts and ends, the bookends to a life of doing something—getting married and having babies, traveling, making money or a thousand pursuits and hobbies, some honorable, some not so much. For many people, Maggie included, earning a living while helping or doing for others was the way to go. Not because she was a saint, but because the work made her satisfied and happy by being worthwhile. The pay good enough. Not everybody in America appreciated the country's military, but Maggie thought a majority did. Most understood what Maggie and so many millions of others had sworn to sacrifice; what so many millions of dead and wounded Americans had already given.

Do your job, Colonel, a voice inside said. The people who live along the Colorado River are counting on you to save their homes and families. They know you're a woman. They know you have an artificial hand. And they know you have a bad back and just crashed in a helicopter. So what? They know you lost your mother, your F-15, and the experimental weapon. They don't care. You, madam, are all they have. They're depending on you. Act like a warrior, Maggie Black: That's what America pays her soldiers to do. Now get the hell off your butt and kick some ass.

Whoever the hell that voice was, wherever the hell she came from, Maggie knew the woman was right. Maggie rolled onto her belly again and crawled forward with a good picture in her mind of the river channels, the garlic farm and both drainage ditches. On the topography map, there hadn't been many features to remember.

After ten minutes creeping through field rows, Maggie figured to be close, but she crawled another twenty-five yards before she came to another break in the garlic. Slow-moving water filled the second drainage ditch. Frogs splashed. Wisps of fog rose on the other side. She unholstered her M9 and checked the side-mounted safety. Heading for a confrontation, she wanted her weapon ready. She gripped the semiautomatic in her real hand as she lowered herself carefully into the ditch, her BeBionic holding onto—

Nothing, apparently. She fell into the water, her face splashing beneath the surface, triggering an instinctive grab for purchase from her real hand. In a split second, the M9 was gone. She ducked under three times, searching the muddy bottom. But no luck.

She gave up in less than a minute. Too much soft mud. The current rolled fast near the bottom, too. Her experimental weapon could be launched at any second.

There was no more time to search for her M9, nothing to do but wipe the mud off her face and continue stalking the truck at the end of this ditch. She'd have to figure something, a plan that didn't involve shooting her way in.

Checking the map in her head, Maggie decided she was less than fifty or sixty yards from her target. She couldn't see anything. The field mist had turned into a thin fog. But her previous estimates had been right, so she kept pushing her way through the waist-deep water, her boots and clothes soaked.

Voices froze her. Her pulse jumped. The night became a hundred different sounds as she tried to listen. Frogs, water, rustling wind, her own breathing. She inched forward and squinted through the fog: Only ten yards from the ditch, maybe twenty yards from Maggie, the left front fender of a truck cab emerged from the mist.

"If you have attended to your wound, we should launch the missile," a voice said.

"I probably lost my fucking eye. I'm not losing that M107. I'm going to finish this bandage job, then go find it."

Maggie didn't know what an M107 was, but she could guess who'd done the speaking. The second voice, the baritone, had to be Henry, deserter from the Mexican special forces. The man sounded tougher than a box of nails, not complaining about his injured eye as much as he was telling the other guy—probably Torres—he was going after his M107. Maggie knew the weapon that brought down Billy's Chinook had to be expensive and hard to get. Made sense that an M107 designated some kind of special ops rifle Henry didn't want to leave behind. But she had to wonder how he'd lost the weapon as well as his eyeball. Could they still have Jordan? Hard to believe a newspaper reporter could do that kind of damage to a trained fighter like Henry.

The better news was Henry and Torres weren't ready to launch. Henry's departure from the trailer and the thickening fog encouraged her about reaching the missile without her M9. She might be able to sneak close enough, though not on this line. Lights on the truck illuminated big chunks of the ditch ahead of her.

She'd gotten a good look at the plans for the wooden launch ramp at Torres's place in Yuma, and if she could crawl close to the back of that trailer, reach the missile undetected, Maggie wouldn't need an instruction booklet, maps or even her BlackBerry to shut down that special AGM cruise missile.

She'd built the son-of-a-bitch.

Jordan heard voices. He lifted the gorilla-weight rifle to his shoulder and tried to find either Henry or Torres in the scope. Something was wrong, or more likely he lacked key knowledge. No matter how he rotated dials and rings or searched for buttons and switches, nothing removed total blackness from the rifle scope.

What if he just fired? That should draw Henry and Torres, at least one of them. They'd come look. Might give Maggie time to maneuver, find an off-switch for that missile launch. Of course, the powerful rifle in Jordan's hands wouldn't be the only weapon those two creeps had with them. Jordan might be in for a gun battle. But what was he supposed to do—wait for Henry to shoot her?

He couldn't think of anything better. If he screamed Maggie's name like he did at the chopper, the bad guys would know she might be close. He'd tip them off. Sighting along the side of the barrel, Jordan aimed at a dark chunk of river bank not far from the trailer. He fingered the trigger. Two things he knew—squeeze don't pull and hold the rifle against your shoulder. No space.

The weapon fired.

With the butt firmly against his shoulder, the strong recoil didn't break any bones. The mule kick only knocked him dizzy.

Or maybe it was the train-wreck explosion of sound.

Jordan sat on the ground. He thought he'd been standing. The ease with which Henry handled the weapon had fooled Jordan. Henry had shoulder-fired the light fifty like the handheld cannon was a BB gun, but the pain in Jordan's shoulder nearly debilitated him.

The furrows were drier than her previous crawl, so Maggie hoped fewer amphibians slithered between the tall, spiked rows of garlic. Of surprisingly uniform shape and size, she imagined these clone-like plants would become dried garlic bulbs, individually wrapped in local supermarkets across America.

Her mind cranked in a dozen directions as she worked her way toward the truck and trailer that housed her experimental weapon. Of course her path was based on what she had *seen*, not what she could actually *see*. Having come from the second drainage ditch, she'd crossed back by the cab, turned right and traveled an appropriate distance before wheeling right again. She calculated herself as close to the trailer, but this time from the opposite direction.

A wheel appeared in the white mist—Torres's trailer. She *was* close, but maybe not where she thought. She scurried forward on her hands and knees, slowing when her BeBionic made a splash. In the forced quiet, she heard Torres and Henry talking again.

"We should launch," Torres said.

Maggie's heart rate spiked. The man who stole her missile was so close. But he didn't seem to have heard her splashing.

"Five damn minutes," Henry said. "We brought the gringo so you could kill him with the missile launch, remember? I promise that recovering my weapon won't be half the disaster that idea was."

The man's thick voice carried an edge Maggie had heard before. Visiting friends in a wartime hospital, she'd heard the grit of excruciating pain behind their words, the kind of pain therapy and medication couldn't calm.

"Why not launch first and—"

A rifle report cut off Torres. There'd been a simultaneous flash on her left, a wink in the fog about fifty yards away, as if the shooter hid inside the river channel. The report had been big, too, probably the M107 Henry had mentioned, the weapon that brought down her chopper. If Henry didn't have his M107, that made Jordan the likely shooter. That he was alive qualified as wonderful news, but incredibly he'd provided a perfect diversion. This could be her chance to prevent the U.S. Air Force's experimental bunker-buster from being launched by terrorists.

Time for Maggie to move.

"I'm going to get my rifle back," Henry said. "Take the other panels off the truck while I'm gone. We'll launch as soon as I'm back."

Maggie waited for the sound of someone jumping inside the river channel, the thud finally coming from right behind the trailer. The pungent smell of garlic pervaded her nose and mouth. She might never look at pizza the same way.

Maggie remained still as Torres chased Henry to the river bank. "We need to launch now. Forget the rifle. I will buy you another."

"I'll be back in minutes," Henry said. His voice traveled as he spoke, fading. "You can put on your stupid mask. I know you've been dying to get dressed up all night. Mr. Black Ogre."

Maggie worked her hands and feet like a crab in the mud, then her elbows and knees, everything driving and thrusting forward. Glove or no glove, her BeBionic would need a steam-cleaning after this sludge safari. If she survived.

Straight ahead, emerging from the fog as she crawled forward, Maggie recognized the dogface shape of a truck cab. She'd estimated her position less than perfectly. She sought access to the rear of the trailer, not the cab. No big deal. She'd have to drag herself over another half-dozen rows of garlic.

Forget pizza. She might never eat Italian again.

As she topped the sixth and final raised row of thick garlic, Henry's baritone cut through the silence of the river channel, fifty or sixty yards away.

"Here I come, *gringo*."

Gringo in the riverbed had to be Jordan. She hoped he'd be okay. But stopping that missile launch had to be her first priority, and with Torres slamming one of the cab doors, everything had clicked into place for Colonel Maggie Black.

No one watched the rear of the trailer. This was her chance.

THIRTY

Calling him a *gringo* again was Henry's trick to make Jordan reveal his location. At least that's what Jordan figured. Henry probably wanted the rifle more than Jordan. Or maybe not, depending on how well the bowl-headed bastard was seeing the world through one eye.

Either way, Jordan wouldn't respond. Fat chance, *hombre*. Jordan had read most of what the FBI had dug up about Henry Melancon, and the reporter figured a trained warrior like Henry could sneak around in the fog and high grass like a cobra. Jordan wasn't making a peep. He'd been too lucky. Twice.

Distant sirens provided hope of rescue and a reason to stay hidden, let Maggie do her thing while he kept the most dangerous of the two men hunting him in the river channel. Jordan wasn't taking his aim off that missile. If he had to, and if he could see Maggie would be safe, Jordan planned to blow that AGM sky high.

Not that he was anxious to shoot Henry's rifle again. Jordan's shoulder was killing him. Could be a broken bone after all.

What was that tiny sound?

Jordan figured he didn't have time to turn and shoot,

only to pick up the rock by his hand. And he did, a split-second before multiple sets of pliers grabbed his hair and flipped him backward. His feet kicked at nothing and his one arm waved in the air.

He landed hard on his back, the ground punching his ribs.

Henry crashed on top of him, one of those catcher's-mitt hands going for Jordan's throat, the other pointing a semiautomatic in his face. The big bastard's left eye was bandaged, though bleeding, the white tape wrapped all the way around his ugly head. The way he'd bandaged himself, the one side of his face completely covered with dressing, Henry couldn't see Jordan's rock-carrying fist on its way.

Torres untied the leather straps that crisscrossed his back, freeing a four-foot, tapered wood saw. He'd searched a dozen hardware stores in two states to find the right noisy blade. People had stared as if he were crazy, dragging one saw after another across the floor, whipping the handle, searching for the perfect sound.

Standing beside the Great Spirit's flying gift, wearing the face of Nataska, the Black Ogre, he began to wiggle the saw's tip. He used his wrist to snap the blade back and forth until the perfect, practiced rhythm emerged. The saw's eerie reverberations tingled magically through Torres's spine.

He had fashioned the mask himself, discovered the missile and the water basket and magic of Chaco Cruz, even found this ultimate saw. No longer was Torres but a lonely man with mixed blood. Through magic and the Great Spirit's wishes, he had become Nataska, the fearsome Black Ogre, the Punisher of Wicked Children.

He would teach the white man an unforgettable lesson in justice.

Maggie peeked around a corner of the trailer to check the strange noise, although strange didn't quite cover what sounded like a horror-movie soundtrack. Her chin dropped. Torres wore a glowing, horned alligator mask while his hands wiggled a long carpenter's saw. Darn if the thing didn't make almost musical sounds.

Even through the fog, the kachina's big teeth gleamed phosphorescent purple, Torres posing like a supernatural monster inside the garlic field's eerie white mist. As silly as all his drama was, the costume, those teeth and the discordant, high-pitched saw rose real goose bumps on Maggie's arms.

She clutched the flatbed trailer. What a wacko Asdrubal Torres had turned out to be. Had he always been mentally ill? She hauled herself onto the trailer bed and crawled inside the homemade launch ramp. The thing reminded her of a cage. She wormed between the sturdy wooden braces, Maggie headed topside, her decision being to reach the missile's navigation access panel, a trap door on the CALCM's top, near the front.

Conventional air launched cruise missiles, hers included, carried at least two kinds of navigation, not just a global satellite positioning system receiver. Her CALCM also operated with a TERCOM system—terrain contour matching—that measured the missile's progress along prerecorded maps. Torres would have had to re-program the TERCOM system, or tried to disconnect it.

For safety reasons, Maggie's explosive test missile electronically checked itself every two seconds for all-systems efficacy. If any system showed up less than one hundred percent operational, everything shut down from the turbofan jet engine to the arming device on her bunker-buster. Everything except the special booster rocket her staff had included. Most AGMs didn't use boosters. Hers did because of the weapon's unusual weight and their ultra-low-altitude testing plan.

Bottom line, there were several ways to shut her puppy down.

She stretched to peek above the missile. No sign of Henry by the river channel. And from what Maggie could see and hear of Mr. Black Ogre—why did Henry tease him like that?—Torres still wore his alligator mask and played some Dracula movie death chant on his saw.

Maggie shifted her weight onto one of the ramp's diagonal supports while she reached for the navigation control panel. The access door opened with a heavy-duty, flush-lift ring. Maggie did so with her real fore-finger, the lid snapping back without resistance. Dis-abling the GPS guidance system might be trickier. For Maggie the project manager, hands-on detail work was a thing of the past. Several years.

"I'm back," Henry said. "Let's blow up a dam."

Her hands were wet and slippery from the mud crawl to get there, and Henry's voice startled Maggie so badly, she slipped from her perch. She almost fell, only catching herself at the last instant. Even luckier, Henry didn't bother glancing up inside the launch frame. If Henry had returned, was Jordan dead?

"We must hurry," Torres said. "I hear sirens."

Maggie reached inside the missile's navigation panel. No wire harnesses to rip out, no on-off switches to flick. Well, actually, there was, wasn't there. The quickest way to stop this launch was to reset the GPS settings—something her top engineer called putting the system back to zero. A reset button sounded like it might be on a pinball machine, but pressing a single chrome rolling ball switch allowed the missile's GPS locations—launch and target— to be reprogrammed. TERCOM, the missile's second guidance system that followed maps, needed both a start and finish.

The trailer creaked and groaned as Henry mounted the flatbed near the cab. He held a small device in his hand that had loose wires poking from one end. He opened the missile's access panel by tugging a lift ring. He then attached his wires to something inside, probably her special booster rocket. Unlike most AGM takeoffs from the wing or belly of a plane, this launch would be slow and hesitant until the turbofan jet engine kicked in.

The navigation equipment she worked on lit up Maggie's face.

The booster rocket clicked and hissed. She gasped knowing what came next.

She pushed the reset button. Nothing happened.

The booster rocket fired.

In the corner of her eye, Maggie glimpsed Henry jump from the trailer, his back and butt chased by deflected, blue-white rocket flames. Heat radiated off the tractor cab and warmed the exposed skin on her arms and neck. The missile strained and slid forward.

Again Maggie pushed the reset button. Instead of locking down, which it was supposed to do, the bastard popped right back up. Unnerved by the rocket booster's bone-shaking throbs and shudders, the noise and the heat, she struggled to hold her grip on the wooden ramp and the missile. Part of her wanted to panic when she saw the truck, trailer, and launch frame begin to burn. If those two side trailer panels hadn't been removed near the exhaust, Maggie would already be a crispy critter.

She kicked at the six-by-six wooden cross beam below her and found support, not much, but enough to realize the rolling ball switch beneath Maggie's forefinger wouldn't lock in the DOWN position. She needed to erase the existing GPS program, but the crappy ball switch thing kept popping back up!

Flames licked at Maggie's boots. The missile jerked forward, pulling away from her. Maggie let go of the ramp and snagged hold of the missile's access panel frame to stay with the AGM. She was going for a ride.

She pushed the reset button again. The rolling ball switch popped back out.

Why? Maggie screamed a curse when fire burned her legs. She pushed down on the button again.

The chrome ball switch popped back out. Why wouldn't it stay down?

Looked like thousands of people might die today. If this bunker-buster knocked out Hoover Dam, Las Vegas and much of the Southwest might have to be abandoned for lack of fresh water. Food prices would soar. The economy would slump into depression. Maggie Black would be The Woman Who Destroyed Hoover Dam.

She skidded forward with the launching missile. She held on tight as the nose of the four-ton CALCM left the ramp.

Jordan covered his ears. The rocket booster's white flames gushed from the both sides of the trailer, the light brilliant, the power and noise like passing locomotives. If the undoubtedly clever Maggie Black was correct about the cruise missile's destination, then her three-stage, experimental bunker-buster was on its way to strike an over-capacity Hoover Dam.

Where the hell was Maggie?

He'd lost the rifle, but Jordan felt lucky to have his life. Henry had probably wanted to kill him this time, not only get his rifle back. But once Jordan had unhooked himself from Henry's grip, he'd abandoned the empty rifle and taken off running. Henry had fired a couple of shots with his semiautomatic, but decided against a chase. And why wouldn't he? Both of them knew Jordan could move faster, anywhere, anytime.

Jordan waded into an ankle-deep water nearer the

embankment to get a better view as the cruise missile inched forward, gathering momentum. The rocket flames formed a bright backdrop for the business end of the launch ramp.

The flames turned orange and yellow as the eighteen-wheeler burned, a thick bloom of smoke rising from the engulfed cab and forward portion of the trailer.

The silver missile slid from the billowing smoke amid fingers of fire. The ground beneath his feet vibrated, the water puddles shaking.

Where was Maggie? If the missile had launched, Torres or Henry must have killed her. His gut wrenched. Was Dr. Strangelove with a smile really gone? Even if she survived, the experiment being launched had to finish her career. No matter where the missile ended up, or what it hit. And if the weapon did blow up Hoover Dam, kill thousands of people?

The missile inched off the ramp.

Jordan gasped. Maggie hung from the missile's side, her feet dangling.

THIRTY-ONE

Maybe too late, Maggie remembered what was wrong. Forgetting tiny work details must be what happened to good employees when they shifted to management. As the boss, Maggie hadn't worked on the CALCM's navigation systems with her own hands since the first few months of the program, over five years ago. Maggie's work had been about current and future budgets, personnel acquisition and management, not to mention weekly, monthly, quarterly, and annual progress reports.

What she'd forgotten up there in top management is that to work the reset button, you had to *hold down* the ball switch, not push it. Hold it down for three full seconds. On the fourth tick, the GPS navigation reset to zero.

Three full seconds.

That was a big problem, a period of time that wasn't going to work for Maggie Black, former combat pilot, daughter of engineer Sean and deceased mother Jane, Lieutenant Colonel in the United States Air Force, third-degree brown belt in Shotokan style karate, friend of Franny the bartender and her daughter Gina. No way Maggie could press that ball switch down and hang around for three seconds. The missile was on its way into the sky. She had maybe one, maybe two seconds before she either burst into flames or took off to the clouds.

Booster flames burned the skin above her boots and socks. The heat was unbearable.

Maggie gripped the edge of the navigation access panel with her BeBionic fingers, held down the rolling ball reset switch with her opposed thumb, then locked her myoelectric hand in the current tripod grip position.

The AGM missile was five yards off the ramp. In mid-air, Maggie disconnected herself from her left arm's rod and artificial forearm assembly. She fell, leaving behind her twelve-thousand dollar, multi-articulating compliant hand and power supply, the fingers locked on the navigation access panel with her BeBionic thumb holding down the rolling ball reset switch.

For however long it freaking took.

Tumbling toward the river channel, Maggie smelled burning hair.

Which oddly made her think of cooking.

And for sure, Maggie wanted to try making real *beouf bourguignon* one day, maybe Julia Child's recipe with all the classic ingredients. Her mother had often prepared a decent beef stew with red wine Maggie had loved as a child, and she'd tasted the genuine stuff once on leave in Paris. But the chef at her French place in El Centro refused to serve the dish, claiming American beef was too inferior, so years had passed since she'd enjoyed those incredible flavors—beef simmered in pinot noir wine with butter, bacon, mushrooms, and pearl onions. The wine and beef went so well together, and Maggie wanted to fill up on that stew without all the potatoes, carrots, and chunks of celery included in Mom's recipe.

This was of course a strange thing to consider as she sailed through the Arizona air, Maggie headed for a hard landing with two legs, two elbows, but only one hand to catch herself. Yes, definitely a strange contemplation, except the classy French dish would be perfect to impress a handsome young man; an intelligent and kind man she wanted to show appreciation and friendship for; a man like the one running below her now, Jordan Scott dancing over rocks and bushes with his hands extended, checking his position against her intended path like a baseball outfielder chasing a fly ball. Though Maggie wasn't falling from that high an altitude, maybe ten or twelve feet above the river channel, she could easily snap her neck or break her back, and wasn't it wonderful and rather thrilling that her new lover wanted to help. She had an excellent, if unusual view.

Maybe Maggie should rethink her opinion on age differences, love and romance. How often had that four-letter word shown up in her life? She'd fallen hard for Billy Payton at seventeen years old, but she'd gotten over the son-of-a-bitch quickly after discovering how many other female pilots he'd slept with that semester. The list wasn't long, but it was a list. Also, she'd been strongly attracted—infatuated?—with the Australian during the stateside portion of her rehab, but Maggie wanted no part of moving south of the equator when the Aussie asked after getting orders to head home. Was that love? Probably not, or she would have gone. Since then, she'd taken occasional lovers, but no one who lasted. No one to really love. And she had to admit, even with a good friend around like Franny, more and more often Maggie was lonely. Everything in nature asked her, what was more important than love? And if love did finally show up again in a person's life, should anything else matter?

Maggie and Jordan arrived on the same spot at the same moment, Jordan tripping and falling beneath her as she crashed from the sky. Her butt and thigh slammed him in the back, shoulder and neck. Jordan had absorbed some of Maggie's momentum, but also taken a bad hit and buried himself in the mud, Maggie on top.

She rolled him onto his back. His face was bloody. He gasped soundlessly.

She yanked on his belt, lifting his hips from the wet ground and refilling his empty lungs. Their collision had knocked the wind from him.

She offered him her left elbow as a lever to tug himself from the mud, and he showed no hesitation using her arm without a hand.

They sat together on higher ground watching the cruise missile climb straight up, the booster rocket still in charge. She prayed her BeBionic hand stayed attached to the ball switch long enough.

"Are you all right?" he said.

"I'm burned, but alive," she said. "How about you? Your shoulder looks bad. And your face."

"I got rifle-butted. I see you lost your artificial hand."

"And you lost a tooth. At least my hand's attached to the missile. Resetting the GPS, I hope."

"So the missile's not headed for Hoover?"

"Keep your fingers crossed."

One hundred feet in the air, pointed nearly straight skyward, the CALCM booster's exhaust lit up twenty acres of a commercial garlic farm. Maggie had held onto the missile long enough in mid-air to acquire an excellent sense of what a rocket ride into the clouds might feel like. Good thing she'd gotten herself unhooked.

She rubbed her left elbow with its empty fitting. "It'll take me two years to save enough for another BeBionic."

"Maybe not after the world reads my story—Colonel Maggie and the Black Kachina. What a tale I have to tell."

The flame from the booster fizzled and trailed off to nothing, darkening the garlic fields again. Thanks to Maggie's fail-safe efficacy system, which had determined the missile had no GPS setting, the turbofan jet engine failed to fire. With a barely audible swishing of air, the cruise missile with Maggie's experimental weapon tumbled back toward earth. Because of Maggie's shut-down system, it wouldn't go boom either.

"I don't see Torres and Henry," she said, "but there are sirens and emergency lights headed this way. Dollars to donuts it's the FBI's Special Bastard in Charge."

"Who?"

"Daley."

"Oh." Jordan tugged on her real arm. "But let's stay

quiet until they get here, okay? Henry might still be in the neighborhood."

Maggie nodded. "Yeah, okay. I lost my pistol. And I'm all out of fight anyway."

Jordan smiled. "I doubt it. Colonel Maggie Black, out of fight? I couldn't believe my eyes when I saw you on that cruise missile blasting off. Oh, man, Maggie, if I only had a camera, we'd both be headed for fame and fortune. It could easily happen still, although a little video would be awesome. Can you imagine the views your missile ride would attract as a ten-second spot on YouTube?"

They stared into each other's eyes, Maggie shaking her head at his crazy talk but feeling very special inside. Maybe real love took longer to develop, more time together, more trust, more everything than what she felt right this minute for Jordan. But she was *in love.* In love with Jordan Scott, ace news reporter, grand catcher of falling women.

She needed to see where this relationship went.

They wrapped their arms around one another.

Torres let Henry walk ahead. Flames from the burning truck painted orange fingers onto the horizon. Torres spread his feet in the water channel and donned once again the mask of Nataska. They had trudged over two miles toward a prearranged meeting spot five hundred yards from Mexico. But this place where Torres stood now was where his Cahuilla ancestors had come to fill the magic basket. This is where he belonged.

"Why are you stopping?" Henry said. "We have to hurry."

Torres breathed deeply, filling his lungs with clean, rain-washed air. He was cold and tired, wounded by Henry's stubbornness. Had his friend listened to reason and ignored the gun, Torres might have accomplished the task Nataska and the Great Spirit had assigned him. He thought he had won, running away, seeing the missile launch into the sky.

And then the missile had fallen into darkness.

"Listen to me!" Henry said. "We have to hurry. My friends won't wait forever. We're already late."

Torres pictured the primitive world of his ancestors, a vista of simple beauty along the shores of ancient Lake Cahuilla.

"Asshole!"

Asdrubal Torres heard a swishing sound.

THIRTY-TWO

The flashing red and blue lights worked closer. She and Jordan only had a minute or two left alone. What did she want to say to him? Anything? The wind gusted. A patch of clouds had spread into pieces, and the night sky popped with stars and planets again, flashbulbs in the blackness above the Colorado River channel. The croaking of frogs became a steady chorus.

She touched a bump on her head. Her knee had gotten twisted when she landed on top of Jordan. Her back was sore as hell, but that had pretty much been the story of her life since the airplane crash in Germany. She'd also lost her M9 Beretta and probably her BeBionic hand. Expensive, but nothing serious considering she and Jordan were still breathing. Not to mention that her lost and dangerous experimental weapon lay a few hundred yards away, the explosives undetonated and easily recoverable.

"Hey," she said. "Did you poke Henry in the eye and take his rifle?"

"I sure as hell did. I don't know how, but I did. That sucker had me around the neck, too, choking me. I thought I was a dead man."

"I'm impressed."

"Yeah, well, I read a lot of Jack Reacher novels. Plus, I'm fast on my feet. I basically ran away every time."

She remembered Billy. "Maybe we should go get Billy. I left him with the Chinook."

"The general was good ten minutes ago when I talked to him, found out where you'd gone," Jordan said. "Looks to me like emergency lights are down by the chopper right now. There'll be FBI and local cops around us in seconds."

Maggie squeezed Jordan's hand. "So listen, Jordan, old pal. When you write your next big story about all of this, you know, our adventure together, you won't mind leaving out a few details, right?"

"What do you mean?"

The ground below Maggie turned wobbly. "For instance, exactly how my bunker-buster could have cracked open Hoover Dam to make a breach, perhaps releasing nine trillion gallons of water on an unsuspecting public—see, that would be a matter of extreme national security. I mean, you understand, right? We can't give our enemies such detailed information about our vulnerabilities, nor frighten the American people over—"

He held up his hand. "Stop. Fat chance I'm keeping this story a secret. You have to know that, right? You and I, Hoover Dam and your experimental, three-stage bunker-buster cruise missile are going to be page one, national news for a week. Maybe around the world. You saved the United States of America from a human and economic disaster."

He stared at her. There was a light in those blue eyes she really liked.

"Maggie, this will always be the biggest story of my life. I'm not sitting on any part of it."

Maggie and the entire U.S. Air Force would be shamed if every fact and mistake came out. More importantly, the people, homes and businesses all along the Colorado River would suffer economically if the threat were dramatized. America's enemies could use the information to imagine and plan their own attack.

"Listen, Jordan, Hoover Dam's possible breach, how Torres and Henry almost figured a way to bring the dam down, that's all classified information as of this minute. National security."

"Ever hear the term freedom of the press?"

"We made a deal, remember?"

"We made a deal on—"

"Is that you down there, Colonel Black?"

Maggie recognized Daley's voice. She glanced at the channel bank where a throng of mostly men stared back. In addition to FBI Special Agent Chip Daley and Billy, who wore a new bandage on his head, a dozen plainclothes agents and uniformed police positioned themselves behind the two bulldogs. Well, Billy was a bulldog. Daley was more like a Chihuahua. Everybody including the Special Bastard in Charge had a weapon drawn.

"It's me, Special Agent," Maggie said. "Everything's under control down here."

"We made a deal on the information you gave me," Jordan said. His voice was loud, maybe the reporter in him upset. "Sure. But I found out plenty of things from Henry and Torres myself. I went head-to-head with a trained killer, got kidnapped, shot at, beaten up, and barely escaped getting buried up to my neck like Chief Reynaldo. I have my own story, Colonel Maggie Black, and I don't need your permission to write about Hoover Dam. I know what I know, and you can't stop me."

Gee, she'd really fired the guy up. Mr. First Amendment. She turned and called up to Daley. "Are you listening to this, Special Agent?"

"Yes, Colonel, I am. Sounded to me—and to the Air Force general beside me, I might add—it sounded to us like that reporter threatened to reveal secrets of vital national importance. Information that could strike at the heart of our American way of life."

What a windbag. "He sure the hell did," Maggie said. "I believe we have no recourse but to arrest him."

Jordan's mouth opened. His blue eyes melted staring at her.

Maggie winced with guilt.

Daley tossed something toward them. "Be my guest, Colonel Black."

Shiny and silver, the chrome-plated steel handcuffs reflected red lights from a nearby emergency vehicle.

* * *

Maggie closed her eyes and pretended to be asleep as Jordan walked into her hospital room. When he'd called her an hour ago, wanting to come see her, Maggie had sent Franny and Billy home for the day, then washed and brushed the few wisps of hair that projected from her cranial bandages. She also swiped on lipstick and a touch of mascara.

She smiled realizing how anxious she was to see him. More than two full days had passed. He'd been writing stories from San Diego. Appearing on radio and television shows. Mr. Celebrity.

She opened her eyes when he sat. "What happened to your neck?"

"Nothing." Jordan held a digital camera. "Mind if I get a couple of shots, Colonel? Your fans would love to see what their hero looks like after her awesome missile ride. All we have now is that stock Air Force—"

"Up yours, Mr. Reporter. And put that camera away or I'm calling the guard."

"—Air Force head shot. Come on, Maggie."

"No way. And don't tell me your neck is nothing. You're braced up like it's broken."

"Only one vertebrae. And it's cracked a little, not broken."

"When I landed on you?"

"Yup."

Thanks to Jordan's front-page stories—now in syndication throughout the *Sun-Times* newspaper group and regurgitated by the wire services and worldwide media outlets—pretty much everybody on earth knew about

U.S. Air Force Lieutenant Colonel Maggie Black. They knew where and what she'd been holding on to when the cruise missile took off, what brand of Irish whiskey she enjoyed, and wholeheartedly believed Maggie had wrestled that cruise missile from the sky like a rodeo champ. Jordan was such a storyteller. He was definitely in the right profession.

Maggie's threats to Jordan's freedom had gone afoul when *The New York Times* scooped him the very next day. They'd printed everything, even the lost weapon's potential to damage Hoover Dam, and everything the Air Force had done wrong. Maggie had no proof, but *The Times* source had to have been Daley, or at least one of his men. There had been no use trying to pressure Jordan after that.

She pushed on the mattress with her heels, sliding her butt higher on the bed. She wore a long and modest blue cotton nightgown, the left sleeve cut off to match her missing forearm and hand. Her black-gloved BeBionic had been recovered from her crashed CALCM, and was being repaired in the United Kingdom.

They'd call her Stumpy for a while.

"Any news to feed me?" Jordan said.

She glared at him. Always working. "No comment."

"What's the matter?"

"Are you going to write about the water basket, *toloaches*, and Chaco Cruz in an upcoming story?" she said.

"Maybe. But it's weird stuff. Sounds crazy, really."

"You wrote how much I like my Bushmills," she said.

"I thought that was weird."

"That bothered you, huh? What I gather, specific liquor brands add to a warrior's legend, Maggie. I think you should trust me on this."

"Right." The colonel shook her bandaged head, then winced. Maggie's exploits in retrieving her experimental weapon had earned her a concussion, damaged hearing, second-degree burns on her legs, neck, and right arm, plus a patch of third-degree burns above her left ankle— burn treatment being the main reason she was still in the hospital. "Damn, Jordan, you're the world's biggest bull shitter."

He grinned.

"My staff will put a copy of the final FBI report in the mail to you," she said, "provided you tell no one where you got it."

"Thanks."

"Are we off the record?" she said.

He shrugged. "Whatever you want."

She sipped her water. "I do have news for you, but let's make this one from government sources, okay? Not military. The FBI won't be out with it for a while, although who knows. I heard Daley and *The New York Times* are chummy."

"I gathered. How about a highly placed, gorgeous, and sexually attractive government source."

"Hey." She glanced toward the guard, then glared at Jordan. "You want the news or not?"

"Oh, give it to me, baby, give it to me."

She changed the glare to a serious one. "I don't like

that word applied to me.”

He stared. “Baby?”

“Yes.”

“Really?”

“Yes.”

He nodded. “Okay, you got it, Colonel. Now please. What’s the news?”

“I *am* serious,” she said. “Next time it’s a punch in the nose.”

He grimaced. “Yes, ma’am.”

“They caught Henry last night trying to slip across the border into Mexico,” she said.

“Who caught him? Daley?”

“No,” Maggie said. “Mexico’s FES—the *Fuerzas Especiales*. The people he deserted after killing his commanding officer.”

“Uh oh for Henry. How about Torres?”

“No word on him. Daley’s Mexican contacts say they’re putting the screws to Henry, trying to—”

“They might be putting the screws to him literally.”

“—but so far, Henry hasn’t said anything about his ex-partner.”

“They didn’t seem to get along that well when I was around,” Jordan said. “Henry barely put up with him near the end.”

“I heard bickering, too.”

“If justice rules,” Jordan said. “Henry killed that murdering bastard Torres under a no-witness policy, and no one will ever find the body.”

THIRTY-THREE

At first, Torres was not certain if he were awake or dreaming. His body was numb and frozen in place. The top left side of his head thundered with pain. Minutes of semi-consciousness passed before he understood why his hands could not touch himself.

A tickling sensation inside his nose told him not to succumb to panic. Facing certain tortuous death, a warrior needed to remain silent and to occupy his mind with pleasant thoughts. To do otherwise, say to worry about the ants exploring his nostrils, would only risk screaming madness. He needed to concentrate on the new perspective he had gained of the world. At eye level, the earth was large and colorful, a bewildering, beautiful place. The dwarfed trees were cartoonish giants. The pale blue blooms of a nearby *palo verde* bush matched the sky on a summer day.

Self-reflection also took his mind off bugs, and these hours turned into days made his approaching death seem quite natural. Had he spent his brief moments on earth in a worthy cause? Chosen the best path?
Torres spit a beetle from his mouth. Other bugs choked his throat and bit his tongue and foraged in his sinuses.

His head crawled with tiny beasts.

But what difference did anything or anyone really make? In the end, when the wheel of eternity rotated past these decades and these centuries, what truly had been personally accomplished? Honestly, do not people's lives, loves, and constructions each slip effortlessly into the past, forgotten by all who struggle presently?

Of course. And since all paths end in destruction and the great mystery of death, what matters only is the journey. This, Torres's mother taught him early. People must all choose a path with heart. To be happy, and at one with the Great Spirit, humans must walk a road that helps others—a trail of service.

With all his might, he had tried to recreate Lake Cahuilla for his people. He'd put forth the maximum effort of his heart and spirit. And perhaps even in his failure some small things might change for the Cahuilla. Exactly what, he couldn't imagine. Except that a few would tell his story. The story of Asdrubal Torres and the black ogre kachina, Nataska. His quest for revenge against the white man.

The pain inside his head and throat became difficult to withstand in silence. He struggled to breathe because fanged and clawed insects crowded his air passages, eating him from the inside out. Was this his ultimate purpose, Great Spirit? To feed the bugs of the desert? His heart trembled inside his chest. His bones shook and he sensed madness at the back of his neck, whispering the availability of her pleasures.

Fear was an ugly emotion; one he had not known well

until this moment. Fear robbed him of spirit and faith. He wanted to scream, "Why me, Great Spirit? Why must I die now, and in such a cruel manner? My hands and feet frozen in the soil like a tree root. What have I done to deserve such a death?"

Torres could hear the Creator's answer, too: "Why *not* you? Are you above human weakness? Are you so special that you cannot stumble across a piece of bad luck? Are you incapable of mistakes?"

The answer, of course, was no. He was human and therefore subject to distraction, error, disease, and ill fortune. He needed to listen to the voice of faith, the voice that said there was some greater purpose at work. He was stuck in the earth like a fat worm for a very important reason, and when the time was proper, the Great Spirit would show him why.

Maggie shuddered thinking what poor Chief Reynaldo had gone through. She couldn't totally imagine, thank God. She refused to think hard about it, either: Stuck in the ground like that, insects eating you. "How's the chief doing?" she said.

A different nurse brought a covered dinner into the room. Maggie didn't want to know what tonight's menu included, maybe a sign her health had improved. She was starved for something good to eat. Something with spices, at least a freaking *hint* of flavor. First time in two days she'd been hungry.

"He has one or two more surgeries left, but Chief

Reynaldo is back at work," Jordan said. "He's lecturing news reporters and selling baskets, jewelry, and T-shirts on his new website, Cahuilla Country. Never saw a man enjoy his fifteen minutes of fame more—or use it better. He told me he'll have to take one particular medicine forever because of all the stuff they couldn't remove from his lungs."

"Yuk," Maggie said.

"But his Cahuilla tribe is scoring big, every dollar going to a new education fund for the reservation's children."

"That's fantastic," Maggie said.

"Let me ask you a weird question, Maggie. Do you think Torres might have really tapped into some special power? I mean, how the hell did he wind up hiking exactly where he'd see your cruise missile fall from the sky?"

"It can only be coincidence."

"Or how about, only one other time in its eighty-year history has Lake Mead been filled to capacity, and yet Torres discovers a weapon of mass destruction that might attack the dam at exactly the moment the spillways get stuck?"

Maggie stared at him. "I don't know what to say. But I don't think—"

"How about my great grandfather's basket? How can we disregard all of these—"

"Okay, okay," Maggie said. "As they say in those old cowboy movies you like, I get your drift. But the theory is pure horse crap."

Jordan grinned at her. "Maybe. I guess you could just as easily say the Great Spirit designed all of those events so that you and I would meet."

Maggie liked that idea, she and Jordan part of a grand design. Even better, she liked that Jordan would think and say the words out loud. She grinned. "I refuse to accept that we needed Asdrubal Torres to get together, although I see nothing wrong with having something going on with the Great Spirit."

"Torres did have something going, I think," Jordan said. "Too many weird and unaccountable things happened."

"Torres was a murderer," Maggie said. "The FBI says he killed two Cahuilla teenagers the same day I lost my missile. Plus, those guards at the All-American Canal were shot with Torres' pistol. Young men with families. And his own father, murdered. Still, maybe you're right. You know in a way it *will* be the Great Spirit who eventually grants Asdrubal Torres his wish."

"What do you mean?" Jordan asked.

"Hoover Dam...crumbling. It's a matter of time, really. My father showed me a Bureau of Land Management report once. It seems even the BLM admits America's system of dams, canals, and levees controlling the Colorado River is only a temporary fix. That's the word they used. *Temporary.*"

"You're saying Lake Cahuilla will refill all by itself one day? A natural event?"

Jordan may have suffered a broken vertebra, but Maggie had never seen him look better. She suspected the joy and confidence on his face had been hidden a long time. He was proud of himself: All over the world, people read his stories.

"Lake Cahuilla refilled over and over—thousands of times during the last half-million years," Maggie said. "One giant earthquake is all it's going to take."

Falling asleep that night in her El Centro hospital room, Maggie hoped she'd have the flying dream again, the one where she soared between white clouds in a blue sky. One reason, she loved the sensations of flying, which the dream delivered, and two, Maggie was curious if she'd still wake up sad, feeling less than a whole person. Truth was, she was better than whole, better than normal. Her myoelectric, programmable BeBionic hand enabled some tasks a human hand couldn't manage, such as preventing the launch of a deadly missile. Quite logically, that made Colonel Maggie Black special herself.

Weeks later, Maggie seared the last four beef cubes in olive oil and bacon lard while she listened to Jordan singing in the shower. Hard to say which crispy, crackling noise she enjoyed more, although her version of Julia Child's *beouf borguingnon* had to be a better imitation of the original than Jordan Scott's account of "We Belong Together" by Mariah Carey.

She changed the finger-setting on her newly rebuilt BeBionic, improving her grip on the iron kitchen pincers she'd found in a drawer. She and Jordan had picked up her rebuilt artificial hand in London the day before yesterday. Now in Paris for the rest of the week, they'd rented a one-bedroom apartment on Rue Balzac, two blocks from the Champs-Elysees and Maggie's favorite wartime hangout, the Café George V. They'd eaten lunch there earlier under a warm sun and fluffy clouds, a respite between shopping for Maggie's beef stew ingredients.

She removed the last of the beef cubes and set them on top of the bacon pieces—lardons, Julia called them. The roomy apartment was a financial deal, twice the space you could get from any hotel in this neighborhood at half the price. The main room's two-story plaster ceiling carried a crystal chandelier; the walk-through windows opened onto a balcony you could stand on and smoke; and most importantly, the open-planned living area included a newly refurbished kitchen with a fancy gas stove and refrigerator. As soon as the BeBionic people had given Maggie a pickup date, she'd planned the trip with Jordan. Paris and cooking the man *beouf borguingnon* had been on the program since day one.

While she'd been falling through the air, actually.

She tossed her sliced onions and mushrooms into the hot oil. They would brown quickly, so she kept her gaze on them, the iron pincers poised and ready to flip the veggies in a hurry. Maggie had to be back at work on Monday, but that was a good thing. The old cruise AGM with her experimental bunker-buster hadn't been badly damaged, and would be reassembled and ready to test again in a few months. Maggie's special weapon program was back up and running. Both she and General Billy had survived all Air Force and congressional purge attempts so far.

"Hey, Colonel!" Jordan had slipped up behind her.

Maggie wheeled in his direction, the iron pincers held high, forcing him backward, making him dance away. Like that first morning after spending the night together, Jordan's wet hair dripped onto his broad shoulders and only a towel at the waist covered his naked, right-from-the-shower, body.

"Put some clothes on if you want to hang around in my kitchen," Maggie said. "And you'd better not drop that towel like you did before." She aimed the pincers strategically. "Or we'll be dining on sausage tonight, not stew."

ABOUT THE AUTHOR

Former *Los Angeles Times* reporter Jack Getze is Fiction Editor for Anthony nominated *Spinetingler Magazine*, one of the internet's oldest websites for noir, crime and horror short stories. His award-winning Austin Carr mystery series is published by Down & Out Books, including the latest, *Big Shoes*, which won Deadly Ink's David Award for Best Mystery of 2015. His short fiction has appeared in *A Twist of Noir*, *Beat to a Pulp*, *The Big Adios* and several anthologies.

http://austincarrscrimediary.blogspot.com/

www.ingramcontent.com/pod-product-compliance
Lightning Source LLC
Chambersburg PA
CBHW051644180726
48284CB00006B/1859